QUEER AND ALONE

QUEER AND ALONE

JAMES STRAHS

Whiskey Tit
NYC | VT

Queer and Alone was originally published by PAJ Books in 1988, and is republished with permission of Jim Strahs and Emma Strahs.

This book was produced using PressBooks.com, and PDF rendering was done by PrinceXML.

Contents

I have forwarded to my publisher this memoir by the late D.F., having unearthed it from his effects. There are those who will ask, "Just who is this guy," etcetera, and I, being nothing like him in manner or morals, can be of no help. However, in a very learned work by W.H. McNeill called *Plagues and Peoples*, there is a fragment that speaks to his condition: "Any prolonged slackening of career opportunities for the peasant surplus – in cities, armies, or by migration to some frontier region – soon had the effect of ponding excess population back in the villages. To forestall rural overpopulation, alternative careers had to involve high death rates, yet without deterring large numbers of men and women from accepting the risks involved... the probable upshot of leaving home." It is assumed no one will attempt to book passage based on the information herein contained.

1

Roman Curse

I was in Rome when I was told I was to die. Well, it made me sick just to think about it. And I had been having such a wonderful time that winter under those balmy Latin skies. I never even thought of leaving for the north and the land of the midnight sun. You might say I was hounded out of town. But better let me give you a few of the details.

I had eaten brussels sprouts for «lunch» the previous afternoon. Now this is a dish I just detest. To my mind it is no more than a foul-smelling, thick bit of greenery which no sauce can really elevate. I know it must be related to the thistle family of plants. But never mind; no more of the *nouvelle cuisine* for now.

She was an ordinary *signora* of the working class of that country. Her husband would see me walking in the gardens and greet me with native affection. A peasant, really. I am speaking of the woman who told me I was to die. I was living in a sparsely furnished little room in an ever-so-ordinary little villa overlooking the Eternal City. It was there she graced me with that absolutely pedestrian augury. It's really a very silly thing to say to another person. And a shot from the blue! "The sooner the better," she said. Can you imagine that? I mean, really, what an incredible thing to say! I'm afraid I was forced to let her go even though I did need her to launder the linen, wipe up the horrible red dust which blew in my window and empty the shell ash-tray. Little things but so important to our sense of well-being.

She began, innocently enough, by warning me that all my associates would betray me and I would soon find myself alone in a queer land, homeless and heartbroken. Oh, maybe she was just another innocent psychic but I don't care. She couldn't have known anything of my past. I'm sure none of that got into the Italian papers. Not that they wouldn't print it if they could; they'll print anything. Don't you remember the pictures of that actress's severed head lying by the side of the highway? They can be so tasteless, these journalists.

Anyway, I took her willingness to talk as a sign of native friendliness. But it's so hard to tell with foreigners. This is why I talked to her in the first place. The old bag, I said to myself, needs a good dry-cleaning. Like many women of her race, like women of most races, all women really, she emitted an odor. I bid her "good-day" and was about to leave for the palace when, taking my hand, she cast a soulful gaze upon me. I said nothing, being dumbfound in wonderment. She said: "Why are you here, Mister Desmond? Why have you come to our city? *Signor* Desmond, what do you want from us? What have we done to harm you? Why do you not return to your homeland?"

I turned sympathetic and muttered something about the climate, the pines, the ruins and fountains and steps. The art. Perhaps I should have gone to Florence or Verona. I am afraid she, like most simple people, the poor and down-trodden, those who labor with their hands to earn their daily bread, did not understand the power of art. She tightened her grip and said: "You will die soon, Mister Desmond, the sooner the better."

A smell of fermenting milk rose up from her every crack and crevice. She made her eyes twinkle in the morning sunlight. It was something most extra-ordinary, quite a neat little trick, almost cinematic in its magical effect. I politely freed my hand and crossed to open a window. She couldn't have been part of a «hit-squad». That was just too far-fetched. And she couldn't possibly have heard of me in connection with what happened stateside. I was never mentioned anywhere as being anything more than a material witness. A whiff of eucalyptus wafted in on the breeze. I told her right then and there that her services would no longer be required.

By the way, my name is not Mister Desmond but Desmond Farrquahr. And that is my given name. I just hate people who make them up as they go along. And let me say right here and now that I have nothing but nothing to do with the world of work. I have just enough money to get along and that is that. It's a trust. I've never had to worry about the simple fact of survival the way so many do today. Call me lucky but that is who I am.

I told her right then and there that her services would no longer be required. She shrugged her shoulders and shuffled out of the room. She left me quite alone and somewhat the sadder for the experience. Not that I cared. Two weeks later I left that holy city to continue my travels. I took a taxi to the railroad station which was crowded with people leaving town. The train ride north was very exciting. We went up the west coast where the souls of the poets themselves dwell in the mists off the sea. So many painters have done such lovely watercolors of these shores. We rolled on through the night. Empty rail yards in the arc light, a slim volume of my favorite poetry. I had a comfortable little *couchette*. I feel that travel makes one so much more fit for ordinary life.

I believe our first stop was Dijon, a well-situated city in France, famous for its mustard and its hams. I didn't «rest» there. I sat finishing my breakfast on a siding and then we continued. Twelve hours later I was in Bremen-town, that city of musicians. I took a streetcar to Bremerhaven where I took a room in a picturesque though seedy old «flop-house», the sort of place a sailor «sleeps it off». In a matter of days I found my Captain and within the week I boarded a steamer bound for Hong Kong by way of the Cape of Good Hope. That's just how easy it is though it happens so much faster on paper. And «bad cess to her» is what I thought as I stood at last on the gangplank, about that woman who had told me that horrible thing.

2

Captain and Crew

The Captain was a jolly, round-faced, fat-lipped and calculating Oriental of indeterminate origin. The vessel itself, the Hohenstauffen, was of mixed crew and Liberian registry. Eventually I asked the Captain how it had come to pass he'd be skippering some «kraut tub» in a «tax dodge» but he just laughed and told me name and nationality mean little on the high sea. He must have known of what he spoke though it wasn't much of a ship. In order to steady her in a storm they had to hoist a ragged little sail amidships. And the bulkheads went to flaking paint. But never mind. It was all vintage steamship à la Troost and so very, very Weimar.

I trust I'm not proceeding too wildly for you to keep up. I got on a big boat at this point in time, the Hohenstauffen, a merchantman of convenient registry, the Captain of which was an indeterminate Oriental with a calculating air, and off we steamed for Hong Kong with a clutch of fellow-travellers. You see, I travel very lightly with never more than my hands and pockets full of gear. I carry: a) folding money; b) a simple yet elegant carpet bag full of shirts and notions, socks, underwear, ties, clasps, slippers, toilet and such-like articles; c) a leather folding case containing three carefully pressed chocolate-brown three-piece suits; d) a thin briefcase for papers and writing materials, mechanical pencil and lead, pen, ink and blotter, envelopes and a folding postage scale; e) a medical shoulder satchel containing a stethoscope for listening, a silver hammer for reflexes, drugs and potions, teas and ointments and such and f) a shopping bag for odds and ends. Little more. That's really enough unless you intend to jog or dance or play the grande dame.

He, the Captain, immediately invited me to his pilot-house, sort of his lounge on the bridge, where we sat for the longest time drinking a smoky dark tea and talking of this and that, waiting for clearance from the harbor-master of all people. We watched the tugs jockey for position in the dusk amongst the tankers and the trawlers, the liners and the dredgers. Bremen, our port of embarkation, is such a busy place. The year I sailed she handled four point five four million tons of metric cargo from the U.S. of A. alone. And though badly damaged in the war, this old Hanseatic city is still the brewspot for Beck's, that king of beers Europeans love. It's the one with the key on the bottle. It's the only German you need know at this point.

I remember the night before I was so savagely beaten by that hired assassin in Cowloon. That's in China, sort of a Hong Kong suburb at the end of the voyage. I was at a dinner party in the sea-front estate of the late Harold J. Hung, a wealthy Sino-industrialist. There we sat overlooking the delicately lit shallow blue pool of Hung's private lake, watched by graceful pagodas, crossed by willow-draped causeways and moon bridges, discussing, of all things, religion in the modern world. At least that's what I thought. And it's not because I'm somebody that I was there. I went with a friend and they didn't know me from adam or any other of the hoi polloi, no matter how hoity-toity. And of course I'm well educated so I had no fear of the social snub, so deadly and hurtful to those of us forced to suffer low birth.

The atmosphere was quite gay and it's possible I just may have been able to see a bit of my own collar-bone when I said to someone: "Well, dearie, remember, they can only communicate with words in grammatic sequence even though they be capable, as is everywhere supposed, of making non-verbal signals in order to initiate some sort of 'dirty-work' in the minds of those even more feeble, ignorant and class-ridden than themselves. To themselves it's just plop, plop, plop, word after word after word, piled tower-like upward in an ever mounting babble of incomprehensibility, absolutely un-disintegrated and un-annealed by the black heat of sleep or even the lesser mental ineptitude of logical disorientation, like so many chocolate bricks of Babylon. In a word, it's process, process, process," I concluded, in no way intending to insinuate anything arcane or culty.

All this must have been apropos of something said in conversation. I can't be expected to remember everything across this great a distance. Such a literate crowd, really, I could barely understand myself. And then, expanding my notion to include the movement of mind itself, I heard myself saying: "Without this they are quite helpless. They can't travel, inter-connect, digest their food, move their bowels, maintain an erect attitude. . . . It's total paralysis."

A hush settled over the room where I sat drinking a pink burgundy from a crystal goblet, the sort that crack on your teeth should you bite without thought. I failed, for some reason, to recognize the silence for one of embarrassment. How could they fail but be fascinated, I said to myself. I thought for a moment to speak again but Hung himself, my host, the millionaire Hong Kong industrialist, Harold J., quite a mensch, really, took my arm and whispered: «Dis Clist pidgin no brong ploper dis chop-stick dinner, my flinde, talkie-talk too maash!» His speech was so heavily accented as to be unintelligible if you weren't listening. Of course, I had been social-drinking and was somewhat heated. Everyone seemed so witty and such beautiful women. A table-mate, the luscious Miss Coy, was almost more than I could bear. And then I understood. Here in the East my discourse was taken as just so much first-world hoo-doo, of no more interest than the lives of the saints. So I took the cue from my host and let some others take center stage to speak of things which took their interest. I don't know why I mention it.

I merely wish to add that I have often thought, since my voyage to Hong Kong, since my beating and hospitalization, since my subsequent flight across the Pacific to sunny California and my current career in Hollywood, of what that poor, wretched, over-worked Roman domestic woman had said to me.

And please don't think this a funny book, make-believe or imaginary travelling. Or even composite boudoir farce. Although it be true that a certain tedium has played its part. Oh, you know what I mean, those slow things people do when you watch them, the annoyance of the inevitable that is taking me to my death, those small indications of future activity, the announcements of monotony to come, an advertised action fulfilled in each excruciating detail: the check-out girl with five small items and a slippery plastic bag; a man beginning to dial a number on the telephone: the commencement of a backward count at a given digit, absolutely determinate, ten, nine, eight, seven, etc. They have a saying in farm country and I just know you'll allow it here: about as pleasant as being corn-holed by the vet! No matter what sort of «attractive packaging» disguise it, no matter how removed one's «radio hook-up». Only a man who has been hurt as deeply as I and who has seen the fatherland so forsaken and justice so vilified can speak on an occasion such as this with words that are the blood of the heart and the essence of truth. But all this is yet to happen; it is not yet here at the tip of my tale.

Needless to say there were others, other travel-rats seeking some steerage to adventure, aboard our boat, the Hohenstauffen, a scheduled freighter carrying machinery and electronic hardware to the less industrialized corners of the world. Not that we were in any way at the helm. All the quarters were roughly equal, all of us staying in a class I would describe as «purser». Oh, I hope you didn't think I meant we were travelling third class and peeling potatoes with live chickens! I wouldn't do that to save my life. In fact, some of us were quite well off. I, however, have always been a man of moderate means. But I will say this much for myself, I have always done the very best with what I have been left. Which is a real American virtue and one of which I think we can all be proud. Call it individualism but we've got it.

We ate our meals together at the Captain's table in the officer's mess. A few took tea of chilly afternoons in a section of the lounge. And there was a bar there where those of us who did drank liquor. Not all were going all the way to Hong Kong but others aboard were to cruise the duration.

Our purser was an Anglo-Italic, Fred Summerhill by name. He was quite personable and given over to the sottish life. I have reason to believe he had been shanghaied. It was he who mixed so many of the drinks which were drunk and we all owe him for his silent and somewhat selfless service. There was a short fat man named Barker who looked like the violent type, someone who couldn't take a ribbing. I had nothing to do with him. Anyway, he «kept to himself», as they say, and debarked in Capetown. There was a degenerate young entrepreneur from Berlin who sought to recover from a nervous disorder right before our eyes. He never said a word and decided to stay in Bombay. And then there was Levis Chase with his pretty little girlfriend Mary-Gay. They were young and in love and would spoon forever on the poop. I could have watched them for hours.

Then there was Cayman, little more than a parvenu from Key Biscayne or Boca Raton, a man of perfectly deadly jocosity. Not that he was really old, fifty or fifty-five, the prime of life really. From the first day out he would hang on the bar and grumble at every decent remark: "Ha, ha, ha, that's a good one. Do you know any more funny stories." They, the Caymen, Ernest and his charming wife Nanette, were two who quite took my fancy at first. Actually it was Nanette who was of the two much the more active and attractive and out to wile the hours away. Being a «typical husband», he was more often than not the stick in the mud and the gin-soaked blanket. They had retired somewhat early and now travelled the world in search of mild curiosity and civilized personal adventure. That is what they told me and it seemed to be true. I took them to be a cut above the common lot. I thought they'd be sage and sober company on the swells. Little did I know there is little that is compelling in the everyday life of the drunken. I'll tell you right now it turned slightly ugly in the end. By the time we reached the Malay Peninsula it was all a bit fishy. It has all turned so sad and so desperate for so many. Nevertheless, we spent many a carefree hour on the rails, many a blind afternoon of seagulls, tumblers and giggling, watching the ever changing thrash and wash of wild-life left in our wake as we pushed through this latitude and that, such and such a current.

There is a funny story about Levis Chase and Mary-Gay. It seems they had a devil of a time a few days out for apparently he had forgotten his supply of prophylactic device in his rush to embark. And she wouldn't or couldn't use an «insect» or a «plunger» or whatever they call those things women insert for safety. He ran about the boat for days wildly trying to borrow or devise some easement as it were. You can imagine how palsied we were with mirth at our thoughts of his predicament.

But beyond these bits of broad farce I was bored witless and quite adrift in my psyche. I would lie awake nights in my cabin dreading the dreams I knew would follow my fall into lifeless sleep. There I would rest, stationary and prone, staring blankly at the darkened porthole, feeling cold and empty inside, listening to the slosh of water about our hull, clear as a sound effect. There would I lie while the water washed we sleeping sailors at our fitful snoozing, trying in idleness to recapture some of the mystery of the great adventure I had known as a younger man, the great adventure of life which had already shown me so much pain and sorrow, had revealed such an ugly slice of myself, my smallness, my aberrant ways, my willful lack of faith, an adventure through so much violence and death which had taken everything good and innocent and beautiful and ground it into the dust beneath my feet. And there it would stay until scuffed again by some unfriendly shoe.

And here I was headed for Hong Kong, fleshpot of the East, where life was relatively cheap and families slept ten and twelve to a bed. Oh, of course I was excited and nervous. Maybe even a little scared. And I imagine I was a little angry, strange as that may sound, for I had had none of these doubts in Rome. Nor even in Calabria. Coming up through the welded-steel superstructure of the ship, up through the grills and grates and slip-joints which held this old girl together, were the lyrics of a popular song. It came up from a shortwave in the stoke-hold where the crew hung their hammocks and did whatever it is crew does at this point in a voyage: something to the effect the singer was mean and twisted and his phone unlisted. Ah, the common folk, I'd think, and their simple lyric cantankerousness. I'd light another cigarette and file my nails to the quick. Then, at long last, I'd fall into a fitful slumber as a multicolored dawn broke on the water.

A few short hours later I'd spring awake, ready for another day. My heavy heart would perchance be lightened by the sight of another yellow sun. I'd make my toilet and rush to the dining room where Xing Ling, the cook, would stand poised with the porridge pot, about to throw the last of it down to the porpoise. In the nick of time I'd stay his hand and, with jovial cursing beneath his breath, he'd re-heat and serve it into my bowl piping hot. Then a waiter would bring it along with hot buttered toast, juice from the citrus group, a rasher of bacon or a speck of ham, a cut of cold smoked fish, a mess of scrambled eggs and all the hot coffee I could drink. I, needless to say, would dive in to my ears. Old Xing Ling would look over fondly and say: "Ha ha, he is a hungry man." And then he'd laugh. But one's appetite is always augmented by the sea air.

The dishwashers would be laughing too and slapping their thighs over that day's best joke. I must be honest about these people and admit every day's best joke had to do with the size of some man's cumbersome member and the comic atmosphere surrounding its insertion into the inferior world of the woman. You see, these people aren't like us and neither high nor low makes any distinction between subjects fit for conversation and those better left to the nether regions of remote imagination. Why, it's not unusual for the novice listener, in the hands of a clever raconteur, to find himself led along quite blindly by the silly, droll little recitation until suddenly, plop, plop, he'd find himself staring point blank into the contents of this or that person's chamber pot.   Not that I speak Chinese with any fluency whatsoever. Just what I've been able to pick up off the radio and from friends. I'm sure their language, as old and as venerable as it is, is just as much cattle-slobber as our own.

Oh, we had running water and indoor plumbing; don't think this vessel was some «Bombay stinker» or «Filipino ferry-boat» or something of that ilk. But these men were simple laborers from a cruder, earthier culture than our own, full of arcane rituals of sanitation, a weakened sense of the fecal taboo and, on the community level, longstanding sewer beds in dire need of ultra-modern septic engineering. This must be one of the things the United Nations is trying to accomplish. Why, I'm willing to bet some of those guys never even used a «flusher» until after they'd signed on this cruise. As children they were, no doubt, encouraged to «do it» in the winter wheat or the rape seed paddy where grand-dad at that moment was «haulin' oats», part and parcel of that sometimes deadly roulette, human fertilization. As you clearly must see, there are absolutely no secrets on the ships at sea.

In any case we became quite friendly. When we finally arrived in Hong Kong harbor and I descended the gangplank for the last time they, to a man, shouted from the stern: "Good-bye, Mr. Des." And then they laughed and slapped themselves. I pride myself on just this sort of human touch.

Back in the mess they began to smoke and play cards while they peeled their potatoes and diced their onions. I would relax at my table and smoke cigarettes over cup after cup of coffee, two sorely hurtful habits I have since entirely abandoned. It is in my heart always to issue the strictest warning to all young people, teenage girls in particular, to never, never pick up those deadly white coffin nails! I just know I could get through to them, to even the most abandoned.

From there I made my way to the pilot house where it seemed the Captain awaited me amidst numberless charts and globes and sextant-type of navigational tool. And there was a small but interesting collection of books there, all in strange miniature versions. Most seemed technical manuals, tables of vectors, conversions and isoscelations, rigging handbooks, celestial negotiation, boiler maintenance in Spanish. I found a Shakespeare the size of your pocket but it was in German. And an edition of the Cantos no bigger than an infant's rubber shoe. He must have had close relations of the first kind with one of those marvelous private printing families so active these days in Europe and New England. But then, maybe they belonged to the owners.

The Captain would offer me a chair and then take one himself at a lacquered driftwood coffee-table with a green glass cover. He was very polite. Too polite, some would say. Everything was bolted to the floor, of course, so that it wouldn't float away should the ship sink. He would begin a typical séance by pouring the musky dark tea into thick-walled mugs of white porcelain, old, thick-lipped cups you no longer find attractive, from a large, floral pot with his short, fat fingers. Then, after settling back into his chair and cradling his mug on his stomach he would begin to converse in the most formal pidgin I've ever heard. Obviously I've cleaned it up quite a bit. For example, out of the blue he'd ask me: "So, Mr. Desmond, in your country, history is but a construct?" Have you ever noticed how foreigners will do that, begin a chat on the most absurdly elevated level? It's because they don't really speak our language. I'd just begin to improvise and mumble: "Yes, it is invented as it passes with precious little regard for the function of this particular intellection let alone its adherence to the form of truth herself; in sum, short-sighted, self-serving and contentedly complacent, and in your country," I'd ask, because he was being so polite.

He'd arch his eyebrows one at a time and say: "You mean here on my big boat?" Then he'd laugh and begin thumbing through a magazine without bothering to pick it up off the glass-topped coffee-table and closer to his eyes. He'd thumb with a big open-armed gesture for me to see, stopping at some large color photo or a small black and white snap-shot. Perhaps he'd indicate with his index finger. He'd show me a picture of a hunchback, for instance, or a battle scene from some brush-fire war, a current event or a flip-book full of sheiks, presidents, bosomy starlets and half-naked accident victims. It was really quite random and I don't mind saying I did not get the point at the time. I, being as I am persistently if not belligerently lineal and pedestrian, would say in turn: "Well, all right, what about history here on your big boat?" He'd laugh again his silly laugh and say: "Oh, there is no history here, just location and climate, cruising speed, a clean deck and order down below." I'm paraphrasing of course. For though his pidgin was terse and lucid, it lacked standard grammar and pronunciation.

"Your log?" I'd ask.

"My log? You want to see it?" he'd respond cheerfully. He was nothing if not cheerful. Then he'd cross the room on his muscular little bow-legs and fetch me a leather bound volume neatly inscribed with an absolutely indecipherable character, something blocky and vaguely pictographic. His face would light with a completely innocent smile and he'd say: "You can't read this, can you? Hee, hee, hee, very few people can read this. But that's okay, it's just climate and location, cruising speed, wind velocity, order in the court, hee, hee, hee." I swear, it was idiot-city out there sometimes. Absolutely infuriating. But far be it from me to back-seat drive thirteen thousand tons of German machinery cutting through the water.

I'd accept another mug of murky tea and lay the leather-bound log on the table-top. I had only to consider the alternatives to my present interview in order to take my punishment like a man: watching the gulls dive for jetsam with Ernest and Nanette Cayman; attempting to help Levis Chase find some copulatory envelope in which to sheath his member. I could just imagine the scene in their stateroom. She'd be sprawled on her back, her legs raised and spread above her like eagle wings, her porcine little slit dripping and pulsing with the beat of her heart under her enormous breasts, rolling and sloshing about on her chest as our ship slashed into the crests of waves, her eager, twitching finger poised for selfish pleasure. And he, he'd be rummaging through his chest of drawers for a piece of goat rubber or veal appendix. I'm dead sure it was rather sad. I invited him into my stateroom one afternoon for sherry and said to him quite confidentially: "Look, Levis, old boy, why don't you just knock up the dear young thing and have done with it. I understand the medical facilities in Hong Kong are first-rate." His face registered disbelief so I went further. "What I mean is," I ventured, "why not go all the way. Or even better, why not dump your silly little «boy-dough» just inside the tradesman's entrance, as they say. Your normal, healthy volunteer can stand that sort of penetration without undo trauma. You know what I mean, her back door, the dirt track, the bread rack. Do you follow me at all?" I was fairly desperate to communicate anything at this point. I had worked myself into quite a slather. Well, he looked at me as if I were the queerest thing he had ever seen on this man's earth. He soon stopped coming by for sherry which was perfectly all right with me for, by that time, I was in it up to my ears with Miss Deborah Springman, a fellow passenger, and I had come to despise sherry.

So the Captain and I would sip from our mugs and settle quite peaceably into the rhythm of the sea. We slipped between England and France, slid past Spain and out of the North Atlantic into warmer waters off the west coast of Africa. This took a few days. But just think how difficult it would be in an airplane. In any case, we sailed and we sailed and left the bulk of Europe bobbing in our wake. There seems to be little for a Captain to do on a modern sailing vessel given a crew worth salt and a head of steam.

To pass the hours, I proffered the Captain some bits of my personal history, the sort of spontaneous anecdotal generosity one often encounters in a solitary voyageur. I remember relating the singularly droll tale of my first sexual encounter, thinking that he, as a man of the world and old naval hand, would enjoy its telling. I was but a boy of thirteen when my Uncle Louis took me to the whorehouse across the river from where he lived in Southern Ohio. He was the adopted son of my mother's mother's sister who had married a Mister Wilifred Leclerque from Terre Haute and lived with him on the outskirts of Newport, Ohio. Bewildering as it seems, Louis's adopted father somehow insinuated himself into the mainstream of middle-western wealth and the family has never slid from this elevated ground. My own father died at my low birth and left me the «little man» in our house of seven women.

En tout cas, there was a whorehouse across the river where I was ushered into the chamber of a young Kentucky woman not much older than myself but «born to trot» as they say down there. She then initiated me into the book of masculine knowledge, the pages of the mystery of which still leaf freely in the hoary recesses of my mind. She took my hands in her hands and put them on her breasts, just visible beneath her flimsy silk kimono, an island pajamas in the East. She then looked down on me with her large, moist and heavily-lidded eyes and said: "These are the fruits of the flesh for the up-keep of a hungry man," or something to that effect. She then bid me squeeze and fondle the cute little things with their hard, brown nubbins until my interest seemed to flag. At that time she un-zippered my fly and dropped my trousers over my knees. She put my soft and still-hooded «toy» in to her amazingly pliant and charmingly painted mouth where she sucked and chewed until, at long last, it «stood tall». It was the biggest little erection this lad had ever seen. Slipping the hood back off the bulb and holding its length firmly in both hands, she said: "This is your joy-stick." She lifted her nightie and revealed her lithe and naked torso. She lay back on her bed then and, bending her knees, showed me her moist and fleshy «plop box», mid-south patois for girly thing, under its filmy black shag. She cocked her head and drawled: "Y'all fly me home, okay?" I remember her words quite distinctly, for it was at that moment that I came off on her bedsheet and satin slippers. She cursed me then for soiling her linen and I believe Uncle Louis gave her extra money for the clean-up. On the way home he teased me for being a «screw-ball hot-shot» but that didn't bother me. I love her today with all the intensity of that boy so many years ago at the confluence of the Ohio and the Mississippi.

However, it was years before I gained the control necessary for adequate penetration and my full potential for pleasuring was not reached until I had myself circumcised at the age of twenty-eight. And let me just add, that with all my advantages, I still hold the sex education of grammar students to be of paramount importance in our Republic. I wished to indicate with this story that I have had relations with women of all walks of life, some from the very best segments of our society. And I have found several of them to be most intriguing. Of course the risk of disease is so great these days there is no doubt voluntary continence is a station on the road of success. And, as you see, I've been around and am most emphatically not a Johnny-born-yesterday.

Perhaps the Captain could grasp my point but at times he would seem to doze in his chair. He would wake with a start and turn a page in the magazine. He would thumb and mumble very sympathetically: "Ah, yes, very good, very good. Many stories, very bad." I don't believe that he quite understood that I was, in this situation, merely seeking to avoid the mundane negativity implicit in middle-class sensitivity, to by-pass this negativity in order to achieve as quickly and directly as possible a more profound cancellation of the mechanistic and the sour-mash schools of thought. But he was considerate if not comprehending and we got on famously.

When the Captain was called to other duties, as he occasionally was, to the navigation of a shoal, perhaps or to some ceremonial responsibility inherent in his captaincy, or to the settlement of a grievance from one of the crew (a mixed lot of waterfront third-worlders from the major deep-ports,) I'd amble away to the lounge, a well-windowed affair abaft. There I would find the Caymen, glasses in their hands, solid smiles across their lips. Old man Cayman rolled the liquid in his tumbler and mumbled "ha, ha, ha. . . ." Nanette would perhaps be perched upon the piano humming softly to herself some song of torchlight, stardust and dark wine. She was a dreadfully lonely and neurotic woman but quite successfully integrated into society. Ernest clapped my shoulder by way of greeting and breasted me yet again with another of his silly punning conundrums. At this point we were neither close nor involved the way we would eventually become. But relationships are so difficult to avoid in these days of avid tourism.

"Picture this," he'd begin, "picture this if you would." Then he'd pucker up like the man on the box of oatmeal, sputtering a bit in his effort to affect correct pronunciation. He'd twinkle in the eye at this point and nudge me in the ribs most unpleasantly. "Picture this," he'd begin again, "a black guy and a white guy were in a night-club with two Eastern babes, maybe one Okinawan and one Manchurian, okay, jay-naked save for solid lucite stiletto-heeled shoes and floor-length Russian sable coats with silver-fox trim." We'd have taken a table with a view of the sea while he continued his riddle. Obviously he'd been up the whole night through working on his set-piece, this little slag-heap of verbiage. How these people fancy themselves, especially when «under the influence». I'd steal a glance at Nanette, seeking any sort of solace or escape. She'd smile coyly and recross her legs. They were quite well preserved despite her crow's-feet. She dressed in a modern version of the pre-war style: abbreviated bee-hive below and yards of flounce on top.

Cayman continued then after an appreciative glance at Nanette's recrossing: "Now these guys in the night-club were the sort of men who'd cozy up to rich women, women who'd give anything for a good time. They'd pleasure them, if you know what I mean, show them a good time in exchange for favors, money, things like that. I don't know if you've ever run across this sort in your travels. You've been around, you must have seen them." He paused for a moment and put a finger to the corner of his eye.

"Well, anyway," he'd say, "these yellow babes were rich. They each had a roll of fifties in the pockets of their minks as thick as a widow's wrist, maybe a couple of grand each just for drinks and cabs and gratuities and suchlike. So, to make a long story short, a gun goes off in the middle of the dance floor where a mixed crowd is dancing to beat the band. We don't need to know who shoots it off. The white guy jumps up on his chair and the darky dives under the table. Now, what I want to know is, what made the jig go low?" He paused.

"Jig-go-low, get it?"

He would back away slightly and chuckle under his breath, more like a forced exhale, searching my face for a reaction. Then he'd make a move to chuck me on the upper arm but truncate the gesture in midair.

"That's all right," he claimed lamely, "it's a lousy joke anyway."

Really, he needn't have told me of its quality! It's just not the sort of story one would tell really educated people. And it's only in North America that the pun is seen as indicative of intelligence, culture and refinement. Puerile beyond belief is how I would describe it. But what was I to do? We were virtual prisoners on the high seas and it seemed as if forever. In actual fact it was only four February, nineteen seventy-nine.

I attempted to tidy up the conversation by saying: "Well, that may well be what you called them back in nineteen thirty-three but now-a-days we call them pimps." I did not intend my reference to their ages to be in the least pejorative. And given my feelings, I assure you, it was anything but.

"Pimp, oh my!" said Nanette, perking her head upon her smooth white shoulders. Her attention would decline should the conversation not be of interest.

"A hateful species, I agree," I said cheerfully, "but not beyond comprehension in our present day and age."

"That's it exactly," she said with meaning, leaning slightly across the table so as to seem closer to my thought. "You must be very bright. Were you well educated?"

I was somewhat taken aback by such a frankly personal question but admitted to having received a primary sort of schooling from small religious institutions in the northeast of the country.

"Oh, that's all right," said Cayman.

"Oh, no, we shan't hold that against you," added Nanette, "but do go on with what you were saying and complete your thought."

I could see as well as you they were baiting me with flattery in order to «bring me out» but I continued nonetheless to expound some of the unformed thoughts knocking about my brain at that moment.

"Well," I said crisply, "our pimp could be such a man as would prefer to live proudly with his substantial faults rather than meekly squeak by on his meagre virtues, thinking great vice exposed to the open air of public regard to be so much more attractive than modest virtue closeted and left to grow limp and turgid. . . ." Or something to that effect.

"Right, limp is no good," commented Cayman, though I doubt he had even bothered to follow my exposition.

"And turgid is terrible," added Nan.

We were sitting at a small, glass-topped cafe-table. Through its transparent surface I watched Nanette repeatedly cross her legs, exposing and re-exposing for just a flash the soft, white flesh of her inner thigh. Then she said: "What an exciting idea. And what fun to search out this hidden virtue in such a man. What a good deed that would be."

We were all quite still for several moments, sensing, perhaps, Nanette had more to say. Then she said in a girlish voice: " I remember I read a book in nineteen thirty-three. I remember a girl receives a telegram from her best but flippant girlfriend who was to marry a man named Burden and left a day early for the wedding. She's kidnapped off the platform by a bogus groom-to-be, in fact a golden-boy gone bad. Need I go further."

"Not really dear," Cayman cut in quickly. But it had no effect on Nanette. She seemed to be in something of a trance.

"He's really a wife killer who nabs the girl because she suspects his true character. They all get married in the end except the girlfriend. She seems to be taking the next boat for Europe to recover her spirits. It's really low, a mass of crude cliché and even cruder violence. But I must say I enjoyed it."

She smiled at me and I could see Cayman himself was modelling his face from dumb pleasure to a painful grimace with some rapidity. Unfortunately I was forced to leave the table at this point. I wanted to say, "take care lest he be all bad," but felt there was a grey exudation just beginning to ooze from my brow. Sheer imagination, I'm sure. I mean, I don't think anyone could see it. The grey exudation. I excused myself and went straight to my bunk. I slept for the next seventeen or eighteen hours and woke as the day broke sunny and bright through my porthole the next day.

We were sailing just off the coast of the Spanish Sahara which remained hidden beyond the curve of the earth. After breakfast the Captain said we would soon see land and a few moments later there it was, just above the horizon. My insides leapt at this first sight of Africa. Perhaps it was blackest Senegal about Dakar but it was hard to tell from our dim view of tree-clad hills. We kept this land in sight until we anchored off Monrovia, the first stop in our voyage.

3

Monrovia

From our anchorage behind the massive stone breakwater we saw the proud Liberian capital shimmering that evening as the sun went down behind us. This was our ship's port of registry and, as such, must have had special significance to each and every one of us aboard her. It appeared to be a busy little place but no Port of New York. A sultry breeze came off the land which is no surprise considering our latitude. Little reed dinghies vied with old red tugboats in a natty little competition for our attention. I thought perhaps the little brown boys aboard these boats would scuba for shiny coins and indeed threw quite a tidy sum of Italian lira into the wash. But this was all so much foolish generosity for later I was told the water be too deep and murky for diving. The Captain told me he had been in radio contact with a local dry-docker for, apparently, our vessel was in need of some repair. Somehow sea water was leaking into one of the forward holds even though our ship was double-hulled in sheets of steel. I had not seen the leak myself as it was below the water-line where cargo and crew were kept. The Captain said one of his men had awakened soaked in salt-water, an experience which had left him quite shaken and the superstitious crew itself on pins and needles. Our hatches had been battened and bulkheads sealed so we were in no immediate danger. The Captain further said that speedy and skillful repair was a key to success on the modern ocean. The old adage about stitches and nines came to my mind and I decided that there was no time like the present to fix it up. Not that I had that much influence with the Captain or had any real say in this business. I was not there in a decision-making capacity. The sea was calm and we made no contact with the natives that night.

I woke the next morning with the feeling I had escaped some cruel and unusual fate. It must have been something in my dreams which so harrowed me. Probably some freakish combination of tribal drums and nautical bells. What a shame to have reached my age and still not have one's nights to one's self, I thought, to have come this far to find, in fact, there is an odor to one's toe.

After my customary breakfast I was informed by Freddo, our purser, of an impending visit to the city. We had been granted a special dispensation by the Chief of Customs to pass the entire day ashore as a body. I thought at the time it had been granted as a favor to our Captain but have since discovered it to have been the first of many bribes paid by Cayman to have his way in the third world.

As soon as I reached the Captain's quarters I found we were to go ashore immediately in a special launch chartered for this occasion. A gaggle of us gathered amidships and waited in the rising sun while the launch came about and lines were belayed. Then with happy shouts of «all ashore» we scrambled down a catwalk into a small native «moto-boat» which ferried us to the shores of the dark continent.

On the docks huge, fat women, strangely postured and strangely gaited, moved with baskets of fruit and nuts balanced on their heads. Stevedores chanted powerful pagan work songs as they unloaded the steaming holds of huge, black freighters. At first we clustered on the quay like clumsy birds, but then we crossed the St. Paul and headed for the center of town. Ashmun Boulevard is quite a handsome thoroughfare.

We could see the Nimba Mountains in the distance as we climbed up the slight incline toward the beautiful antebellum City Hall. The men you see on the streets here are very handsome. They remind me so of the great dark-skinned actors we have in our own cinema back home. We moved for a while as a group. Quite a spectacle, I'm afraid. The natives gawked as if we were naked. Children giggled and hid behind their mama's skirts. Then as a body we all stopped and stood on the street corner under the hot African sun as if frozen in some foreign frame of mind.

The Captain, who had been tailing along behind us, excused himself at this point for a rendezvous with the dry-docker. I, with

several others of us in tow, headed straight for the nearest movie
theatre. I had correctly diagnosed our problem as one of orientation
and I find the cinema a «specific» when it comes to cases of incipient
culture shock. We hurried up Ashmun, took a right on Firestone and
there found the Loew's Luxor, a grand old film palace of the golden
age. What a hang-over!

They were showing propaganda movies that afternoon with
mixed casts of Europeans and Africans. What a relief to get in out of
the blinding sunlight. And it was air-conditioned. And both films were
in English, which is the official language here. What a stroke of luck!

The first film was called Smoke Scene and starred a local man
called John Boxer and a French girl named Josette Jacqueline, a
fetching little minx. They walked about town in a openly miscegenous
relationship until shot from ambush by a misguided Boer up from
the south. Many wept openly but I believe in saving my tears for
physiologic necessity such as dust on the iris. Whatever could they have
had in mind when they made this one?

The other film was called Camera Land and featured tourists who
come to Africa to hunt, two American marriages, young and mixed.
I can't believe they ever agreed to do something so freighted with
problem. Needless to say it made no sense whatsoever. But the sheer
art of that is not insignificant. Often I think it is the art of propaganda
herself, her muse, her ugly and phlegmatic muse. But jump into it they
did and I was embarrassed from word go. They meet in the deepest
darkest jungle and, after a spate of «honest» talk, start right in swapping
partners and tasting the dainties of intra-racial delight. Of course their
relationships are purely physical to begin with but later descend to love
and guilt and hypocrisy. The soft-core scenes are mildly interesting if
you go that way but I do find such phrases as «dark sausage», «brown
jug» and «blond roots» totally gratuitous and unnecessary, not to speak
of tasteless. The two whites stay in an hotel room to fornicate in
extremely painful and self-conscious positions whereas the «others» do
it quickly in the most inexplicable locale, for instance, in a public park
behind a tree.

Sprinkled into this kettle of adventure are interminable
conversations, such a cinematic short-cut. In order to conform to the

conventional morality of the town, the players would ceremoniously re-couple and meet to eat in the hotel dining room. It seems the black male was socialist and the white boy venture/capitalist. The black girl was amoral and cunning whereas the white was a slave to her passions. Can you believe it? John's wife, Joanny, would introduce a random element into the table-talk and then Mara, black Bob's beautiful blond bed-mate, would complain of a «latin buzz».   Then the two males, John and Bob, would wander off into the town for their perfectly tedious verbal intercourse. They were interviews, really, with the black expounding a theory of historical inevitability and the white spouting something which he eventually calls a system of technically precise good fortune. It was really quite droll at times. I have no idea what the people behind this film had in mind when they put the whole thing together. But like most other projects in showbiz, it probably had, au coeur, some detrimental sexual intrigue.

Brock Compton, a perfectly obnoxious fellow-traveller from Long Island who was bald as a bowling-ball and covered in herringbone, suddenly began shouting at the top of his lungs: "What do they think they're doing? Who do they think they are?" I swear he must have crawled up a tie-line in Bremerhaven! Just to be classed with that sort gives me dropsy. A real entertainment-junkie, it turns out. Cayman leaned over and stage-whispered: "Mr. Macy and Mr. Gimble." Everyone giggled until we were all quite silly for a hundred different reasons. And it was too much noise. All the real patrons wanted was more skin on the screen. Nanette sat next to me and repeatedly rubbed her knee against my thigh. I could have sworn she did it on purpose. It was most distracting.

Eventually they go on safari.   Mara begins to complain of her love dandy's brutal behavior against a background of growling lionry. Joanny bemoans chronic innocence and callow «lack of interest» on the part of John, who needed «time between sessions». Modern script-writers just don't understand the function of fear in everyday sexuality. I thought this would be the perfect spot to inject some totally brave female hormone into the flick, some fantasy «skirt-to-skirt», but apparently the producer thought otherwise. Even when the males walked off all alone into the bush with their guns, the women merely sat about the campfire drinking herb tea and bitched softly. Maybe there's some taboo.

Well then, meanwhile, out in the bush, push comes to shove and they are charged by a male hippopotamus, the African water-horse. Bob is blind-sided and dies in disbelief. John straggles back into camp with a bent barrel and tells a story so shaggy he becomes immediately and incontrovertibly suspect. Neither Mara nor Joanny seem to care in the least; perhaps this is the seed of a «real relationship». We leave them driving away with the crumpled black body on the roof-rack to seek some sort of modern justice and understanding in the post-colonial city, to deal with the law and the assurance companies. So much for realism. They also showed a short subject called The Complete Canine which I don't remember.

We ate an early dinner in the Chinese restaurant just across the street. The service was good but abrupt and the food adequate, though too highly dosed with meat-   tenderizer.   After dinner we went to a place, a brown-brick structure stuccoed over with ochre plaster. This was called a Transit Hall where we were to await transportation back to the ferry. We were served a mocha coffee in small earthenware cups by a group of young boys in khaki shorts. We sat on rough wooden benches just outside the door. The boys then stood behind us ready to serve our thirst.

The landscape was flat and dusty, a few plane trees the only relief. There were the mountains in the distance, of course, and the jungle in the valleys. But this plateau was flat and dusty from the foot-pad of people. Yet there stood in front of the Transit Hall five enormous rocks of some smooth, hard mineral substance. They were transported there from, of all places, Zanzibar. They might, in fact, have been meteorite. We were told they were there transported by a local tribal leader quite popular with the people, quite recently killed by the government police. The boys seemed quite upset and there came tears into their eyes, the eyes of several of those more sensitive among them, as they told this story in a strangely-shared sing-song shanty, staccato and up-beat. They spoke briefly of a scheme, a plot, something devilish, to make him «killable». That's the term they used. I meant to question the boys further but we were rapidly herded on to a taxi-bus for a bumpy and dusty ride back to the shuttle-skiff.

This sad story was touchingly told by these little boys. They were Mandingo boys, Muslims. They looked like good boys. Their parents had worked for peanuts on the Firestone Plantation, a million acres of good rubber jungle. They lived on a simple diet of rice, cassava, yams and okra, ceci beans and ground nuts. Oh, sure, it's easy to see how different we are. But isn't it better to stress the underlying unity, our common quest for happiness, even if these boys do turn saboteur. I'll go along with natural disaster, but many of our troubles are man-made, created by our own ignorance, greed and irresponsible action. I may not know how to fight it but I do know there is a direct confrontation with the universality of our predicament waiting for us somewhere down the pike.

These boys embodied, it seems to me, the noblest human qualities of honesty, sincerity and good heart. These simple virtues will never result from money or be produced by machines. Only the mind itself can produce these attitudes. This mental development is not easy nor can it be produced quickly. It requires brave and consistent adherence to truth even in the midst of dishonesty and competitive aggression. They must have come from loving homes. When we recognize the basic goodness in the outlook these boys shared, a true sense of compassion becomes possible and, eventually, a natural, non-commercial reality presents herself.

On board the skiff, Cayman made his way to my side where I huddled beneath the helmsman's rudder. He moved alongside a rower and said: "Look, forget the black guy and the white guy. Then say the Chinese girls are Egyptians or Lebanese or anything but keep the gunshot. So now the story is there's two leather-necks and an army guy, still bar-boys but crack soldiers, sitting in a night-club with the two new babes, big tits, wide hips, real grooves. Bang, the gun goes off, the marines jump up on top of the table, the army guy hits the deck. And so now the punch line goes: "So why'd the G.I. go low?"

He paused for a moment to assess my reaction. Well, he got none from me, I assure you. Then he said, somewhat wistfully: "Dive under the table? Is that better? Never mind. I guess you'd have to write it out and no one would ever do that." Sometimes I think the pathetic old gentleman was trying, in his own twisted way, to communicate with me. But I doubt it.

Perhaps my forced smile was a trifle too warm and understanding for the next thing I knew he was telling me how the buffalo still ruled the great mid-western prairie, though they were stiffer now with joint disease. Hundreds will die in a harsh winter. He told me they no longer ran in herds; they were mostly solitaires living in wood. Can you imagine, he said they lived in wood-lined burrows and watched the news on TV. Then his little wife came up out of the dark and blathered how fish had crawled up out of the Atlantic, up on our pilgrim shores, those self-same hordes of virgin cod our forefathers saw and beat to death with sticks when first they crossed the great water which separated our country from civilized life. She went on about the violent life of birds and the brand new crop on Peter Cooper's New Amsterdam farm, how a fat woman can imitate a mail-box. She said she was attempting some point of absolute immutability. My, they were strange. I had had no idea they were quite so loony. And they were impossible to escape once they began in earnest.

I experienced an attack of violent nausea and vomited my dinner off the stern of the skiff into the sea-green water. The helmsman, a handsome older man, looked askance but the Caymen gave over their flotsamous gab in favor of the more immediate comfort of a cold compress, a snatch of Nanette's slip torn from under her skirt and applied to my brow.

As it turned out my skiff-board discomfiture signalled some graver illness, bespoke as well by my ghostly color and shrivelling flesh. I practically lost consciousness, falling back into Nanette Cayman's lap and listening to the regular cadence of the rowers' labor, the regular dip, pull, lift and skim of their oars in the water. I meant to ask why we were not motorized but could hardly lift my head to inquire. I assume it was to save a few piddling jugs of gasoline.

Several of the brawny rowers gingerly hoisted me aboard when finally we reached our ship. In a great to-do of whispers and shouts I was taken to my stateroom on a make-shift pallet. There Nanette stripped me of my clothing and bathed me in cool water until I fell off into a fitful sleep. I was raving, she told me later, about all sorts of animals, a common subject in dreams, about chickens, pigs and snakes and long corridors of incarcerated females, criminally insane. I remember her still, her smell, her touch, her presence, just as dawn was breaking in, whispering into my ear and running a cool terry about my torso.

Perhaps in that long night of fever and vomiting I gave her some window into the nightmare which haunts me, the charnel-house of my private knowledge where the very tissues of my physical being struggled to survive. She sang a little snatch of song in my ear and then I fell off into a somewhat more peaceful sleep. I woke the next day trying to find the words by which to thank her. And for what, I asked myself!

The sad truth of the matter was that I was a tortured poor soul on the very brink of instability. And there is nothing more comforting than a cool rag for the near mad. Oh, I don't worry about going crazy anymore; I know I'd remember enough to make other arrangements. But images of my previous life, my wild youth as an unqualified wastrel, innumerable imagined injustices and presumed slights coursed through my tattered rag-bag brain like a liquid formed from mustard seeds!

What fools we mortals be, I thought. Perhaps she had noticed some flaw in my form during our enforced intimacy, some small blotch in my make-up which she might inadvertently blow up into malicious gossip. I am less than perfect, after all. I felt compelled, within reason and as an intelligent being, to explain everything, even snips glimpsed in transpiration, to any other such intelligent being who should happen to perceive them, if only to prevent misunderstanding. Beyond that I felt perfectly covered and envisioned no special effort of dissimulation vis-à-vis Nanette. The very notion she might «have the goods» on me was the furthest thing from my mind.

After breakfasting as usual and seeking out my accustomed meeting with the Captain, and having found him to be otherwise occupied with what repairs were possible to our ship, I searched for Nanette but found she had already gone ashore with Cayman to procure woven baskets or whatever other native curios she and he could locate. They were avid consumers. No event of moment went by without some memorial purchase.

No, I don't think of my indisposition as representing in any manner the very first signs of a tell-tale ship-board relationship. It is just that this sudden uncustomary sequence of events jarred my frazzled equilibrium and left me in a terrible state. I retired directly to my room where I wiled away her hours ashore smoking and staring out my porthole. But then, suddenly my teeth would clench and my hands would convulsively clutch at the bed coverings. I was terrified. I felt an innocent though deadly force of nature was seeking vengeance on me for some imagined crime, some human misstep, something crazy escaped from the fate of my friends back in the states, from Winnwood, scene of all those terrible things which shall forever go unmentioned.. I had become quite distracted from my thoughts of «the tale written in smoke» by the rigors of travel and such droll company, but now it returned with savage vigor.

Such then is the power of sufficient metaphor to hold you and mold you and ultimately do you down and treat you unfairly. It's amazing the ramifications aren't more extensive and profound. But then when you think about it, perhaps they are.

4

Xtian Host

To the man at sea the horizon appears a perfect circle but on land it bumps up due to topographic irregularities. By the time we reached Africa I had forgotten just how irregular it could be. In Rome, I seemed always to be in a valley looking up at steeples or on a bluff looking down on churches. Then I was on a train in the winter which is a rather extreme lack of perspective. Even with electric light it is a disordered way of looking at things, so framed and mono-dimensional. Then there were the various hotels, the North Sea docks, the large German workers, and at last aboard the boat. We sailed and we sailed until I found myself at the Transit House, flat yellow dust at my feet, savanna planted plateau in the middle distance and mountains on the horizon. And at this point in the story I am back on the boat staring out the porthole at the perfect circle of horizon.

During this time I met several interesting people. One was a ship's Captain of indeterminate Eastern ancestry, little more than a slave to his line and his log. Two others were Ernest and Nanette Cayman, retired-capital types. In a moment I shall speak of a certain Miss Springman and a gentleman of the cloth who drew me from my «study» and into another tawdry bout of active negativity. Our boat was anchored in the harbor at Monrovia. We were headed for Hong Kong. While travelling I experienced great mental anguish which I trust is not too, too transparent. I felt I was fleeing some extra-ordinary fate awaiting me in my native land. Yet I continuously displayed all the tell-tale signs of home-sickness. Well, I freely admit that experience has never been my strong suit.

Oh, where do people go in this small world? Where could we even begin to hide. Myself, I can't disappear for an instant even though it be my fondest desire. My perception remains a constant and sequential hell peopled on an endless tape stretched off into the measureable distance and curving over the horizon, that self-same perfectly absurd shared illusion chez nous. (Any Captain on any vessel sailing any of the seven seas will tell you the same story.) Now a different sort of a fellow may have sought some relief from such a prison of consciousness in sexual excess or drug abuse, some obsessive behavior, a twitch perhaps, roaming hands or a tic, a binding fetish, anything to escape this continuous drone of neural notification that is such a characteristic of the real world. But my road is not such a road.

With my new-found friends, the Caymen, ashore purchasing native artifact, I was left to my own device aboard the boat and fell easy prey to all manner of fellow passenger. There was a cleric there, a meaty sort of fellow with backward collar, named Murchison. He was in his late forties or his early fifties. It's so hard to tell with a man of cloth. Anyway, he was a real spook and, I suspect, in secret, a «torch». That is, I suspicioned him a closet-arsonist, not that I had a scrap of evidence. And not a word of my suspicions did I breath to a soul aboard. I'm sure he lived in constant fear he would wake one morning with his faith in tatters and some dim reflection of his shenanigans in the dailies. And don't think they don't fight back, that sort. More than once he'd breasted me in some brutal exchange of language.

Miss Deborah Springman was another such. She was the serious young lady on board the boat. What a horror. And thick as a thief with the reform pastor. One day she'd take canvas and easel to the tip of the bow and pose with her bristling little brush for all who wished to ogle her, clad only in the scantiest of South Pacific bikini. And they thought themselves so moral. Well, the possibility for sin seemed endless to me.

Needless to say I was very, very careful when it came to my dealings with the both of them. For all I knew they were «unwittings» or professional entrappers or both. So many were in those troubled times. They both believed, for obscure reasons known best to those who actually profess the Xtian fellowship, that, if they, by any chance, found me alone and unoccupied, I must wish, out of some primordial necessity, to take them on in an ersatz emotional partnership and tote them about in a disgusting dependency relationship like so much leather luggage. Or worse! In the case of Miss Springman there was no doubt she wished in the depths of her mind to engage me in one or more of the infinite varieties of erotic intimacy. I tried to keep a moderate and reasoned distance from the good girl but when I realized her fantasy of our encounter perhaps involved the manipulation of fecal debris, today's most common degeneracy, I just about flipped my lid. Can't you just imagine me pushing her «black apples» about those rolling decks in a deadly game of scatological shuffleboard! It's just a good thing for her she never asked me to perform my «palsied little waltz» in her bed-pan. I would have given her an ear full. And if I'm any judge of character she probably had me footnoted for sheet of saranwrap and plastic flat-ware. Little did they know how distasteful I found their company.

Now I know that nothing is important enough to keep a secret. (No matter how hard one try. As I said to Rory as he lay dying in that Hong Kong tea-house: "My darling Rory, what do you want, just another showbiz funeral, a regular «finnegan's wake»?" Of course, I was really bawling my eyes out but I wouldn't let him see it for all the stew in China.) Well, Deborah was, naturally enough, taking her virginal brush with egocentric incest to an early grave, sad as it seems. I don't want to go into it here, no more than to sketch it in the boldest strokes: the Vienna triangel. It seems mom wouldn't «put out» and pop didn't want to break the law and go with an «illegal», so the child suffered. An absolute fantasy in this sort of situation, I assure you. Nothing more, nothing less. Oh, woe to the selfish Hausfrau! But why carp, I always say. And the good cleric, it seems, just couldn't keep it in his pants. His apostolic turkey's neck, that is. It has always been thus and so with this churchy type. All manner of perfectly ordinary, perfectly nice, well-mannered and well-preserved, attractive and virtuous middle-class lady has fallen to the carpet upon hearing his latest sermon of Sunday-morning potency. He'd worked the Dearborn area of Michigan in his youth until he drank his way to the Los Angeles area. Hollywood took him to her bosom but, at some critical juncture, he seems to have fallen short of her hopes for him. Hence he was sent on this long vacation with a side order of missionary activity. May the good lord have mercy on the infidel! He finally disappeared in a cloud of circumstance outside a cafe after we had docked on the Island of Bali.

I put it all down to the intoxication of his faith. Listening to this man ramble I remembered just how autocratic and godless monotheism could be, in fact had always been, especially in its messianic and evangelical modes, religion's juvenilia. Because, of course, he wasn't speaking merely for himself as an individual, but, I am sure, spoke as a real and true representative member of all Xtian sects and creeds everywhere professed. Even more, I feel he spoke for all one-godded people the world over.

Oh, these preachers can't help themselves when they meet liberal agnostic free-thinkers such as myself. He would approach me where I sat on my chaisse-longue with, say, Gibbon or Virgil or Dante or Plato, say I'd been once more re-reading "The Symposium" or another of the perennial favorites, say it were a more modern classic, say Kierkegaard or Tsao Hsueh-Chin or the later Isherwood, and begin his spiel, shifting his weight from heel to toe, toe to heel, foot to foot and back again. I don't know what he could possibly have hoped to accomplish with this purely physical maneuver. After all, the only issue between «us», on any meaningful level, was the very life of the mind herself. Well, I'll admit I am less than blameless. I stuck it to the old boy more than once, to the hilt of my powers of rational thought. For, as we well know, «freedom of religion» is a two-way street.

"Consider an alternative," I'd say, "much in the mode of the noble Hindoo savage. Or the lowest Toltec, Aztec or Inca stone-mason on the shores of Lago Titicaca or at work on Cuzco, that "uniformed one-storied city in worked-stone," unlimited in his possibilities for a hopeful fate, rich in the fruit of his function itself. It's just so obvious monotheism and its obverse only serve the central state and never the differentiated individual."

"Or think on the model of polar diffraction," I'd adventure, "the way the poles diffract energy, E, for instance, under the heat of the night-time sun and the pressure of a globe pining for a «big bang», say MC, the face of god become manifest, clearly appearing to those attuned to the beauty of these light waves under spells of fatigue and disorientation when fear is forgotten for an instant or perceived in stupor or intoxication or the pernicious influence of repeating decimal or syncopation's inducement to swoon or the spiral cascade of a garden hose or the strobbing of a double tinkler or some half forgotten hammer blow to the head or neck or chops, just by way of instance." Oh, wasn't I just drunk with myself when I said that. Really, I was so distracted I hardly said what I said.

He'd counter me then with some piece of sacral misinformation, some tidbit of pathos concerning the function of a ministerial busy-body in the wretchedness which surrounds us, something akin to: «He would have died on a bench in the park had I not drug him into the rector's cellar to expire.»

I mean, really, how pretentious. And to think they preach this gibberish. My anger was tapped by this nth degree of pomposity and I'll admit to battering him about his theological front. "«I am the Lord»," I said, "«thy God», we are forced to say, is merely the feeble rally-cry of a desperate and lonely desert chieftain, hell bent on sexual domination, cursing in advance the frightful earth on which he stood in fear, dessicate and infecund." I'm sick of these imitation adults dressed in sports clothing, weekend gear, treating thought as a full-time hobby. I mean, I love the passive and leisurely thought of the middle class, but such indulgence inevitably leads to sexual possession.

I'm not one to brag but by this time the man was in a wretched state and I had yet to square my argument. Not that I am in any way proud of having caused his wretchedness because I don't think I did. But I do quite fancy myself in logical discourse. Perhaps I realized my goading and gibing had been too «flesh-biting» and withering for the old man so I turned my interrogative upon Miss Springman who sat beside him like a swami on his face.

I barely had time to say, "picture if you would a Xtian host on the threshold of great carnage and the vagaries of one-eyed blood-lust", when she flared up and accused me of being an impotent buffoon bandying phrases and mixing metaphors to the detriment of organized religion and to the personal pain of a very sweet, very pious man who, if he were not able to help a body, would never cause him harm. Well, it was certainly no concern of mine that this semi-sainted prelate grasped at any opportunity afforded to lead by self-appointment certain sad souls through this our little club-med of disenchantment. Then she called me selfish and obstructionist and, to add slander to insult, something only a mother could love. Well, I sorely wanted to leap to my feet shouting «point-of-order» but merely gripped my flat-wear more tightly and held my tongue.

Furthermore, she continued, she was not my mother nor did she wish to be. She was quite right, of course, but I thought the statement of it rather gratuitous. She appeared before me, she said, as an ordinary American girl seeking only personal salvation and intellectual stimulation. Well, I could hardly keep from giggling when she dragged out that clinker. She had no interest in my sort of negativity, she claimed, and if I chose to «get physical» she would immediately call the purser who, she was sure, had my number. Well, she was wrong about that. He didn't care what I did.

We all remained silent for a moment and then I said: "I deplore this tendency on the part of the children of wealthy people to invest authority in ticket-takers. Not that the purser is not a fine gentleman and a personal friend," I declared, "but I will not have him waved about above my head as if he were a club." This conversation took place, you may remember, in the harbor at Monrovia, full of ships whistling and tooting, while awaiting necessary repair to our prow. The Captain himself returned shortly after we had finished with each other. He called us together in the dining room, the Caymen had returned on the same punt, and announced that for some strange reason which he was at a loss to explain we would not be able to obtain the mechanical and technical services which we so urgently required here in Liberia and were therefore forced by circumstances to set sail post-haste for Capetown where he fervently hoped we would get what we wanted.

But before the Captain returned and made this announcement I summoned some energies from my small reserve and concluded my argument with that opiated pair huddled in a darkening corner of the ship's lounge like dead powder puffs.

"Let's face it," I said without undue malice, "the early proto-Xtians, your forbearers, pre-Constantineans, they weren't actually persecuted, thrown to the lions and dismembered, tortured and molested in the way that we read about in fairy books. Oh, there were those who got themselves thrown to lions, of course; your average Roman loved a blood sport, a savage game of skill and endurance pitting man against man and man against beast and even beast against man if necessary to change a critical vote in the forum. Who doesn't. And, naturally enough, some of the self-same poor and victimized rubes just happened to be proto-Xtians. The important point to keep in mind is that these blood-sports only accidentally involved the «seeds» of these past-time fanatico-religionists. Isn't it just as crucial to give unto Caesar at least half the dust beneath his tawny sandal? And let's face it. They weren't all that innocent. They were all, in some subtle way or another, opposed to the imperial notion of, what shall I say, secular statehood? Not to speak of godless empire. Let us not mince words. We can suppose this to be true of these people as it was certainly true of the followers of the first Jesus of Nazareth. It was his hench-man, we are led to believe, who flipped the original two-headed coin. So it seems to me grossly inaccurate to describe the sanguine pass-times of the Roman public as an organized persecution of a particular people with sectarian tendency. And anyway," I added, "I have it on the best authority those burrows of theirs weren't the only dirt works they engineered."

"And," I concluded, just to put a tad of yeast into the sticky brew, "all they really had for sale were the hearsay recitations of an overweight Palestinian youth." They glared at me balefully but as they were more or less silent I considered the issue closed. Only later did I feel a trifle guilty at what I had done and then only after this same Deborah had forced me, in my rooms in Hong Kong, to pay the price of my weakness. But having sufficiently indicated my good intentions I felt no further call to reform my behavior.

We hoisted anchor on the evening of that same day and sailed out of the harbor we had so recently entered. It seemed a bit strange to be leaving so suddenly, rather Arab-folding-his-tent like, like thieves in the night, and silently slipping away. Of course there were no coast-guard watch-men and we were as free as the birds to come and go as we pleased but I felt it strange somehow. I had hoped for another day ashore to chat up the natives and gather tourist type information but, alas, it was not to be. The Caymen had procured a whole lot of good stuff, masks made of real rubber, the head of Vasco de Gama done in bone, some jars of pickled nursehound and dogfish, local delicacies. We plotted a southerly course. It began to rain so we were all confined to interior spaces.

5

Social Mechanics

It was a sad crew steaming out of the harbor that night, disheartened by the inability or callous unwillingness of the local iron-workers to accomplish our repairs. Eventually, however, this turn of events brought us all closer together both for better and for worse.

We were approaching the equator now, something I had never done before, sailing just off the continental shelf at the bottom of the slope. Such a sad coast, so much jungle. Who knows what «witches» have cast unlucky spells on those trees, have spun that mist in which the gulls wheel endlessly, have troubled the free spirits in the shrubbery, what aunts and uncles of what «gods» whizzed round those distant snow-capped mountain peaks. Even an «infra-red» photo from a «space-shot» would reveal mysterious patches of murky purple heat in those mountain breeches, perhaps systematizing this piece of anarchist real estate for the development of a valuable mineral slick.

We hoped to reach Capetown by the end of the week but all feared we would grind to a halt right here broken down and becalmed on a foreign and hostile patch of water. Or worse, be taken in a storm with the boilers cold, the screws unspinning. There is no ship so sturdy, so subtly engineered for balance between rigidity and flex, that it cannot be snapped in two amidships or swamped with killer waves as it flounders helpless, unable to face the evil blast. Or driven aground on a shoal to capsize in shallow water on sharp rocks and be beaten into fragments by towering surf.

We took to wearing our Mae Wests everywhere, to breakfast, to lunch, to dinner, to bed. Tensions were heightened almost to the breaking point. Some sought relief in alcohol, others in native hemp, some in transcendental alienation, many in sexual promiscuity. More of which in a moment. The Captain attempted to reassure us in a combination of mime and pidgin, a factor which increased anxiety and drove some of the less stable to the very edge of panic behavior. He would clutch his throat and hold his nose up high, as if out of the water, pant and gag and say: "No worry too much, no sinky tonight, go Davy Jones Locker." Then he would laugh his silly high pitched laugh as the women's knees parted and the men stepped to the bar.

I was going to tell you in lurid detail of the sexual events which took place those nights when we all feared the end was near but have decided to avoid the subject as distracting and as marring a generally higher tone attempted herein. Suffice it to say sexual excess became, overnight, the rule rather than the exception and the Master of Novelty was at the helm.

Our Captain remained disturbed by something which had transpired while in port at Monrovia and seemed to emerge rather unwillingly from his more private quarters. He remained aloof from us for several days. I wondered for a time what could be the cause of this strange behavior in an essentially easy-going and imperturbable man such as the Captain was. I eventually thought he had suffered some racial slur though I assure you I have no concrete notion of his experience. Perhaps it was just an unlucky combination of words passed within his earshot. When I was finally able to speak with him several days later he was quite recovered from whatever real or imagined event had affected him. In any case, he was most inarticulate. Perhaps he was more worried than he seemed about our little floating home-away-from-home.

Well, I was depressed, to say the least. But, and thank god in his high heaven for this, I had a good book by G.G. Coulton which I read to wile away a few of those tedious nautical hours. He said: "When we realize that here is a subject on which every man must be more or less prejudiced (unless he be trying to get through life without any even approximately clear working theory of life in his head), then we can attach far less importance to a man's prejudices, which are more or less inevitable, than to his attempts at disguise, which are unnecessary."

Mary-Gay Cumberland, you remember, the girlfriend, came to me the very next night dressed only in mid-thigh laced-silk stockings held up by very dainty colored garters and a little tasteful Hollywood bra under her terry robe. Any old negligée is so much more sensible for a girl than useless gym shorts, provocative or not. I say this for she would work out in the spa and then stop by chat, always talking some nonsense about «wanting company». I'm not «girl-crazy» like some I've known but was, of course, sympathetic. As always, the conversation came round to her troubles. She complained quite cheerfully about this and that in her life: her complexion, the selection of magazines in the commissary, the «conceitedness» of Deborah Springman, how «weird» the Captain was, how her older brothers had tormented her when she was a child. Of Levis, her boy-friend, and his inability to bring either the dear child or himself to any sense of bestial satiety. Actually she seemed to sense the potential for a primitive bliss which she feared was somewhat lacking from her own sensory menu. Not that I in any way presented myself as a specialist. God knows I'm not. Oh, I know the major theoretical works and have some rudimentary clinical experience, but little actual practice in the field.

Well, anyway, it seems Levis would get enormously tumescent, as red as a large dog, and parade his hardware about their small stateroom which was only slightly larger than mine. She led me down there by the hand after consuming almost all that was left of my selection of Spanish sherries, giggling like the little silly she could become. They were just down the hall. And I don't approve of this noise-making in the corridors when others are trying to sleep, just minding their own business in their own little cubby-holes. I know for certain that several such incidents had been reported to the purser by the various wet-blankets on board. But I smoothed them right over with my usual mix of suave assurance and tact. It was not for nothing I was known on board as the peacemaker.

There lay Levis, sprawled on their mussy bed in a drunken stupor, quite larger than life and obviously in pain, moaning and groaning and seeming to clutch at himself pathetically in the truncated gestural grammar of the blotto. I'm not going to claim there wasn't a factor of blur in so much of what was done during those days of fear. Mary-Gay fell on the bed then and looked up at me so beseechingly with those beautiful blue eyes of hers I ask myself now if anyone could have refused her request, as whimsical as it was. I mean any ordinary person with normal moral equipment. And wouldn't I be guilty of a callous deception did I not tell you precisely what did transpire?

Well, I'm only going to say Levis finally achieved «relief» of some sort. But, my lord, at what a price. Afterwards he and I had a long talk and worked a lot of the kinks out of a troublesome relationship for he arrived angry and embarrassed and abrupt the next morning at breakfast and that didn't look good. But I think that now is probably no time to start griping about idiocyncracies of personality, about who can give as good as they get. It is most certainly not the sort of behavior I would have expected from him, having regarded a few of his antics from the night before. He didn't seem to care what I did to his «darling's precious» that night. I mean, he wasn't keeping Victoria's secret to himself at all, rather was he rubbing my face in it. But Mary-Gay proved herself to be the selfless and generous person I have always thought her to be. In her role as hostess she saw to it that each of us felt himself to be both clever and welcome. And this is no small accomplishment. It is so difficult to find the right «topic of conversation» in mixed company. One always seems to be groping in the dark, seeking some grounding in the «common denominator».

In any case, once one has actually witnessed first-hand the intimate rippling force which lies sleeping within a young lady of her character's well-springs, there is a bond forged which survives any amount of idle slander and generic gossip. Let them talk till they turn blue in the face. I have nothing to hide and could stand naked before my maker even today. On this, and all other confidential questions, my lips are sealed forever. She appeared at breakfast the next day quite radiantly happy and seemingly in good health. He, as was mentioned, had an attitude problem which was causing him to sit apart and say the most ridiculous things to Miss Springman, etc. So I feel I was justified in doing them a good turn. Of course certain types will say, as they always do, that I'm just «jerking-off the dogs», but I don't care. We remained quite close for the better part of the journey. Mary-Gay and I never again did mention our adventure into social mechanics. But it's not surprising as we were so totally cut off from normal intercourse, being a ship at sea.

There is only one other incident I will mention in passing. And in truth it is much less an incident than a trifling episode in my ongoing tussles with Nanette. Some people just hit it off, no matter how wrong headed it may be, and then want to sweep it under the rug when they get back from the convention or the cruise or whatever. This isn't right! These are the vital sign and nothing, virtue and reputation or an old man's money, should come before them. We all know the tale of the twentieth century, the young wife, the drifting «floater» in blue-jeans perched on the fender of a hay rake, the innocent jug of lemonade, the steaming August afternoon, the generations of boredom, the casual caress of his buttocks. . . . This drama need not be sketched to its fulfillment on the spreading acres of violated domesticity and the surging fluids of random travel, as tell-tale an error as Thursday the thirty-second. Suffice it to say Nanette came to visit me late one night, coy, curious and in search of what she called a «favor». She knocked softly on the door. They all knew I couldn't sleep. I threw the bolt and there she stood, for all the world like a little bird up on tiptoes.

"Why, Nanette, whatever do you want," I asked, incredulous to see her before me in heavy mascara and a sable cowl. Something about face creams. This woman was such a case of impeccable vanity. And she would do absolutely anything to save herself a wrinkle. And I mean anything.

I showed her what tonics and lotions I had arrayed on my make-up table. It wasn't really all that generous a selection but then liquid is so heavy for a traveller to carry. She sniffed at this jar and that, aloofly denigrating all the commercial preparations. I think this is carrying snootiness too far. Many brands currently available are more than good enough for her face or arm or torso or flank as well as anybody else's. But by her silence you could see she always thought nothing good enough for herself.

Then she began speaking of a «secret formula», druidy mumbo-jumbo about turning hand-cream to face-cream at the open end of the arching rod of the slippery elm shoot, something that magically appears in the bottom of your wash basin early in the morning. I was dressed in my best silk dressing gown, one that hung in perfect folds right down to the middle of my knee. She wasn't at all good looking. Quite a hag, really. Oh, not that she didn't have that absent surface attraction which is so common in younger women and so successfully mimicked by desperate women in their middle-ages. She hummed a little tune then while she continued her inspection. I stood there a little mortified for her and the hour of the night. Not that I had anything else to do. But I certainly didn't want to be compromised into companionship.

Suddenly I saw her staring at me in the mirror and she said with some aggravation that in her memory we had come to some understanding over dinner and that I seemed completely amnesiac. I, naturally, remembered nothing from our dinner save loose talk and my normal wit. But amnesiac I was not.

"That isn't what you want, then," she asked with a totally false air of assumption. I didn't, at this point, wish her to be angry with me. But I found myself frozen in her glare and actually unable to move. It was most disconcerting. Perhaps it was just that I was really quite stripped emotionally and absolutely too vulnerable to risk any bold or clumsy movement. I guess she could have killed me in such a helpless moment but not even Nanette was that reckless. Though maybe she just didn't have the nerve. It's just a thought I have in retrospect. There wasn't really murder in the air. We were just discussing moisturizers.

She told me later that this treatment properly procured and applied and left on the skin for twenty-four to thirty-six hours can save a person ten years of painful, disfiguring and unkind aging. She offered me money but I told her quite simply of my independent wealth and left it at that without even bothering to go into the details of her misconception.

I know this may sound dreadful but it's really not that bad. I didn't mind her being selfish. And there are worse people in this cold, cruel world. And even if she had done something wrong, I would have forgiven her. After all, she wasn't a bore like her dreadful husband. Him! I wouldn't give him the time of day. We chatted a bit about art and politics and then she left with a «some other time then» thrown over her shoulder. That was just to cover her retreat all the way back to the larger stateroom she shared with Cayman on a much better deck. I certainly had shown her she couldn't push me around and have her way with me. And it was to stand me in good stead for the rest of our acquaintance.

This is but a small fraction of the total number of such incidents which took place during those torrid times with their associated fear of death by drowning. I half blame the Captain for this callous sexuality which I feel he helped bring on with his dumb show of watery death. But, good golly, people go through this sort of thing all the time. And I'm just happy no one was hurt by it all. So often today people are hurt so badly by sex and all its associated vainglorious pomp and ceremony. And there's love-sickness. Then nobody's happy and more often than not some pin-head goes berserker with a car and a secretary and that's it, they call in the hostage negotiators and the men with earphones and high-powered rifles. So I long ago decided one in the hand is worth two in the bush.

6

Radio War

Miss Springman came by my table at lunch the very next day and said, without any provocation at all: "Look, Desmond, or whatever your name is, I don't know who you are and I don't know who you think you are and I don't care but the walls are thin between these cabins so I know what you're up to, what you do and with whom you do it when you're up all night claiming you can't sleep." I concluded two things from what she said: 1) her cabin abutted mine on the other corridor and 2) she had been listening to and remembering my table-talk.

She interrupted herself at this point to lean in quite close to my face. So close, in fact, I half feared an attack. I was eating a fish, one of the deck hands whom I had befriended had caught it off the fo'c's'le just that morning, and I remember quite accidentally breathing the smell of it into her nostrils as she approached. She backed off slightly and then continued her tirade.

"Don't try anything like that with me, you understand, you dirty bum. I've got your number. You're idle and bored and you think you can fiddle with people just like a car radio. Well, try it with me and you'll fry, buster, I warn you. I don't forgive and I don't forget."

It was terrible to hear her driven to such extremity of hard feeling against me. And she spoke with that charming flat tonality of the simple folk of America, that coy and fetching way they articulate in their pathetic little attempts at communication, saying «weedone» when they mean in standard English «we don't own» or some other such indecipherable inanity, then laughing that hideous laugh they laugh like so much leisure pork in pig-tails.

And right away I started thinking she had said: "I don't defecate and I don't fatigue." But of course she hadn't; I just heard it that way.

And I had had no idea she stayed up nights listening at the plumbing for the latest gurgle let off by my toilet in this terrible sinkhole of flesh in which we fool mortals dwell. She must be a chronic self-abuser, I thought to myself; a very dangerous type. I determined right then and there to catch her out at it red-handed if an opportunity presented itself. Which, naturally, it did. In due time. I don't know what she expected me to do, lucubrate to a tape-recording of her tarnished past? I have never traveled with a more disagreeable group of people. But then people always say this when they're on the road to nowhere.

By now it was late February and we inched our way southward down the west coast of Africa toward Capetown. Fortunately the weather was fine but every new cloud on the horizon would provoke another attack of anxiety. For instance, they had run out of lemons at the bar and there was some talk of scurvy. Whenever we'd see another ship on the horizon we'd raise and lower a little flag on the stern, a way of saying «hello» when out at sea. I wandered by the pilot house where the Captain hung on to the edge of his instruments.

"What's wrong," I asked with concern, fearing he too would go down before his ship. He was apparently still upset by something which had transpired in Monrovia. Monrovia happens to be the place where his ship was registered so I thought perhaps it had something to do with that. I asked him. I said:

"Is it anything official? Do we hoist the Jolly Roger?" The Captain smiled for the first time that day and said:

"Jolly Rodger, very funny." So I was happy for that, that at least I could still make him smile if not laugh out loud. I feel it is such a pressing need for talented people, artistic types, people with entertainment in their blood, to provide whatever comic relief possible for those in positions of authority, to lighten the burden of those saddled by terrible life and death responsibilities with a song or a joke or even a sultry little dance. He was silent for a time as we watched the sea do what she does and then he said:

"Give me one good English sentence, one sentence, and I'll fix them." I thought this highly unlikely not to speak of unusual and questioned him further but he would not or could not elaborate at that moment. But it was an enlightenment in and of itself to see that even such an exalted personage as the Captain could sink to the common cry for vengeance.

Later I gave him the following problem: «There was a hole there then the size, say, of one's thumb and forefinger wrapped about the shoulders of a pear.» Apropos of nothing in particular, really, but speaking, perhaps, reams on my situation. I had no idea at the time what use he would make of this.

You see, I thought at the time that the skull itself was nothing but a mass of emotional scar tissue enclosing three concentric core of functioning cellular activity, cellular activity whose action was intelligence. The outermost core apprehended fact; the second core contained a worried world of logic, math, our everyday comings and goings-on; and the third core, the brain itself, where fact was manipulated and transmuted by raw nervous power. This third core was always uncontrolled and in it was the real and actual anarchic movement of intelligence, the frankenstein, the man overboard. And here was the capacity for reaching out and seizing speech somewhere in the second year of life. So I was very tolerant of the Captain and his asinine little language lessons.

We continued our transit down the west coast. The sad coast, as so many of us began to call her. It took a good number of days, far more than most of us were prepared to spend. We, those of us who had managed to hold on to our good-humor, were smoking and drinking in the lounge one night not long after dinner, listening to the short-wave, when in walks the purser with two prostitutes he had smuggled aboard in Monrovia. I guess I wasn't the only trouble-maker on this ship! Well, we let out a collective gasp and several of the weak-kneed and fainter-hearted amongst us left the room. Miss Springman strode out on her little alligator boots but Nanette stayed and showed what a real lady can do when faced with a difficult social situation. She befriended the two hapless women in a shake of her little head, had them drinking at our table and practically eating out of my hand. It really was a whole new kind of party after that. I spent hours in their little broom-closet of a cabin trying to get them to open up about themselves, attempting to question them on their social backgrounds, but they did not appear interested. They passed amongst us with that easy grace that is the mark of true professionals.

There was a civil war going on in Chad just inland from where we sailed. This is what we learned from the wireless. Chad is a vast territory stretching from the Sahara Desert to the forests of Central Africa. From what we heard it is impossibly riven by ethnic, religious and political conflict. Despite potential underground wealth, the capitalist projection for the economy has failed to flower and remains somewhat stunted in the midst of fourteen years of civil warfare. Chad entered our history when she was first colonized by France at the turn of the century. Foreign occupation and military domination were sensibly accepted by the farmers and traders of the south in return for protection from occasional raiding and pillaging from the nomadic camel-raisers of the north. The northern organization, especially the Toubous of the Tibesti region, took arms against the Europeans, that old invitation to genocide. The French recruited their puppet officials and troops from the southern Saras, many of whom accepted the Catholic yoke. Professional colonial hands call this policy «doubling», a practice still in use throughout the world by those involved in popular manipulation and, even, in personal defense. Of course its most egregious instance is with the American adventure in Viet-Nam. With just a fraction more «real work» in the short run one can eliminate the genuinely bothersome necessity of further and seemingly endless out-lay of labor and, instead and indeed, «lay there in the moonshine» and see others as they would have you see themselves, comme on dire, and capitalize therein on this very basic move in diplomatic jujitsu. Some hesitate, again the mealy-mouthed and the hyper-apostatized, to involve themselves in this simple procedure because of the initial necessity for the outlay of innocent blood but, believe me, the dividends are extra-ordinary. One added benefit on the colonial level is the possibility to double or in some cases triple one's sphere of graft and taxation.

The first French puppet show after «independence» was directed by a man called François Albrecht from a suburb of Lyons and involved a local man called Tombalbaye. The lid was blown by the publication of some secretly printed memoirs by pre-colonial guerilla heros leading to a Muslim rebellion in sixty-four and the creation of the Chad National Liberation Front two years later. This was called Frolinat and «doubled» by a man called Siddick. The situation could not be stabilized without heavy reliance on French troops and «advisers».

Tombalbaye secretly opposed the French policy of «doubling» and was killed in a military coup in seventy-five. He was accused of economic errors and an attempted «authentication» of all the country's peoples. True or not, these ideas were made up in western Europe. His successor, General Felix Malloum, accepted the yoke of «reconciliation» and «disorientation» of the northern rebels into small bands but they were no more under his control than before. A piece of contiguous real-estate called the Aouzou strip was seized by Libya who then threw increasing support behind the northern Moslem nomads. The French increased their military support.

The situation deteriorated rapidly in seventy-seven and seventy-eight with the Frolinat group led by Goukouni Queddei advancing southward and the French increasingly disenchanted with the régime they had protected for so long. In a last-ditch effort to retain power, Malloum signed an agreement with the «mercurial» former Frolinat leader Hissene Habre, a secret, chameleon-like lone operator who can wheel and deal with absolutely anyone. Ideology is not involved. Habre arrived a month later to take up the post of Prime Minister with a bodyguard of two hundred and fifty armed men.

Hissene Habre used his first months in the new post to gather followers from the Moslems in the National army which soon began disintegrating along ethnic lines. Just as we passed, with the main body of Frolinat forces led by Goukouni Queddei advancing southward with Libyan support, fighting broke out between Habre's forces and the demoralized Sara troops loyal to Malloum. Saras began leaving the north and Moslems fled northward from the south. The French, outnumbered, intervened here and there to damp down the fighting but are not, apparently, trying to prop up the government.

What we see here, of course, is the «re-doubling» of the French by the Libyans, the French having lost some of their classic taste for sang froid. And the Libyans, thereby, leave themselves open to the «missing trick» manoeuvre by the successors to the French «sphere of influence», i.e., our boys back in the bloody Med.

It was all so messy and needless. Some of us took to going down to the radio shack night after night with the prostitutes and drugs and alcohol. I was ready to slap faces. But in retrospect that party takes on a very different significance from that which I then lent it . I see in it the almost childlike transparency of those people who, when miffed over something like their inability to praise me on my most recent remark, became socially helpless, unable even for a moment to dissemble a cordiality they did not feel. When hardship penetrates worldly veneer, every exchange, intimate or no, is governed by a gloomy arriere pensée. They lacked the necessary grace of hypocrisy without being saved from its vices. This will squelch a good time every time. It was shameless and I soon stopped altogether but not before I learned more than I wanted to know about radio war in Africa. Algerian supported Polisario were still fighting the Hassans of Morocco. South African troops were passing from Namibia, the old South West African Protectorate, into Angola, raiding. I just got so confused. It seemed as if the colonial fabric of the entire continent were about to unravel. And all for man's unsatisfied ambition for economic progress, so aggravated by a framework of dogmatic notions of «democratic institution». I think this is what the late Kennedy was trying to tell us just before he died.

It was returning late one night from one of these soirée télégraphique that I saw Miss Springman sitting on a padded deck-chair outside the salon, her elbow at her stomach, her hand at her ear fiddling about with a gold ring through her lobe, her head cocked and her lips slightly pouting, much in the manner of the auto-girls in the industrial north of Italy. I passed her by without a word. Not so much as a sideways glance. I just cut her dead. I know this must have hurt her deeply but I had been drinking and was feeling ever so carefree and vicious. Anyway, so many women wish to be taken for prostitutes and then demand a lady's treatment afterwards. I wasn't going to take any chances with this little chippie.

I went up to her the very next morning after breakfast and said: "Why, Deborah, you seem to have my expression on your face." Then

I made a big smile with my mouth hoping against hope she could grasp, somehow, the fact that my statement was humorous in intent even if she were incapable of delving the humor itself. Predictably, she looked hurt. I simply turned on my heel and went about my business.

Later, in the course of our luncheon, I happened to say: "Well, Deborah, what is the deep structure of this sentence: «The cold chicken was then thrown into the hot fire.» I hoped to show her in this way that though I was definitely not interested in her or in her «nasty condition», I was not unfriendly nor above discussion on certain seminal subjects. She left the room in tears and I must say I feared the momentary censure of my fellow-travellers. No matter how right you may in your heart feel, it is not right to send a girl away from table in tears. You must know by now that I adhere to a ultra-strict moral stance and am absolutely merciless when it comes to «self-criticism». So I certainly saw how it would be possible for one of the diners to think I had committed a social gaffe. But the tenor of opinion was yet with me. We all peaceably commenced again eating the sausage and fish had so thoughtfully prepared by the cook.

But please don't think these remarks gratuitous or unrelated to the actual transpiration of our prior verbal intercourse. Don't think them sarcastic cracks tossed in the face of a meal-mate. I mean, it was not the same thing at all as yelling «your mother's bum» at a latent schizoid matricide in order to provoke some sort of more or less violent behavioral reaction in a crowded movie theatre. I'm not that way. It was a retort apropos of the general drift of conversation. We had taken on live stock in Monrovia in the form of certain cackling pullet. In due time their livers reached our tables chopped as a appetizer. Miss Springman complained of their tasting somehow strange to her, greasy and unclean. She was such a fussy eater.

"It tastes of the barnyard itself," she complained. I was perhaps too full of myself and said:

"Peradventure it be brain damage and chicken shit you taste or some prior state of existence as the fowl mutate into swine." I could observe her mind through her eyes, the windows in her skull, rise up and flutter about like a flock of gulls on a parade ground in an early morning rainstorm when disturbed by an erratically ambling pedestrian.

"Perhaps you would prefer fingers of beef for your lunch," I suggested. "Let us discover the Chinese word for finger and holler it up to the cook through the ventilation system." I was being quite gay, playing out my life as jolly old Uncle Desmond, quite oblivious, quite unconcerned, quite me, in fact, for my appetite had returned for the first time since I had vomited on to the water off the skiff taking us out of Monrovia and had had that chilling scene with Nanette. Then I said what I have said I said: "Well, Deborah, what is the deep structure of this sentence: «The cold chicken was then thrown into the hot fire.»"

She left but was back before we had finished our meal, freshly made up, not a sign of our struggle and her tears. You might have thought she thought herself the source of the 87 rivers of forgetfulness. What I had said to her had had about as much effect as a ball of wax shot from a pop gun into a concrete culvert. I just gave her a stare that let her know in no uncertain terms she would never get under my skin. It was then she started stomping about the dining room in those absurd, alligator, cowboy toe-shoes she wore, looking like she were suddenly «Miss Society» with the «good word» hanging off her bottom lip like slobber. Words flew wildly. As at Winnwood, I lost some of my self-control and in my desire to make the basic situation clear my emotion burst forth in a deluge of angry sounds, desperate exaggerations, wild objurgations. Some of those assembled turned from me as from a man lost. Nanette cattily summed up the scene by saying sardonically: "Desmond wants a divorce." I'll get her later, I said to myself. It was all much simpler than anyone would admit. There was no need for anger or for shouting. When you cannot do anything about an objective situation and you are unwilling to face this fact, all the subjective furies will be unleashed to wreak havoc. But the facts are not altered. I swear, I still think she did something unnatural when she was out of the room. And the way she moved! Like a donkey smelt a grass snake on a high pass. Such an obvious play for attention. I just pushed my custard aside and left the table.

7

Girl-Trouble

I know what you're going to say: girl-trouble! A young thing's sneaker and crumpled sock glimpsed in a mud-room and «boing», the boy is gone on the titanic love-boat death-wish of imaginary gratification. Well, that's just not the case here. And anyway, the very notions of «girl» and «boy», the pink and blue cultural commodities, are all too rapidly replaced by «bidder A» and «bidder B» before these infantile players ever survive the holocaust of American adolescence. Why should I care which way the wind blows when all I care about is how it vents my stateroom.

Old man Cayman was speaking to me again. He feared, I believe, he would be forced by circumstances to remain aboard our vessel for the duration of our cruise. And, in fact, he did. Only death would have separated him from his dear Nanette and she had found quite a few things to pique her interest. But she was the one, I think, who made him stay. It was for his health she said. Now there was an empty set! She once said to me: "Do you need something for the pain? Because, if you do, really, Ernest sounds just like. . . no. Not sounds like, I mean, has access to the most outrageous collection of drugs." And she was right. I saw it myself. He later suggested that perhaps I had helped myself to something that wasn't mine but I know for certain it was the purser, Freddo Summerhill because. . .well, never mind. This time he had some screwball idea about mercury-vapor autos, to be made of a super lightweight titanium alloy yet to be developed.

"Lightbulbs for cars," he'd say, "highway lightbulbs. All conduits will be flexible and uniform. All connections will be self-locking and easy-release. After the manufacturing process there will be no further maintenance involved. All a mechanic needs to carry is his toothbrush."

I, of course, thought him absolutely mad with that madness absolutely unique to the small workshops of suburban North America. We were gazing out to sea, leaning on a stretch of starboard rail.

"But do you know what the key is, the hard science," he asked me earnestly.

"No, what," I ventured.

"A better physical description of light," he answered, "a new conception."

"Maybe it's in lasers," I suggested wanly. I'm sure he intended it to be something comparable to the discovery of Sumerian batteries in Iraq in 1936.

"No, not there, that's just a feat; there's no new conception there. But we have started, haven't we?" I wanted to say «who we» but instead I said "have we?" He said:

"Why us, of course, you and I. That's where all great ideas get off the ground, when two people get together in a face to face interchange." I assured him I had no competence and little interest in the field he had chosen for our dialogue. I suggested that perhaps the First Mate or even the Telegraph Ensign would pull more weight within his sphere of activity. I couldn't think of anything less appetizing than collaboration with his sort.

"Oh, no, no, no," he concluded, "I need somebody like you, happy-go-lucky. Anyway, we're only a Chinese puzzle away from a solution." He seemed to want me to think about it, silly dreamer. But for the life of me I could not remember what it was, a Chinese puzzle. The only picture which came to my mind was a child poised before a television screen. I just know if you scratched him deeply there would be a stark, raving bourgeois humanist.

I'd certainly gotten myself into a pickle with those two. I sought now to avoid them at every turn but they were hunting me like a mama and papa armadillo after some tiny spider in the spines of the sweet mescal plant. Can you blame me! My god, they were even more demanding than I.

For instance, I'd be in the billiards room and they'd find me out there. Nanette would hoist a shapely hip upon the table (she was quite well put together despite her age) and bid us boys shoot about her with our sticks. Such a lovely body on such an old hag, almost youthful. And he'd run on oblivious, building elaborate puns or forecasting market movements and trends in tangibles. Anything to escape, I'd say to myself. I'd talk and talk and do impersonations.

And the horrible snit I'd be left with after each encounter. And still they did not stop. I was on deck once throwing the «black slug», as they say in showbiz, into this ghastly and nightmarish soup they call my life when Cayman came up behind me saying:

"Well, well, here we are." He clapped me on the back quite painfully and intoned: "Des, my boy, I guess it's pot-belly or hunchback for you." It is true I had been indulging in a slouched posture when he approached, leaning over the rail the way one must. And I straightened right up. Then he hit my left arm with the knuckle of his crooked over right index finger directly between my deltoid muscle and the head of my biceps.

"Hickory dickory doc," he chimed, "the mouse ran up the clock. What time is it?" he'd grin, feigning sociability. It just happened to be eight bells or whatever navy-time but I said one, playing his silly game, hoping for some respite from his aggression.

"That's right," he'd assure me, "you're a regular whiz-kid!" It's a wonder I didn't develop character armour or something worse being around him all the time. I'd turn to face him through this volley of punches only to find his face twisted up into a hideous mockery of a grin. He'd say:

"Watch my face, I'm going to change my mind." It was impossible to talk to him. He just wouldn't listen. Then he'd add in his dreadful monotone:

"All I'm asking from you is the motivating simplicity, you understand, nothing fancy-pants." Then he'd saunter off down the deck singing: "Free of disease, free of disease, a monkey died for me!" It's really too bad, don't you think. I mean, I don't think he was another Howard Head or Edwin Lear or Hughes Tool or those people in Outer Space, Inc. No big genius inventor/Ivan the Terrible to tear holes in the fabric of business as it is done today. Believe me, I tried to be polite. I imagine also, as a person who cares about people, I felt a very real sympathy for his condition, he being so queer and alone.

One more thing about the trip down to the Cape. Old man Cayman began spending more and more of his time, finally whole days at a stretch, holed up in his suite unfit for human company. According to Nanette he fell first into a sulk and then to a fit of reckless wantonness of which she would be the unfortunate object. She told me, in great detail, how he would force her to parade about their room for what seemed hours in various sexual accessories available in any large department store. And high-heeled shoes, of course. All those things that should have gone out with the wheel as a medium of communication. Then he would seek to be-spot her in the most humiliating fashion. From here it was not far to a sort of demented schizoid catatonia into which he would often sink. In this state he was really only a jazzed-up stinky vegetable who could do little more than read the newspaper, smoke a smelly cigar and telex his broker.

When he was, as previously described, confined, his wife and I would stroll about the decks, sometimes arm in arm, perhaps shuffle-boarding or stopping in the lounge for a drink, going to the kitchen for a tea in the warm rain which often washed us. She would clutch at my right arm and lean her little head against my shoulder. Considering the wet spray there was nothing unusual about this sort or physical contact.

"Oh, Des," she'd say, "This is so civilized." Sometimes she'd walk me to my cabin and have me remove all my wet clothing behind a screen before tucking me into bed and sitting on the edge of the coverlet. It was all I could do, sometimes, to avoid the danger of a «certain intimacy». She'd lean close to my ear in the most conspiratorial manner and whisper:

"Oh, Des, I wish sometimes, crazy as it sounds, that we were married, lived together, did everything together. But we aren't, darling, and we never will be. And you know, Des, I'm worried. I am very terribly worried."

"And what, pray tell, worries you, Nanette," I'd whisper in return. She'd pause and draw back, fixing me with her little eyes:

"About him, of course, I feel I must save you from his wrath. He can be absurdly violent and cunning when he feels himself crossed."

"Save me from his wrath," I exclaimed, "I can't imagine anyone saving me from anything. What a silly notion, Nanette." I'd roll myself over hoping she'd be moved to massage my lower back, my sciatica having flared some, but she became abstracted and spoke no further words. In a moment she stood up and we'd part in a flurry of little smacky kisses. I'd read then, waiting to fall into my disturbed sleep. But deep in my heart I too was now worried. But just a tad.

Of course some people will whisper of sublimated sexual urges etcetera but I won't have any of that ruining my social life. I will go whither I would with whomsoever takes my fancy irregardless of common gossip and slander.

Well, old man Cayman must have been reading the wind with his finger for he was on me with renewed fervor the very next day. After some inanities about the weather and the pummelling I had come to expect for him he said, in a rather matter-of-fact voice:

"Look, Farrquahr or whatever your name is, what kind of people do you come from? What kind of folks turn out a boy like you? You're not like any of our three kids." I began to speak rather quickly of my Uncle Louis, my martyred father, my sainted though oft-sullied mother, but he cut me off and said:

"Look, stay away from my wife." Lord, was I shocked. And my first thought was that he must be horrid with anger. I was totally taken aback by what he had said, almost knocked overboard by the violence of his suggestion. Not that he seemed upset in any way, in fact he was calm. He was still smiling. Then, seeing the shock of consternation, I'm sure, across my face, he attempted to indicate his jocular intention by cuffing me behind the elbow of my left arm. His touch must have shocked me for I blurted:

"I am not just another piss-ass faggot to boss around," misunderstanding him apparently for he immediately corrected me.

"That's pick-ass, Des, you must understand." Then he made an obscene gesture, tweezing together his thumb and forefinger and abstracting from his buttocks.

"I like you," he continued, "you're an intelligent guy. No offense intended."

"I am intelligent, that's true," I stammered, thinking perhaps a note of sincerity would crack his shell somewhat. But he was a harder nut than just common decency. He fixed me with his eyes and said, as if he were talking to a child:

"Look, Bunny, I don't know about your father and mother but I'll tell you something about here. You want to work or go fly a toy airplane? I'm asking you seriously. You listen to me. We ride fast so you want a bite of the big red apple or you want to sit in your chair and wait for the green light? What? Like I said, we go get dinner. You want something to eat, you help. If you're going to work here, you've got to know what I'm saying."

His fixed smile was so disarming I didn't know what to say much less what he had said. It must have had to do with the project he'd thought up for us. So you can see by this time I was already suffering from their never ending conceit about themselves. And then he was gone down the deck, jumping up beside the hawse-pipe stanchion and clicking his heels. The sea was blowing up a bit but we didn't need to worry since we were so close to safe harbor. Or so I thought.

But how was I to take what he had said to me. He couldn't be serious about me and his wife, no matter what she'd told him. And certainly that was no job offer, that babble about work and food. Then what did he mean? Surely he couldn't have though my intentions in any way dishonorable. And besides, he hardly ever paid her any attention or catered to the more delicate side of her nature. On the whole I thought him a rustic and a bore. I mean, could he have meant to say I shouldn't see her? Did he really expect me to respect so antique a personal prerogative as privacy?

8

Capetown

I must say Capetown was all we expected and more. So much more. She seemed to have so much poise for a city so far from civilization. One morning, seventeen days out of Liberia, I finally spotted her smokestacks on the horizon, her downtown silhouette against the enormous mass of the Table Mountains and, in the foreground, Robben Island, where she keeps all of her illegals.

They, the Caymen, were talking of getting off here and taking their own chances on the «dark» continent. I half hoped they would so I could be about my own tale in something like solitude. However, it was not to be. As it turned out, we became separated at a very fortuitous moment. The Captain called us to the dining room where he announced the vessel had been accepted for repair by a Capetown dry-docker. We all gave a little cheer for one tends to identify with something so large as a ship, don't you think? But it would be necessary to abandon ship and go ashore for three or four days while they breamed her bottom or whatever they do, steeved her bowsprit, whatever, for our easy steerage. Just as well, I thought. We were to be lodged in private homes. Arrangements had been made through the Ministry of Tourism and since we were all, save the Captain, white and personable, there was no problem. He'd stay on the bridge, I guessed, and eat with the workmen. All were bidden return to stateroom and pack for the stay. What excitement, I said to myself.

Here we pulled right up to a long pier and walked down a gangplank. You come in so much higher that way, so much to be preferred to coming in at sea level in a small boat which is such a bitch. We all carried our gear so we had to go through customs but they were very nice. It turned out I was to stay alone with a certain Mr. Smuts and his family which was fine by me. I just love a family group. He's not, by the way, the Mr. Smuts but just another Mr. Smuts. He and his wife and nineteen year old daughter lived on the outskirts of town, one of the more fashionable suburbs on the road to Stellenbosch, Africa's Princeton. They have a simply beautiful home overlooking False Bay, just on the other side of the Cape of Good Hope itself. Off to the left is a lovely shot of the Hottentot Holland range of mountains.

They, the Smuts, had me met at the dock by a chauffeur, a very sweet young coloured named Steve. There he was standing at the gate with a little hand-lettered sign saying «Farrquahr». I said good-bye to one and all. We agreed to meet somewhere en masse, at an eatery to be chosen at random by dear Nanette. She whispered hastily as I kissed her on the cheek that she would come to me, to wait in my rooms. It was the first hint I'd had that I was to have more than one room. She said:

"Oh, darling, they'll treat you very well. They think you're one of us. I didn't have the nerve to tell them I have no idea who you are." Again, I didn't have the foggiest idea what she was talking about. We drove away through the crowded streets that might have been the very streets trod by Mahatma Gandhi himself during his extended stay in this community of souls. But I think he spent most of his time inland on all kinds of minority business. There are, in fact, over half a million Indian sub-continentals down here somewhere.

It took over half an hour to get out to where they live. Steve didn't talk much. He seemed shy and innocent, qualities I found very charmingly mated in him. We stopped several times so police officers could look into the car to see if I was all right. They had been having, I understand, some industrial disturbances of late, caused, no doubt, by the disturbing influence of outside agitators slipping liberal notions to workers in battery factories. I found the national police so handsome in their paramilitary get-ups. They'd smile and gesture in my direction. Oh, things were hopping down here with so many people interested in blowing it to smithereens.

The Smuts house itself was a sprawling single-story ranch affair with a long driveway crawling up the front lawn. Beautiful jacaranda trees grew on the sheltered side of the house. There was no one in sight when we arrived save an old gardener trimming some privet hedge. Then Mr. and Mrs. Smuts came out the front and walked toward the limousine as Steve opened the door for me. They seemed fairly friendly. Mr. Smuts and I shook hands. He asked me how I liked the weather in his country. I told him it was a lovely day and from what I had seen this part of Africa was one of the fairest to behold. And I only meant the landscape itself. Oh, Mrs. Smuts was handsome, but about the fairest part I know nothing. You never do with that sort of woman. Anyway, he seemed pleased. He was kind of gruff and outgoing. He wore a sports shirt buttoned to the neck and decorated with a string tie. He was hatless but wore handsome hand-tooled western boots of cowhide. He looked to be fifty-five or so and was greying at the temples.

Mrs. Smuts was not greying and wore a pleated skirt over a cotton blouse. That is, the blouse was tucked into a skirt. I hope you don't misunderstand me. Her eyes were light blue pools of purest irrationality. Quite fetching, really. She could trace her relatives to the Indian wars in the northeast of America. They must play a lot of tennis to have those delicious tans, I thought to myself. And when we walked around to the back of the house I saw the tennis court. So I was right about that because I could just see her in a little tennis skirt.

The grounds were beautiful and very well kept. There was a small pond in one shaded corner bridged by an arc of stone springbok leaping. They told me it was a miniature of the Oppenheimer memorial in Johannesburg. It was so precious poised there in the greenery. The mountains loomed above our heads. Plane trees appeared on the near horizon. Finally this African landscape drives me mad. I was so relieved when they finally invited me inside for a cup of tea.

They seemed like nice enough people. Though you can never tell and I've learned to be wary about this sort of thing. I never put all my cards on the table right away. After I get to know somebody, though, I'm as open as can be. Some say extraordinarily open. I'll show them everything I've got and breast not knave nor deuce. However, this is very seldom necessary. But It always feels so stiff to be thrown into a new social situation like this. And this is why manners are so important.

They help to carry us over our fear and our ignorance and the possible pain and pleasure this can bring to those around us.

They told me their daughter Tess was shopping in the city but would return in time for dinner. We had a pleasant enough cup of tea. I don't think we discussed a thing except the service itself. Oh, you know what I mean. I would say, «what a lovely cup, wherever did you get it?» Then she would say, «yes, bone china from Holland. We are very proud.» And he would say, «and cost a pretty penny, too.» Things like that. Manners again. They just keep coming up. And they can't teach enough of them in our schools these days. You're never too old and seldom too young to learn a few more, either, and get along with just anybody. That's what I think.

Shortly I was shown to my rooms to await dinner which was at eight. I lay down on the bed and fell into a deep sleep. While in this sleep I dreamt of a horrible bull elephant goring, tusks flashing in a tumult, the rearing, the roar. It was a horror. And to think that they hunt and kill these magnificent beasts and made piano keys out of their teeth. In the Kruger National Park, in the northeast corner of the country, armed gamekeepers scour the jungle in search of poachers but it's not enough. If I had any, I'd give all my money to the fund to preserve and protect all the great beasts, at land, on the sea, and in the air. I awoke at six forty-five in time to shower and dress for dinner.

Dinner was very pleasant. Their daughter was there and turned out to be a ravishing dark-haired, dark-eyed young beauty in a nicely tapered worsted shift breathing just a hint of bosom. And that small touch of sophistication can be so telling on the tone of an evening. I didn't underestimate it a bit. Her mother was in a short, simple organza gown. We were served by a man and a woman, Africans from the look of them, in dark grey uniforms.

Tess was not only beautiful but also homey and down to earth, such a rare combination. And I found myself quite bewitched by her feminine appeal. However, she was not talkative. Neither she nor her mother seemed capable of any but the most basic sort of conversation such as «pass the butter, if you would» and «they say a green vegetable is very good for you.» But I wasn't bothered at all nor did I have any negative feelings. Up in my rooms I had taken just a tad of amphetamine as it always makes me just a little more charming and brings out the lighter side. My doctor prescribed it for me to deal with a minor weight problem I seemed to be having. So I had no trouble at all launching into a conversation with the table at large. The problem was, then, their lack of desire to chat even if it's only aimless. It seems to be a South African characteristic. They are a serious and no-nonsense people. I heard that more than once down there. And I must say the young Miss Smuts used it to great advantage. I knew right then she could have me eating right out of her hand.

We were served a salad first and then a soup. The salad was crisp and green with a mild «herb and cheese» vinegar and oil dressing. The soup seemed a beef stock with added fruits and vegetables. The fruits seemed strange to me in a soup so I asked Mrs. Smuts about them. She said that it was very difficult to get the native cooks to leave off putting fruit in the soup since it was an element of their tribal cookery. She paused for quite a while so I went on to tell them how thankful I was they had taken me in off my broken boat and were bedding me and boarding me so thoughtfully. They nodded their heads as if they agreed with every word I was saying.

We were served quite a nice dry red wine with our steak. It was grown right in their region, called the garden spot of southern Africa. Everyone continually assured me it was very much a beautiful part of the world. A silence ensued a previous pause and my host became uncomfortable. He pushed back his chair and asked if I would like to hear something of how they mine their diamonds down there. He said:

"We're very proud of our country, you know."

"Oh, that's nice," I said though I'll admit I'm not really a nationalism fan.

"Yes," broke in Mrs. Smuts, "it is very much a beautiful part of the world."

"Really," I said and then, just to keep things going, added: "I'd just love to hear about the diamonds." Tess laughed and Mrs. Smuts said:

"Oh, everybody loves the diamonds." We all laughed at this. The conversation was becoming positively animated. You could see Tess hung on every word I said. I said:

"You bet!" And then Mrs. Smuts explained that they were not Cape Capetowners.

"We're Johnnies," she explained, "from the Transvaal. Johannesburg."

"Oh," I exclaimed, "that's where the diamonds come from. I was wondering about that."

"Oh, no," Mr. Smuts corrected, "not from there. That's gold country. The diamonds come from Kimberley."

"Oh, I didn't know that. How interesting." It didn't really matter whether I knew or not. I was just being polite, waiting for desert. Watching Tess nod her head. Then I broke in:

"But how do you know if you're from somewhere else?" And then he explained he had been an engineer in his early career before he got into education and research. But he wasn't deterred at all and began again about the diamonds.

"Let me tell you about how we get the diamonds out of the ground," Mr. Smuts continued, "before we forget and you never find out." He was very persistent about this. I had a feeling he was going to tell me no matter what I said. The table fell silent and Mr. Smuts began his story.

"First we blow up a big stick of dynamite down in the ground," he began, "then we haul this diamond-bearing rock up to the surface. It is just called blue ground now, because of its color. When we bring it up, we bring it right away to the cruncher where it is reduced to a little particle the size of this pipe bowl." He picked up a handsome meerschaum from off the table. It looked to be about an inch across to me.

In this crushing process most of the diamonds are released," he continued, "and now we take the crushed ore to rotary washing pans on giant conveyor belts. The ore enters the washing pan at a tangent. Do you know what that means?" He was questioning me to see if I were following his story. Of course I knew what a tangent was. Though I didn't have the vaguest idea what diamonds were doing on one in a washing pan. It could have been a de Beer's brochure for all I knew but I'm sure he had it by heart.

"What I mean to say is that it flows into the pan without disturbing the smooth, circular movement within the pan itself," he explained, "at just the right angle to the circular flow. It is then carried along by a stream of slime and water called puddle. This suspension of slime increases the density of the water so that the stream is able to keep the diamonds in motion but does not allow them to come too near the surface. The upper layers of water continually overflow but the lower layers, with the diamonds, are removed from time to time through a door in the wall of the rotary pan called an exit. By this process ninety-nine per cent of the ore is removed. This ninety-nine per cent is called the tailings and is dumped in large hills called tailings-hills. The remainder is circulated in what is called a Separatory Cone. The water in this cone is made dense with a powdered iron alloy. The lighter particles again fly off and the diamonds sink. The next step is the grease table. A table is covered with a layer of petroleum jelly which has an affinity for diamonds. The whole table is vibrated electrically along the line of feed. The dirt moves across the table but the diamonds stick. The final product is then picked out of the jelly and rubbed by hand. Out of the ten thousand tons of ore which we treat this way every day, we get one pound of stones."

He stopped then and there was a silence at the table. I was awed myself. Just think of it! One pound of stones. But all that work! Was it worth it? It meant, if you could get them out of there, you were a very rich man. And then for a moment I wondered why we all didn't do it like crazy. But then, I'm sure, there would be too many diamonds and they wouldn't be worth a plugged-nickel. And here all the time I thought you just went down in a river bed and started picking them up by the handful. But from the sober silence that followed you'd have thought he'd just read Ecclesiastes. Page 787 in my bible. And what a good-book that is. I sincerely believe it to be the very fountain-head of all true popular music. You remember how it goes: «I say it's empty. Why work in the sun? Generations come and generations go while the earth seems to endure. The sun rises and the sun goes down etcetera. The wind blows south, the wind blows north. Round and round it goes and returns full-circle. All streams run into the sea yet the sea never overflows, back to the place from which it ran it returns to run again. All things are weary and no one can remember why. And there is nothing new under the sun, etcetera.» He goes on and on saying:

«I bothered my mind to understand wisdom and knowledge, madness and folly and I come to see that this too is chasing the wind. For in much wisdom is much vexation. And the more a man knows the more he has to suffer.» So finally he undertook great works.

«I built myself houses and planted vineyards. I made myself gardens and parks and planted all kinds of fruit trees. I bought slaves, male and female and I had my home-born slaves as well. Etcetera.» You can learn so much from an old book like that, even those unfortunate enough to be on the outer edges of society can know all about the wealth of Solomon. And there are so many seminal plots in there, just ripe for the acquisitive mind to pick off.

I broke the silence to say I thought what he had said was quite instructive. Mr. Smuts invited me into the library for a brandy and the two women disappeared to the upper rooms to watch «Dallas» on television. Really, it's one of the most popular shows over here.

The library was very cleverly decorated with books and such, round globes and framed paintings. He spoke quite eloquently of his country's problems worldwide. He cupped his glass below his breast and assumed an awesomely solemn face. I, of course, had no interest in what he had to say. But he seemed to want it off his chest.

He complained of the United States having cut him off from a certain type of sweet crude very highly prized for its easy fracture into gasoline. He said:

"It's like a cowboy not knowing how to handle his gun or walk tall anymore. I say to you, stop displaying this nervousness!" And then I said, naturally enough:

"Oh, no, don't talk to me! They don't have my ear in Washington." I assumed, of course, that he had intended no direct reference to my behavior at that moment which, I can assure you, was utterly beyond blemish. I sat up straight in my chair and didn't even cross my legs. He sat down across from me and leaned in toward my face.

"We have plans afoot to invest in your country, to move our substantial assets into your markets."

"Well, you needn't ask my permission. I'm sure the rules are all set down somewhere in a paper-backed book or information pamphlet." This was obviously just a case of mistaken identity, I said to myself. But so much social intercourse is these days. He leaned in even closer and said:

"Our countries are very similar, you know. You might say that when you hurt us you hurt yourself, for soon we will be like this." And here he enjoined the fingers of one hand with those of the other and shook them before his face. Then he continued:

"The question is one of preserving the values of civilization and culture and progress, of not slipping into darkness, as it were." And then something to the effect that if I thought him staunch I should meet his neighbors. Perhaps he realized how spooky he had become for he then added in a lighter vein:

"We have many precious elements here, highly prized metals and stones, strategic ores even. And we have very powerful friends."

"Oh, I had no idea!" And I really hadn't. Don't think I was just playing dumb to draw him out. I really was. But nevertheless we fell into a rather heavy silence here. The fire crackled in its place. I thought of how little I had to say to a man of his complexion. I prefer all my companions to be at least slightly gay. He crossed to the mantle above the fire and briefly studied the spirits in his glass. Then he blurted:

"You're probably concerned about the black question?" For the life of me at that instant I could not remember what exactly the black question was in any precise phrasing. But then I realized that he was talking about the people down here. I temporized, not wanting to be seen as «out of it» in any way. I said there are those who question directly and those who merely pose a question by their continued peaceable existence or something to that effect. Then, fearing myself to be in much the same position as the consortium of international bankers who afford the «sticky-tape» that holds this entire enterprise together, I said:

"Well, tell me about it." He declined to elaborate on the subject anymore than to say:

"Well, I can't say and you won't see but I can assure you we are moving ahead and there will be changes. However, it is extremely important for you people to bear in mind our determination to preserve the sovereignty of our decision making process." Here he rose to the tips of his toes.

"Wonderful," I said, "I don't think I ever heard that before." I was feeling myself representative of a similar sort of ground-zero position albeit all too true I held at that time no post of governmental responsibility.

"After all," he continued calmly, perhaps too calmly, "you yourself have said the fact that the details of those changes have not yet crystallized, that we are still in the dark as to what the precise objectives and scope of the changes will be, is not as important as the commitment to change itself."

I don't remember ever having said anything like that but then people are always putting words into my mouth. And I am not exactly incapable of such a pretty piece of sophistry. But then I'd defend a body's right to shout fire even on a crowded escalator. Not that anyone would listen to me. The old fellow seemed to have perturbed himself some so I allowed him to complete his thought. He said:

"Well, let me say this. They are all homosexual."

"Who," I stammered, "where?" He must have felt himself on shaky ground apparently for he cut off further inquiry by saying:

"I'll tell you what, let's not discuss anything unpleasant." Well, I know for a fact that what he said couldn't be true because no population is ever more than fifty-one per cent homosexual at any one time.

He went on to say that something called dagga, a drug as far as I could tell, was at the root of both adult and juvenile delinquency, as are the knife, the dice and the dirty girlfriend. He was leaning on the mantel while he gave me these snips from a fuller picture. Then, suddenly, he took a step toward me and said with some vehemence:

"You know, we have some very romantic figures working with us, too, some rather romantic figures. Don't think a pack of greasy pepper-heads can scare us off. You'll see, we are a very resourceful people."

I think he was quite off the wall on this one. It seemed totally fruitless to attempt any further conversation. If only he knew how I had been taught, at the tenderest of ages, everything he thought. And to fear as true a nefarious plot to enslave the world behind a curtain of silence. Thankfully his daughter proved a more reasonable person when she came knocking at the door to my rooms late that same night.

Anyway, I was looking for a chance to escape this Smuts fellow when his hand slipped off the mantel spilling liquor on the hearth rug. While he was on one knee picking up shards of broken glass in some embarrassment and throwing them into the mighty fire he had glowing behind him, I mumbled some gibberish about all people absolutely equally undergoing and eventually surpassing hardship, excused myself and went directly to my rooms. So escape I did.

A short time later there was a gentle knocking at my door. It was Tess asking if I desired refreshment before I slept. I asked her in and she sat on a straight backed chair by the writing table. You may think this situation provocative but in fact it was quite gentle, quite sweet and touching. Eventually she spoke of her great loneliness and desire to see a wider world, perhaps to break into showbiz, there being no theatre as such in South Africa. I had told her I was something of a talent scout. She wore a feathery little dressing gown. It was warm down there still, late in their summer. But more of this in its proper place.

9

Escape from Capetown

Speaking of escape, I must tell you of an incident which occurred the very next morning. Tess had slipped on her gown and left at the first light of day. I slept for two more hours and then went downstairs looking for a decent breakfast or at the very least some palatable coffee when I came upon the old gardener who was trimming the hedges. He came up to me and said:

"My name is Chester Himes and I live here. You tell them from me, master, that if I don't bring these people to justice in my life, my ghost shall return and enter the body of another man and he will try and so on forever until we are all brought to bloody justice, just deserts for this maggoty abomination of a social system." I'm just parroting here. I have no real idea what he was about. He left before I could question him. Can you believe it? I mean really? And I just didn't have the time or the patience to explain it all to the properly constituted authorities. Well, imagine the impudence that took. Even though his statement was somewhat well-phrased. All the same, saying it right out like that! And to a stranger. I mean, I'd never claim to have any commitment to the individual instance of social justice. It's just not done any more. You just end up looking like a fool and not making much money.

I don't know about you but I get so tired of travelling about and was so very happy to have this short stop in so familiar a place as South Africa can be. It was a thoroughly pleasant time though it turned out to be a long two days. Twelve hours more and I would have turned to crime. Oh don't take me seriously because I'm just kidding. I'd never rob a gas station. But I'd just kill for World Peace.

By the way, I discovered in my reading the most interesting thing about some of the natives down here. Apparently among the Victorian Zulu no man would mention the name of the chief of his tribe or even the names of the progenitors of his chief so far as he could remember them. Nor will he utter common words which coincide with or merely resemble in sound tabooed names. Isn't that interesting? For instance, there once was a chief called Langa which means the sun. Hence the name of the sun was changed from langa to gala and so remains to this day though the actual Langa died more than a hundred years ago. I so admire the nameless social anthropologist who penetrated these primitive settings and selflessly rooted out these tidbits of knowledge. When Panda was king of Zululand the word for «a root of a tree» was changed to nezabo because impando was just too close. Again, the word for «lies» and «slander» was altered from amacebo to amakwata because amacebo contains a syllable from the name of Panda's concubine.

These substitutions are not, however, carried so far by the men as by the women who omit every sound even remotely resembling one that occurs in a protected name. At the King's krall, indeed, it is sometimes difficult to understand the speech of the royal wives, the women having a considerable vocabulary pulled from a hat. So the Zulu language of that day could have been said to be double. It's just another reminder that absolute silence is, of old, the wisest policy.

Let's see. I was in something of a pickle out there at the Smuts' house. I don't know how they knew but they seemed to feel Tess had spent the night in my rooms. Also, for some reason, they seemed suspicious of my relation to the help. I heard the Mistress sending the old gardener away right within my earshot. And to think they thought I would mix with their domestics! Mrs. Smuts came up behind me while I was making the coffee I'd found in the kitchen. She didn't seem to like my toying with her pots and pans. It seems to me so easy to read an uncomfortable atmosphere in these tense tourist situations. And I always interpret them in a very sympathetic light. I suspect her brush of animosity had to do with the painful repression of an overwhelming desire to «camp-follow». It's so common with women in a military culture. I don't know. I guess she had motivation galore if one but hunt her head for them. But that's not my job.

In any case she bid me follow her into the drawing room with what dregs of coffee I had managed to squeeze together. On her glass-topped coffee-table was a large picture-book entitled Wildflowers of South Africa but for some silly reason I read it Witchcraft of South Africa which seemed perfectly absurd to me. I sat down on the couch and regarded it again, closer this time, and it still said «witchcraft». Well, no one would publish that, I said to myself. It wasn't until I picked it up off the table and actually held it in my hands that I saw it said «wildflowers». Of course I knew it said «wildflowers» even when my foolish eyes had it saying «witchcraft». I must have been very upset even then. She said, seeing me holding her book:

"Oh, are you interested in wildflowers?" I had to chuckle under my breath as I said:

"No, not really, but they do seem to pop up in the strangest places." Then she asked me why I was chuckling and I just said:

"I wasn't chuckling. I must be suffering some respiratory distress." We were all so near the knuckle out there.

It was then she told me she and Mr. Smuts had been called away on urgent business to the Transvaal and Tess was returning to school in Rhodesia. It would be necessary, she said, to vacate their house this very day.

"My goodness," I said, "I'll have to move to a hotel. What a shame I shan't have another night here." But secretly I wasn't all that upset. I rather enjoyed living in a suitcase. She said she'd give me the name of one that would suit me to a tee but I said no, I'll just stay at the Sheraton or the Hilton or whatever they have down here. She said she'd drive me in herself whenever I was ready. So you see, everything worked out amicably. I was only sorry not to have had a chance to thank Mr. Smuts in person and bid farewell to their daughter. She said this was a pity and not at all possible.

It was a really warm and wonderful visit in the household of some South African native peoples and I was so pleased to have had the experience. We drove into town then in her Mercedes coupe, quite a marvel of precision engineering. By the way, Mrs. Smuts, Beverly, but we never reached a first name familiarity, had a full head of thick, full-bodied hair so I asked her to share her secret. She said it was really quite simple. She bought an avocado at the supermarket and then let it grow quite over-ripe on the top of the refrigerator for from ten to fourteen days. Then she peeled and pitted it, osterized it and rubbed it vigorously into her scalp for five minutes. Twenty minutes later she'd shampoo, rinse and voilà.   A thick, rich head of hair.

We talked of this and that as we drove along. My bags were safely stowed in the boot, their word for trunk. She told me that this car was her very own and that she was extremely fond of it. She and her husband were to go to Johannesburg where he would stay while she went on to their country place outside the city. It was very beautiful and had belonged to her father and his father before him, she said. I said it must be very pleasant to have a country retreat to go to and she said, yes, it was. As we approached the center of town I saw many black people walking right on the same sidewalk, if not exactly arm-in-arm, with white people. And here I had heard that they kept the races totally separate. Well, so much for that piece of misinformation.

She dropped me at the front door of the Cape Hilton and I bid her a fond adieu.   It was such a lovely visit and so sad it was cut short. I just had time to slam the door as she swung her Mercedes out of the drive. I checked in speedily and was shown to my room by a bellhop named Johnson who was, believe this or not, an American negro. I was so happy to be there because I just love room service. I find nothing quite so civilized as having a BLT and fries wheeled in on a zinc salver. It's something you can demand when you go international class.

After lunch I walked to a Krugersbank which is what they call banks down here. I had one of the randsbarons (which is their word for bank officers) sell me some gold coins. I thought since I was here I might just as well get some for souvenirs. But I only bought a pound or so because I didn't want to be weighted down for the rest of my trip. I walked around town for a few hours, totally unafraid, amongst the smiling faces and all those bicycles.

I saw some of their old Dutch houses. They are impossible to describe except to mention their white walls, their gables, their shuttered white windows, their slave quarters. Not that I think you are really interested in any of this. Surely no more than myself. It was just casual tourism close to the hotel, don't worry about that.

I walked to the foot of Adderly Street and saw the van Riebeeck Statue. He is one of their great heros. I don't know what he did but seem to remember hearing somewhere he had found a great pipe of diamonds pushing out through a fissure in the earth somewhere in the Hex River Valley. Later Cayman told me they found so many diamonds at the mouth of the Orange River the market almost collapsed. If it weren't a monopoly it would collapse, he said. He says there are scads of Hope Diamonds all over. But then he liked to hear himself talk.

And it was walking back from the statue that I was attacked so savagely and beaten on the street. Yes, this is a strange story. And I pray to god you don't read this and then start saying South Africa isn't safe for all your friends. Because it isn't really as bad as it seems. Really just another nut with an umbrella. It happened like this:

I had stopped a young lady who seemed to be walking in my direction and sought to question her on certain local customs. Yes, of course, I was chatting her up. I admit this much. And this did lead to that as it will in any conversation. And then, from out of the big blue sky itself, she seemed shocked and offended and began yelling at me in a high pitched Afrikaans. Of course I didn't understand a word and I don't see how anyone could have. But, my isn't the female voice raised in anger a revolting thing to hear! Then a man came up, a big strapping Afrikander of some sort, and she seemed to talk to him while pointing at me and spit and spew a lot of drivel about what I had done. For some silly reason I then attempted to explain myself to him and as I was struggling through these sentences the man came down upon me and began heavily to box my ears with his umbrella. Then he seized me by the arm and tried to drag me down. I clung to a parking meter and was determined to keep my hold even at the risk of breaking my wristbones. The passersby were witnessing the scene, the man swearing at me, dragging and belaboring me, but I remained still. After all, he was strong and I was weak. Don't be a fool and get yourself badly hurt, spoke the wisdom of my heart. Some of the passers-by were moved to pity and exclaimed: "Man, let him alone. Don't beat him. He is not to blame. He is not one of us. He is a degenerate from England." I couldn't really understand them so I can only guess what they said. "No fear," cried the man but he seemed somewhat crestfallen and stopped pummelling me. He let go my arm, swore at me some and then moved away. My heart was beating fast within my breast and I was wondering whether I should ever reach my destination alive. Before I crawled away the man cast an angry look at me and, pointing his finger, growled: "Take care, let me once more see you in Capetown and I shall show you what I do."

I hurried back to my room with my head down and my tail between my legs. Such was the ferocity of my beating. So the physical threat is very real, I repeated to myself for the nth time, and it's brawn over brain again in the capitals of Europe. I was very upset. And to think, I was merely feeling my way through a morass of customs foreign to myself and had, in the process, addressed a frank and honest question to a young lady encountered on a street corner. So what if I were wrong? It had to be as much her fault as my own. I was still in a state of frightening distraction when the phone rang. It was Nanette calling in what seemed to me to be some agitated state.

"Oh, Des, what did you do? I've just had the strangest interview with Mrs. Smuts. She stopped over here to talk to the people we're staying with. What did you say? What did you do?"

"Very little, I assure you," I said impassively. I was quite beyond worrying about my reputation in a town this far away from the «action». And with a woman like Nanette the last thing you wanted to show was any uncertainty or any weakness. She would tell you to go into the garden and eat worms.

"And the tourist board called to ask how soon before our party sailed. And then I found out our repairs had been effected with unexpected, extraordinary really, speed. We sail at dawn."

"Not a moment too soon," I squealed before I could check myself.

"Are you all right, Dessy?" she asked.

"It's nothing. No, I'm marvy, really, " I protested, perhaps a bit weakly.

"In any case," she continued, "we dine tonight at the Modhi Natal. It's Raj continental and I just know you'll love it. You know that Ernest and I are very serious about eating." That would be the curry joint. Blah, blah, blah. I just couldn't listen to her any more and burst into tears.

"I was beaten in the street," I cried, "beaten in the street."

"Don't move, I'll be right over," she responded instantly. She hung up. Actually, I was very happy to have her visit. All this stress had made me feel quite lonely.

Ah, this constantly shifting store-house of character actors we call personality. Getting my ears boxed on a strange street by a stranger certainly did make me wonder, wonder how people suddenly got so much better than me all of a sudden. At times like that I just had to grab hold of myself and remember what this world wants. And I might add, it doesn't much mind how it gets it. Or what sort of messy residue ensues and lingers upon the memory-sheet of it's «climax» emission and subsequent cashiering on the carpet of sound liquid management and fiscal continence. And then you'll say, sure, he feared lest his fluidity be lost playing spillikins in the bedroom. But what are our best years then, our prime? A just solvent bank of sottish memories soon to be overdrawn? And if they but be pleasantly foolish, then what matter whether they transpire in a sweating hair-walled tenement slum or the palace of a burgher? It might sound as if I'm emotionally involved here. But, I must tell you, I'm not. And I'm right in my own way.

I know I have been described as having a pessimistic drag on the social spirit, as suffering a certain «bafflement before evil» which precludes the modest intimacy of casual encounter. I don't think that's true. As for the charge that I'm stupid, well, I don't think I should respond to that sort of slur. But I imagine it is necessary to say a few words on the quality of intelligence contained in these sentiments. For indeed everyone, from the meanest savage and his sour-mash to the epicure and his raw meat, knows something. Knows quite a lot, actually, as much as he need know. A skull full, if you wish. But these «towers of silence», these men of «executive action», whose mentation is piled straight up into the sky, the abode of lucky little gods and their venery, on pi and lineality, seem distinctly Persian in character, where mountain and tomb are analogous. And we have here for reference only the words of the poet, being roughly: «the muscleman will not be converted until he can have houris in paradise.» Ah, the hoarse cry of their strangled masses continuously moving into a deeper voice and a less profound syntax, resolving all questions of value and meaning in terms of «depth of pile.»

But it be an historic inevitability that this sort of emotional indigence will sand-bag out in the end and impoverished will be seen to be poor. We have already witnessed within the soon to be completed decade numberless interpenetrations of opposite, rectifications of name, resolutions of contradiction, even a known instance of negation of negativity herself. It really is a «greater fool» market for the «second gun» theory.

Of course youth will be attracted to this synthetic thought until the realities of commercial and martial intercourse are grasped after which time it will retain mere manipulative value to the users with no perceived attraction or interest to the used. And here, in the actual movement of mind, many will hesitate at the seemingly simple action of mental stacking, this categorical action of putting your known world into a binomial filing cabinet where it will remain safe and be ready for rapid extraction. And those who so reject will then mistakenly proceed toward a blanket rejection of all such rational processing and social mechanization. Will take the easy way out, in other words, and gain much unsightly fat. And who can blame them? I certainly have no vested interest in a fair fight. But let me assure you true movement will not be experienced by those on the road for a day trip or a motor jaunt to the lake country to watch the race wars. And I could care less if you agree with what I'm talking about. I don't think that is really what's at question here. It's not that sort of thing. And I do apologize in advance for when I turn toward the anti-social side. Perhaps it is a crime against the state. In the «troubled sea of wickedness» who has the time to care enough to give the very best for a better life, the reality of failure being such a cramp on la douceur de vivre. Such a shaving, really. But no, I don't think I deserve a big blob on the police blotter for that, not to this day, not for something so simple and misunderstood as a speech impediment.

If you remember I was sitting on the bed in my room at the Cape Hilton waiting for Nanette to come. I had been crying because a man in the street had beat me about the head with his umbrella. This drove me into a bout of crippling subjectivity and speculative thought from which I had scarce recovered when Nanette pushed in the door. She pulled me down on to the bed and lay beside me, pressing her clothing against my body. She was wearing a handsome outfit, a brown and grey fleck worsted twill cut quite nicely on the diagonal with a chiné silk blouse. She pressed her large breasts, quite contained in a large brassière, high up on to my chest just below the neck. She was comfort itself at that moment, small as she was. I can't remember ever having felt a deeper longing for the more profound contact between people. I stood up and straightened the pleats in my trousers as soon as I was able. I walked to the window and said:

"You're not really fair to me, Nanette. You know that, don't you. You shouldn't use me like this, tempt me and take advantage of my weakness."

"We older women really aren't all that attractive, are we, Desmond?" After I had seen everything there was to see out the window, I snapped:

"Don't change the subject." Perhaps I was hungry. She was still on the bed, lying on her stomach. I couldn't help but notice the rear of her knee where her skirt had hiked above her slip.

"Anyway, what attracts me has absolutely nothing to do with the theoretics of attraction." She shifted herself deftly and sat back against two fluffy pillows.

"You do fancy yourself, don't you, Mr. Desmond." I didn't like her using that name. She lit a filtered cigarette and languidly crossed her legs.

"Can you imagine a people so reduced, my dear friend Desmond, so reduced that they live on brown soap and callouses. I do hope you don't have any. They are such a sign of poverty." I did in fact have one on my foot, a small callous as they go, nothing to be ashamed of. I put it down to poor pediatric podiatry and perhaps an early injury to certain bones and ligaments. But why was I wasting this time looking through my shoes.

"Imagine them about their daily lives," she continued, "little iron men in overalls stained black with labor, leathery little women in rayon and polyester, children bound with cord. Oh, if only you could, if only you had that talent. If only you could imagine something that wasn't somehow snarky, Des darling, I'm sure you'd go far."

"I assure you," I retorted sharply, "I'll go no farther than public transport or private carriage can carry me. You know how I abhor walking."

"Oh, you silly, you don't like to walk because your legs are so thin and bandy." She had tweaked me there. How I hated how she turned the conversation sour when I was only interested in cogent repartee.

"I could never properly appreciate an ad hominem," I said coolly.

"You mean ad homo, don't you, Dessy?" With this she got up, crossed the room and casually picked up a very lovely antique blue shaving mug, designed with fetching small black sardines and given to me from my mother's personal collection when I was still a schoolboy. Then she dropped it on to the floor where it shattered into a hundred pieces. It was French from the nineteenth century. It must have cost hundreds. Ah, how these physical objects and events in real time seem to resemble our deeper, inner lives. She touched at the pieces ever so slightly with the toe of her left shoe and said:

"I don't know what to make out of you, Desmond, a mouse trap or a time bomb."

"Make of me! Oh, that's a good one." I could see right from there it was going to be a difficult night before sailing. I almost hoped for some intriguing special event on the television. There was a big Trinatron in the corner of the room. I crossed to it and flipped on the state channel. Our first selection was an information program on the achievements of the South African State in meeting the challenges of the future. Beginning with the work of their famous surgeons, they showed some perfectly revolting footage of an open-heart transplant. With the gurgling and the palpitating I was eventually forced to drop my head between my knees to keep from fainting. Nanette went into the bathroom. I believe she had a bowel movement because when she came out she was dressed only in her slip. She just stood there basking in the after-glow of laxative action. But she was dancing in a plastic bag as far as I was concerned.

The program continued with actual pictures of the atomic test made in their Pacific wastes. They explained in voice-over that these pictures were released at this time to forewarn the world of South Africa's intention to use just such weaponry should international affairs transpire to the detriment of their internal integrity. Of course this was nothing new. We've all known about it for years. Just another annihilation threat, I said to myself. We ordered up some beer and peanuts and settled in for some good telly till dinner time. Cayman was to come by and meet us here. He was «away on business».

Next they showed all about the program for South African cosmonauts. As I understand it there are plans afoot to launch the entire tribe into outer space and give the whole country over to consessionaires who will administer it on a colonial basis. But this is hear-say. The television was getting warmed up now and the colors were quite vivid if not realistic. Nanette had hitched her slip up above her knees but I was firm in my determination to ignore her. There was a feature on the ABC, a fraternal organization dedicated to the old way and stability in the region. The show ended with a demonstration of a brand new invention developed at Wittersrand U., a huge picking machine the size of a field-house which eliminates almost completely the need for agricultural workers. It all goes to show, I suppose, the adaptability of lonely and isolated people when they bond as brothers against intrusive notions.

After this we watched a popular series in which a wife was blamed for her husband's killing because she had inadvertently cursed the earth on which he had been slain. She was put into a psychiatric trance following electro-convulsive therapy in which state the curse was broken but they all discovered that in another existence there is another guilt, more complex, more pernicious. It was so full of commercials! First a car, then a garbage bag, then wine, dog food, burgers, more wine, pain relievers, human scent improvers. By the end of it all Nanette had her hand down in my trousers and forced me to ejaculate into the folds of her lingerie.

"Oh, god, I wish you hadn't done that, Nanette," I said when she had finished with me.

"Oh, don't be mad, Dessy," she cooed, "I know I'm vain. But that's what it's all about. Don't you know that?"

"I know no such thing," I replied archly as I went into the toilet to clean myself. Secretly I wasn't totally displeased but I can't for the life of me imagine what pleasure she could have taken from such a sterile exercise. When I came out she called me to the bed and bid me kiss her. I did and then she whispered that Ernest was on his way up, that he would be there in a matter of seconds. I don't know how she knew. I didn't hear the telephone ring. But I hopped right up and met him as he came through the door.

He walked into the room with that aura of authority one associates with the vice squad and took it in with those big green eyes of his. And there lay Nanette on the rumpled bed, her high-heeled shoes still on her feet, her slip above the tops of her nylon stockings, revealing indeed the straps that led up to her garter belt, something which I hadn't even suspected. And there was a large wet spot on the silk just where it creased itself. And as if I weren't already sufficiently compromised, she lay there smiling a very naughty and insipid smirk. It seemed antique somehow, though undeniably sensual in that torpid atmosphere. Cayman took my arm at the elbow and turned me toward the door. I half expected there to be a shorter, fatter and balding version of himself in the corridor as well as 2 or 3 press photographers.

"Just remember, son," he said in a voice both affected and paternal, "don't get into anything you can't get yourself out of."

"I didn't get into anything," I protested. It was just a little bit humiliating to have him talking to me in that mock-serious tone of voice. We both looked down and noticed I wasn't wearing any shoes. It is strange how embarrassing that can be. I don't know that he suspected anything had been «going on» between Nanette and I, as indeed there hadn't. But a man like that could make something out of nothing. So I told him there had been a freak shower, Nanette had been soaked, we had sent her suit to the valet service, it had just returned and she had somehow spilled a splash of beer into her lap. He seemed to accept this though I assure you I invested nothing in any of the possible responses he could have made. Plausible is a quality of trust to me. In any case he said:

"If you want to hang by your thumbs, kid, I don't care." This sort of flippancy was just what got my dander up. Finally they were very crude and manipulative people who were just taking advantage of my youth, my openness, and enmeshing me in a fabric of half-truth and bad-faith. And I certainly had no desire to get embroiled in a domestic situation. There was a moment's silence. Then Cayman shrugged his shoulders and said:

"Let's eat." Nanette stood up and slipped on her suit. As she straightened her skirt she said:

"Ernest and I will wait downstairs."

"Yeah, we'll wait for you in the oyster bar," Cayman added. So there I was, left high and lonesome. Oh, how to escape her insane novella, I thought, as I looked into the mirror. There seemed to be so little at issue here and yet so much at stake. I dressed quickly and joined them downstairs in the bar.

10

Rory Macallister

It was a beautiful hotel and I mean that. I found Nanette and Ernest sitting at the bar but we took a corner table when I arrived. I ordered a scotch and water. I did need a drink to settle myself, just remembering what a difficult day it had been. Nanette leaned across the table and patted my hand. I glanced at Cayman who looked cool and collected studying the bar decor and personnel. He'd spent his day buying and selling at the stock exchange. Oh, he thought he was so clever. And there she sat, smug as a bumble-bee, waiting for her cut.

"There, there," she said, patting my hand, "it's been a long hard day but it will soon be over and we shall be snug in our beds and deep in sleep." Doddering old amnesiac, I thought to myself. I couldn't believe I was being forced to endure her company. My mind raced through a list of younger, more vivacious acquaintances. Many of them dead already, it was true, too true. What would cause a generation to «dissociate» so, were it not treachery and drugs, then alcohol and fuzzy thinking?

Mercifully there followed a silence of sorts, a lack of conversation at our table, but there was bar-din to keep us occupied: Something music-like from hidden speakers, scads of business men, doctors, lawyers, bankers, executives and theatricals from the music circus on the third floor of the hotel, chatting themselves up, getting to know one another. Then Cayman began mumbling to Nanette, saying he was going to «float a load» on a semi conductor-chip operation. He said:

"They're going merchant on a sixty-four Kay-chip. Be a couple of years before anything comes of it." When I told him I had no idea of what he spoke, and don't to this day, he took it as an excuse to explain the whole tedious affair. Oh, he was a regular manufacturer all right, and part of a real operation, directors of development, newsletters, clipping service, corporate grants' program, all the earmarks of an intelligence operation without the overtones of black-spots and disappearances. And no, I don't think intelligence was, with him, anything more than a hobby. He didn't stop talking, of course, but kept right on as if I would actually try to make some sense out of what he said:

"Of course you know these chips are circuits that form the core of a memory. They make them from crystals of silicon they grow in big vats of pig fat, dope them out about the size of that pimple on your forehead." His very impolite reference was to a blemish above my left brow which I had meant to mask with pancake but had neglected in my haste. He continued despite my rather obvious frown:

"The current generation is 16 Kay, no more, with a lot of loss on the production line. Think about it, one dead cell and you're off your personal best. So apparently what to do is add a few thousand extras, allow random access into the chip and you've got what for, fault tolerance. So now they test as they drop them in the hopper, blow polysilicon fuses on the dead heads and re-route circuits by the other fellers. Even if a couple thou blow, you're still holding sixty-four Kay. It increases the chance of turning out good wafers by a factor of two. And that means big bucks in the market place. Until they go Meg and Kay and change the rules of the game." This «story», possibly about a young farm girl named Kay with multiple personalities who undergoes an ur-catholic transubstantialization routine and lives to play again but to all intents and purposes as two people, she and her sister Meg, much older, much abused, was apparently meant to impress Nanette and I with secondary narrative skills; but it is only recorded here as a primary document in cultural logorrhea. He gave a little chuckle and said:

"Why don't you go twenty-five thousand blind, kid, put a bag over your head and double your money." The man was crudity incarnate as far as I was concerned. To think I would think of throwing good money into something so mechanistic and removed from the operations of my own mind as a big-name-button pee-movie made me want to screech. I couldn't remember when I have been so offended.

"That's about as interesting as a coven of witches flicking their horny fingers and doing the mashed potato," I declared, meaning to lighten the tone and be interesting. I don't forget my social obligations but Cayman ignored me and instead pointed out two men at the end of the bar.

"You see those guys? Well, they're the house dicks. The fat one's the straight guy and the skinny guy's the peeper/entrapper. What a pair."

"However would you know something like that," I asked with just a touch of disbelief. A good question, I thought, but Nanette snapped:

"Dessy, you vixen, don't be rude." Cayman just laughed out of the corner of his mouth and said:

"Ro-me-o and Ju-li-et, can't forgive, can't forget. . ." Such a dumbo, I thought, but of course I couldn't say anything. He'd was out to prove to me that even he had culture. But more on poseurs in a moment. He was going to pay the bar bill in cash but I insisted on signing the check. I just love to charge things to my room. Then, when you get the final bill, it's like a little history of your stay.

We had another drink and waited while a few more of our number arrived, including Miss Springman, of course, with her sketch pad and her little pink sneakers, with her tote bags and her «Je reviens». And she calls herself an artist. Humpf. I'll tell you what kind of an artist she is; an artist of the stained romantic school where the tenderest emotions are painted in ochre streaks on white cotton, an aesthetic only the marriage contract could forgive. And after she'd had a couple of glasses of «old fashion» she began mumbling some totally and perfectly nonsensical blah-blah about believing I had bribed the ensign of the laundry room and had thus engineered the unfortunate and unwashed mix-up in undergarments, not believing for a moment it was a mistake made in the grind of the washer and the drone of the dryer. Of course I threw them in my steamer trunk and forgot them. I didn't want them littering up the floor and making of my chamber a sloven's playpen. I was raised to clean my own room and have not for convenience forgotten all my lessons. But you have to be careful about negativity. Sometimes the eye doesn't even see that «not» and you may be led to think, as Deborah thinks, that I had merely polluted my winter clothing by being a momma's boy. Oh, don't be silly like her. And don't worry, I have moth balls!

Well, that's how we got to the Indian Restaurant just off the bar. It was a little piece of India set down on the coast of Africa. I love the way those India boys decorate their eateries. All that drapery, all that cloth. But our evening turned into such a hideous orgy of indulgence and stupefaction that ultimately I was embarrassed before my new found friends. I mean the waiters. I make it a point to get close to the staff of any establishment. And even if certain owners do object, I feel it improves my digestion. And do you know what's incredible? They were all called Sammy. I'd address one and say: "Sammy, some more lassi and lemon pickle" and another one would jump up and get it. We had such a good laugh over all the mistaken identities. First we ordered a bit of barfi, a true Gujarat delight. Then someone said: "«The Bitter Barf of Dr. Chow»: oh, what a great title for a story about a man eating in an Indian Rest. on the way to China." And some people, Cayman among them because he could only read mysteries, got a little excited and started suggesting certain seminal plot elements. That bothered me a little because, after that, he never failed to approach me with a new one and they were only an effort to get my goat. I don't like to do that, I honestly don't. That's not the way I work. But then I feel this whole tale is compelling enough to want to race to the very end. Let's just leave it to loose talk all along the way.

Now there will be those who say they have never heard of a certain Rory MacAllister. Harumpft. I mentioned him the last time the subject «girl-crazy» came up. And it always did with Rory around. Everything changed for me when he came aboard. I changed from being my crumpled, surly self to someone who could aspire to that yellow velour pleasure ordinary people take in their own grunting fornications. Just that animal hope in the vision of a carrot. Not that I feel anyone's ordinary. But I changed when Rory was there, changed in ways that may be shocking to some, but I swear, if you could have seen the light in this man's eyes he would have taken hold of you as he did of me. Not that night in the restaurant but soon after, when the ship hit the typhoon in the Indian Ocean. Though he would deny it to this day, the man saved my life.

He was Australian which accounts for why he was here. He'd met the purser, Freddo, in a bar and after a lot of winking and drinking, joking and tall stories, he'd bought a ticket and was to be, with all his imperfections, a fellow passenger. And he was here now at the end of the table in the Indian Restaurant. That's where I first laid eyes on this gorgeous human being.   So. I didn't go right up to him or anything obvious. I just studied him from afar at first. And then when I got to know him, «to hell with a lot of bad rubbish» is what I thought. Oh, not him, but all my tawdry troubles up till then. Cayman must have seen me glance in Rory's direction because he then said in a stupidly melodramatic stage whisper:

"New boy on the block, better lock up the hen house." Then some hokus-pokus about critical mass and big bombs eating all smaller bombs until the world was disarmed. There wasn't a death trip around he didn't lay his horny palm upon. So, you see, nothing had changed on that front.

I just can't get in enough of these Rory stories, can I? Well, I didn't put a «blue pencil on my heart» then and I'm not at all embarrassed by my obvious enthusiasm. And if you knew him you'd feel the same way I do. I mean, an absolutely perfect body, a marvelous and touching battlefield of a face, an upper-torso like a splitting wedge. A perfect 28 waist. There is almost a delicious pleasure in my talking about him. I was flattered really, he would take any notice at all of ugly dumpling Desmond. He'd just come from Sun City in the Ciskai and seemed as anxious as I to get off the Cape. And when he winked, you'd want to die. But we, we passengers, were involved in another period of relative excess, a good deal of which was accomplished on shore before our re-embarkation. And Rory was to perform valiantly many of the baser functions aboard which I, for moral reasons, declined to execute.

Let's see, after the barfi we had some of the yogurt drink I spoke of earlier. And Rory was just down the table. I know you know that. Later Rory saved me from being swept overboard in the storm. That is when he saved me with his strength and I am forever grateful.   And sometimes I wish he hadn't. But never mind. It turns out he was a devil of a man with a great wit who knew the territory like the back of his hand. He was such a great help when the police took us into custody. I was absolutely helpless in the face of the rank of uniforms. It was Nanette who had dragged us there. I never said anything about doing anything zany. And the people we saw were marginal at best. My goodness they were goofy, posturing and posing, pursing their lips and rubbing their breasts. I thought they would turn over the taxi but Rory spoke to them. He got them to say the most outrageous things in that funny dialect of theirs. It was a riot. Some men came over. Their names were Cosmas, Nelson, Govan, Walter and Bram. Funny I should remember them at all. But they were sharp dressers and randy as high water. Then some more came and soon there were too many to count. The taxi driver was extremely nervous and I thought for a moment of standing on top of his car and talking to the people, telling them to disperse, go to their homes, store grain everywhere, simple things they say to calm a throng. And that's when the police came. And in such droves. I just went to pieces and started throwing up on all their cars. But I didn't think we were in any trouble. It was the food. The mutton shambhala we had had for dinner, really tasty joints of lamb fairly dripping with fat meat and spice. It never did have a place to settle.

I don't mean to disappoint your interest in the actual police action but I'm afraid I must for I was passed out in the back seat of a police cruiser while Cayman negotiated for our freedom. I suppose he did it with money. It seemed to mean nothing to him though he was anything but generous. Finally they let us off as harmless merrymakers and we went for that awful midnight swim which is also against the rules. We literally crawled back on board. And the customs were a joke. I could have taken out a ton of anything. But I didn't and will not return to S.A. until all those ugly allegations are dropped and publicly rescinded.

11

Storm at Sea

And so we left that vast and comparatively empty country. A short stay and so much like going home at the same time. But it seems so little was accomplished. We sailed at dawn, some of us arriving directly from our wild, funny, exhausting night on the town. The Captain stood by the gangplank looking quite business-like in some tribal robes he had acquired. None of us could stand him any more. In a few days no one could stand anyone. But I'll fill in these blanks as I go along. I just don't have the courage and wherewithal right now.

And the Afrikanders? Hugonauts? Just another pack of rats jumped from sinking flag-ship Europo? Why would I, a tourist, attempt to answer a question like that? What is real independence, anyway? The back and forth of all free movement, the swing from the roundabout to the trees? Or merely a chance to loosen one's tie after a day with one's peers? All my life I've learned it's not that easy and I guess I've learned. But as you know, for I have told you from the outset, I am under medical treatment for a sudden and blinding pain. It's nothing really. And I certainly won't trouble you with more of it than is necessary to understand the setting.

As we sailed out of Table Bay in a pea-soup fog a ghastly ship came up and ran along our lee within inches of our railings. I was standing near the poop with Rory MacAllister. It was in our first hours back on board. We both jumped back in fright. I clutched at his arm and he said to me darkly:

"There's not a soul on board her, Dusty, she must be a ghoster out of Lima; saints have mercy, not a soul. It's a sign from above." He'd taken to calling me Dusty right away, just after I met him in the restaurant. I thought it was so cute I never bothered to correct him.

And he pronounced Lima as in the bean. I was so frightened by the ghoster I was fairly screeching. I'm sure they heard me in the mess.

Anyway, her name was the Van der Deacon, a regular flying Dutchman. I was of a mind to report her incompetent piloting to the proper authorities but it is so hard to get in touch when you're on the high seas.

After she had slipped by and disappeared out the other side of the fog I just crumpled up right there on the deck. Rory reached out and broke my fall with his foot. I think it was the first time he'd touched me. And he was so strong he kept me from smashing my face on the deck. It isn't everyone who's as thoughtful as that. He must have left me there to go and look for help. When I woke up from my swoon I saw my feet were hanging overboard. I had rolled up against the rail and was about to be lost at sea. Then I saw him returning with old man Cayman. They grabbed my arms and pulled me into the lounge before I was swept away. So, you see, right from the start I owed my life to that man Rory; I, who had never known debt.

As we rounded the Cape the seas heaved into thirty foot swells and the twenty-knot wind sent a nasty spray across our bow and awash our rails. Waves crashed over us and «flounder» was the word on everyone's lips. We cowered in the lounge until the sea sickness took up. Then we'd dash out and vomit over the rails in full view of the assembled company. It was so humiliating. No one likes to do that sort of thing in public. It was particularly hard on the ladies for the strong and erratic winds blew their skirts far up over their heads providing profound views of their full exonerated, I'm sure, hind quarters. And by that time half of them no longer had any undergarments to speak of. (Some of the «alpaca» was rather scruffy by this time, caked a bit and matted. Though Nan did her best with what she had, typhoon or no. This is so important in a female person and so unventilated in journals of personal health. All the really big stars know the importance of fluff and bounce.) It's a shame the way we were buffeted about out there, like so much boart from the diamond crusher, like so many loose canon. And to see the women so displayed, bent over the rails and retching. I went down to my stateroom and hung on the toilet bowl for hours.

The Cape of Good Hope is really «itself» in a very real way. There is no mistaking these waters for anywhere else in the world. That's what the old salts say. "All the watery region round about there is much like some noted four corners of a great bed where you meet more fellow travelers than in any other part." And bed it was! When I felt again half-decent I went up on deck and stood staring out on the brute sea. Oh, that rugged sea, so steady and so powerful. I know there is something in the nature of mechanical manipulation about it, not unrelated to the quake and the eruption. But wet! I could tell you. It had all left me so glum and dyspeptic. It always happens when you try to eat anything that «ain't meat and potaters» to you. All those scattered spices and high seas, it was like the Book of Job, that old bible story. And wasn't that a terrible «put-down» on old Job himself. But he did suffer after all, I don't want to say that. For all his hard feelings. I don't know what he thought he'd do with the keys to the kingdom once he got them. Stick them in some slavey's «painted pussy», I suppose. Another freebooting seaman with a gory knocker, I say.

I am forced to admit old man Cayman weathered these trials somewhat better than the average man. His youth was, I understand, not exactly nautical though certainly somewhat tempestuous. This explains, I'm sure, his elegant manner, his genteel veneer, his ability to continuously attribute every error to another. Perhaps it was all sham but it's so difficult to tell in a few short months. He was, of course, totally mad and self-contradictory, but harmless unless you knew him well in which case he could be quite detrimental to other relationships. I feel that he was, at least in part, the key to my unpopularity with the voting majority on board. It was he who applied the «pressure downstairs», as it were. A person like myself is particularly vulnerable to slander. I know they identified me with the brute sea and therefore hated me like a pack horse. But by the third day the storm had made me one with the passengers and out-weighed what they had heard in their minds. I had little fear of the storm itself for I had had experience of similar ones. To tell the absolute truth, I am a good sailor and do not get sea-sick as such. So I could fearlessly move amongst their number, bringing them comfort and good cheer and conveying to them hourly reports of the Captain. The friendship I thus formed stood me, as we shall see, in very good stead. But the real storm was still to come.

Deborah «got romantic» after her regurgitation. Many women do. My god, I wouldn't let that woman near me if she crawled up to my sink while I was shaving. And she was just the sort, albeit innocent, who'd later call you «yellow» as a lover. And how she'd boil if ever you did induce her by force of mind or power of argument to bend, ever so slightly, her little back or lift the protective package of her thigh to any angle whatever, not even touching her ever so modestly with your «reactive finger of doubt». And how could you possibly know before hand that she wouldn't turn out fangy and gray of tooth. There is no way to intelligence a thing like that. She never smiled. She was mumbling through her lips. It sounded like pig under glass, her talking like that.

And yet perhaps I exaggerate. I only know she was a very sick woman when I led her stumbling to her stateroom where I undressed her, meaning to wipe away the throw-up and any harmful bacteria carried there upon. If I hadn't been there she could have passed out on the bathroom floor. I removed her clothing piece by piece and then carried her limp and naked body back to the bed. By this time I had begun to suspect some sort of food poisoning in the curried duck which we had in common partook chez our sub-continental brothers. And please don't get me wrong. I do not mean to accuse these gentlemen of any sort of racially related activity in their apparent attempt to poison the lot of us. For I do believe that all men are born absolutely equal. Though not, indeed, equally and absolutely fireproof. And this, I assure you, I have tested in both squalid and respectable situations. If only we would all realize the cold, cruel and seemingly arbitrary conditions extant at ground zero, as it were. So many unscrupulous sectors of our commonweal operate as mere fluxions of gross national product and have so much to gain from our constant racialist squabbling and infighting. For, indeed, my friends, the republic has rich and powerful enemies who would yet see us bent and broken under the white man's burden.

You take, for instance, the Caymen. Now they didn't believe a single thing they said as far as I could tell, had no concept of virtue nor fear of the law, had never tasted the salty slime of guilt nor the bitter noodle of doubt, and yet they prospered in this environment like sailors-blue by the side of the road. And don't think Ernest thought himself above a bit of pelagian pleasure out there on that float, so tossed and tumbled were we by then. God knows there had been more than a little gamey ram-rodding going on on shore.

You'll remember I made the silly mistake of taking tipsy Deborah to her room where I undressed her and cleaned her trembling and slightly feverish body. It wouldn't be fair to tell you anything of how she appeared in that fervid and unnatural state. And their are ethics involved.   I assure you I have nothing against the profession of male nurse. Many an older man with a massive cardiac arrest will say exactly the same thing. Their delicacy of touch is a model of civilized manipulation. However, she began to wake as I massaged her torso. I didn't want to be there should there be a scene so I left quietly. I knew she wouldn't comprehend my kindness. It must have been that very night Rory first found his way to her boudoir, took advantage of her while she slept the sleep of travellers in the beyond and thus began the illicit congress that was to end so tragically. And this I can prove by eyewitness account. So you can start to think the worst right now.

The storm seemed to last for weeks but I think it was only two days. Some were sick the entire trip and have not recovered to this day. On the second night we were passed by our sister ship in the unabating storm. That's what the Captain said. All I saw was some lights off the starboard bow, sometimes as much as 14 stories above us, then an equal depth below. Quite stunning. Needless to say I wasn't sharing tea and chitchat with him anymore. The Captain. My former good feelings had turned somewhat rancorous. And of course, my relationship with the Caymen had deteriorated to absolute bone meal! I think it was totally their fault. There we were, the three of us, forever fused together like the parts of the innominate bone, like some unbending nuclear family, impotently fused and immobile, bearing weight at an odd angle. Then the storm let up and we cruised innocently enough into the Indian Ocean, bobbing along for all the world like some salted piece of bladder wrack headed for Hong Kong.

Then the next day the fire started in Deborah's bed and spread like burning bushes to her laundry bag and personal papers. There was some slight smoke damage to her clothes closet. And she wore some very fine articles of clothing, I assure you. That very night I happened to leaf through her collection of dresses etc. All of first class materials and from top-notch houses. But more of the events in her bedroom that night in a moment. First this:

I have never approved of sexual adventurism, no matter what guise it takes or how attractive the packaging. Deborah later called it love. Ah, love, that great killer of youth. Poor silly that she was! I myself saw Rory do her over with great gobs of «salivary» easy-off and then with his «thick brush» after the whole thing «blew up in his face.» But more of this in a moment. I must continue my argument as it comes to me. And imagine loving Rory. Why, he was totally immoral with all that innocence of really aggressive guys. And it certainly couldn't have been anything more than class-love, that degenerate specie. As far as I'm concerned love is the single worst plague ever visited on man-kind. Certainly highly placed and well-respected medical doctors estimate that over half of the adult populations of industrialized Western nations suffer from some form of love-sickness, mostly manifesting itself in chronic absenteeism, loss of memory, child abuse and obsessional tendencies. And we wonder why productivity falls and prices skyrocket, why there is tightened international liquidity. If I were put in charge of the drug-testing program for just one year I would revolutionize the business! It's a crime the way this country has been red-lined. Oh, well, it's keep up or keep out where I come from.

The alarm went off when Deb's papers caught fire and we all dove for the lifeboats. One was even lowered. The one to which I happened to have dashed when the siren sounded. It did feel strange to be floating suddenly so calmly on the Indian Ocean in a small wooden boat. They asked me to row but I explained about my bursitis and sat in the back with the Caymen. Deborah went hysterical and began babbling about putting little curtains between us, making our own independent spaces. That young woman was so mad. I just know she was hoping the ship would burn and sink and we'd all lose our lives slowly and painfully. I saw the whole story in the smug little purse of her lips. Then everyone took it up as a privacy issue. I was fairly screaming at Deborah, perched next to me on the same plank of wood. What do you think he meant, I shrieked, when he suggested we go forth and multiply. Some branch of higher arithmetic. I arched my brows to make my point. God knows I wanted to communicate with the woman. I don't know exactly what I meant at the time but I know they heard me back on the boat.

Please excuse me my excessiveness. It is a weakness. But I am a man committed to virtue and the true triumph of right and the rule of law. But even I can see that when I indulge, as I occasionally do, it does my cause a wrong. Let me be perfectly straight with you before we turn again to my grim tale. This isn't the first horrible thing nor will it be the last. Not if we go to war tomorrow and begin killing each other with clubs. Oh, we've all been through a lot, more than we care to admit. Oh, we've all gotten fat and lazy and brutalized by it all. They say I'm a snob but I want to say I am not a snob. I have no political program to speak of. Ladies and gentlemen, I speak to you as a private citizen. I owe no obligation to anyone except my conscience. And seeing as how the life of the mind is all that remains to the bulk of us, I lay these chestnuts in the fire that you may more quickly catch the drift of my wit in these few lines on travel and health. It's just the same old story told the old way. Or it's an old hat worn at an awkward angle. It's just that I can't stand to see the innocent get hurt. Not really. But then, who's really innocent anymore anyway. Oh, I like a practical joke, like a hot wired radio or a short sheet, a burning bag of dog candy. But that's not the same thing.

I just know you're going to underestimate Rory MacAllister in all this because I haven't given him enough exposure in these pages. Rory was rather war-like in his own subtle way. He'd say: "I could beat you to a pulp with one hand tied behind my back." To me! I don't know who he thought he was talking to, the organizer of the American Nazi Movement? And Cayman, so smug and vicious, saying: "This tiger couldn't even stand up if somebody didn't slap on the cuffs." Then he'd wander off, mumbling: "Ha, ha, ha, that's a good one. . . ." Sometimes it was so difficult to know what in the world he was talking about.

Well, I guess we all must husband our genius, mustn't we? Like thick-skinned spies in some unholy war. And if you want something done you just better do it yourself.

And so, as per natural, Deb and Rory became, as they say, regular sex partners. Word of their midnight fornications spread like brushfire through the boat. Even the kitchen help, five or six indeterminate Easterners, whispered phrases such as: «kitchee fun go girlie flick-flock sack whack» and other such inanities. They always reduced everything to its absolute lowest level. I don't know how their wives put up with them.

And Deborah was even more annoying when she began to experience those sweet nothings of orgasm. Something in the climate of the Indian Ocean must have convinced her she wasn't just another tawdry working-girl turning trick beneath the decks. It's all sub-tropical above Madagascar, you know. Perhaps it was those fulsome attentions paid her by the Caymen. She became possessed by an overweening uppityness and grew at times even more insulting. Sometimes I was tempted to give her a good mouth full of my cotton candy, the fluffy stuff of the ultimate put-down. But I stood by the bible and said: Let us shake the dust of it off our flip-flops and let the bones dance which we have broken.

Ah, the time and the telling, the saying and the doing. The days fly by so swiftly on a boat. I am often lulled by the melody of this dignified middle aging which comes over me. When I think of any of them I think of Bucky, which is what I came to call my friend. Cayman, of course, caught wind of it and made nasty fun. He'd yell: "There goes Buck and Dust, the Bobsy twins." But it didn't matter to Bucky who was fortunate enough to have two beautiful children, poor things, and a lovely, though utterly promiscuous, wife back in Sydney.

Now it just so happens I know something of these nocturnal adventures, these private moments Rory and Deb would steal from their fellows. Late one night, as per usual, (perhaps it was that very first night with the storm raging outside, it being difficult to say as there were others,) I could find no rest and so found myself walking silently about the corridors of our great ship in search of distraction from all my cares and woe. And alas I sighted Deborah's door ajar. Thinking her peradventure insomniac and awake and wanting company, I approached closer in order to knock and announce myself. But then I saw a dark figure approaching the sleeping form on the bed and knew it was not Deborah who only wore pastel. Yes, the dark figure was Rory, poised with his hand about to lift the hem of her nightie, she oblivious of him, he oblivious of me. Yes, I stood and watched. What would you have done, pretend it wasn't happening.

The sleeping woman, the sneaking man: it was disgusting. I assure you. I mean it. I'm not being demure. Believe me. Wouldn't it be wonderful if a mature character actor could miraculously appear at this point and assure us that it just didn't happen. But it's not that way anymore. Tight money and mechanization brought on over-cultivation followed by excessive erosion, mob control of food distribution, waste and contamination of organic refuse, chemical fertilization which has not promoted sub-terrestrial organic action, night soil flushed into the sea. Oh, no, no, no! You're going to hear the whole thing. This is well-known to those who appreciate the broad sweep of science, not merely its commercial exploitation.

So I am forced to give it to you as grisly as it be. Does this hesitancy express anything to you? If not, I could get real crisp or rat-tat. Style and pace are so important to me. Can't you see I'd do absolutely anything if I wanted to please you? Rory would say to me, "oh, you old whore," and give me a little push. He was so silly sometimes. And in actual fact he was as mean and selfish a man as I have ever met. He would say really stupid things like, "now that I've gained weight it's much easier to avoid extra-terrestrial affairs," and such phrases as «lustrous as a paint chip». He tried and tried. Secretly I think he was jealous of me but it never came to a head. He was something of a pioneer, really, and pursued everything which took his fancy with the same mad intensity as must have seized our ancestors clearing the virgin forest and killing everything that lived there. Or those who poked the piggy sow of the great Southwest and saw for the last time the Zuni savage. For all the world like the first red man roping an iron horse and tying streamers to his pony's tail.

She was, not surprisingly, naked save for a pair of white silk briefs which she wore to great advantage beneath her nightie. His back was toward me which means I couldn't see him face to face. She, of course, was totally unaware of her predicament. At first anyway. Rory was dressed in a silly gabardine trench coat and sneakers with no socks. But later, moments later, after he had penetrated the outer layers of her negligée defense, she began to respond slightly and I thought I might have been played the fool. I checked behind me but there was no one down the hall. And I didn't know if he knew if she knew. I mean, there was enough doubt involved for me to hear no call from the hollow horn of chivalry. I wasn't about to rush in and flip on the lights. And it looked almost as if they might have staged it. For their own benefit, of course. Now that I think about it, they couldn't possibly have known I was to be there. Also, there was none of that formality, no downstage strings and distorted perspective associated with real manipulation. I imagine they enjoyed it. And I know what you're thinking, he's a peeper and that is terrible to stand there and watch other people as if you were not really there. Or you had not yet arrived. Or you have left already. And by the time you realize this it is already too late. You are watching and there is nothing you can do about it. So why bother, is what I always say. I leaned up against the sill to be more comfortable. You can learn a lot that way. And some people don't really mind. Of course, it's not terribly useful, knowledge-wise, especially since it's really only a mental projection and always will be no matter how seldom you brush your teeth. I mean, you're not there!

Anyway, I wasn't afraid of what might transpire. I'd seen everything by that time. I remember how shocked I was one night when Nanette came to my room well after bedtime. She suggested, with some delicacy, that I ejaculate directly into her make-up jar, a well-formed bottle of some «youth-cream». For an instant I was almost stunned to distraction by the notion she thought the yellow river of love a mere material of manufacture and stammered:

"Why do you ask this of me so coldly, Nanette." I wouldn't have minded half so much if I hadn't known full-well she held controlling interest in one of those snooty cosmetic concerns. I thought perhaps she was jealous of the slight attentions I had paid to Deborah. But then I was always nice to everybody, even though I couldn't really stand any of them and especially not that old bat. Everyone said I tried to talk to too many people at one time in a single voice, as it were.

I certainly shan't attempt to ape in any way the sentiments involved in what I saw, but merely sketch the observable on which all slander is erected in the current frantic Latin of blue euphemism. Everyone will know just exactly what I mean. I begin:

Lifting the night shirt off his fellow cruise-mate's fallen form, he places gently, ever so gently so as not to wake her where she lay curved on her side, her firm hips up, her head thrown back, his mouth's mobility in direct opposition to her wrinkled nugget wrapped in white silk, then pressing in firmly with his blunt dental prober, the deep-kisser. (That he would kiss her there! She must have been paying him. And there is danger of infection in a location like this. So, and later I told this right to Rory's face, he should use one of the modern mouthwashes. Dear!)) She stirred at first not at all but as he continued to probe and then to lift with it , she stirred ever so slightly, her arm slipping down into the warmest place for a sleeper. Then he took out a small but very sharp oyster knife and cut away the silk . . . and I could see everything. It really came to nothing. And fortunately too, for it could have been a perfect «blood bath». I know it was her idea. Finally they threw the sleepy distance-device aside and did it like the animals. Idle experimentation, I said to myself. And now I know why he left home to cruise the world. And as far as she was concerned it was just so much frosting on the cow. I was never fond of her personally. (Though I must say she did not have, at the «core of her activity» a «secret thing», a romanticized conception of her physical reality which, like a new car, you could get in and drive away, but rather an «operative gadget» the workings of which were of as much interest to herself as to my pale eye, spiked or prickled though it may be, for, whereas, many young ladies in other countries put layers of delicious fat on the thing, the average North American's becomes thornier. A psychologist would have nothing to say about this.) I'm sure she is the kind of girl who could take you right up to the end of «shit creek» and then give your «paddle» a nasty little slap. Yes, Rory was a fine specimen of a man. He was, anyway, until two weeks in a Hong Kong stew left him limp and twisted beyond redemption. I found him on a straw mat above a

two-story tea house, little more that an unprotesting mass of puzzled
tissue. He was babbling, senselessly it seemed, about it not being polite
to blow your nose in the petals of a flower, compulsive talk of sticky
fluids, the endless flight of bees.

Of course all the ladies aboard ship eagerly sought his company,
including old lady Cayman. When in my company he put them off
with earnest expressions of private comprehension. And then to me
he would speak of the potential for insidiousness on the distaff side.
However, I know for a fact he had dealings of a carnal nature with a
least three on board the vessel and god knows how many more in our
moments ashore.

Oh, if only we could but stem the tide of affected behavior in this
country at any given moment and discover some disingenuous root for
our human nature other than ball-room dancing. When I made this
suggestion to Nanette she became very catty and said: "But my dear,
you seem to speak with the back of your hands." She could be so flat
and contradictory. And you know as well as I the desire to please is the
origin of all bad taste.

The sun was setting across our deck. We had slowly moved North
and East enough to be in the Bombay orbit. One could almost hear the
sitars and smell the chapatti on the cook fires. The old vedic hymn, a
cut from the «red sequence» of the «First» or «Rig» book, came drifting
into my mind:

The twilight lady has been seen devoted
to the stars staged red in this sky,
as nuns to the goddess in red,
as a courtesan to her lover,
breasts reddened with crayon,
cheating death through saffron years.

These «red annals», of course, be but collections of stock phrases,
stylized gestures, nets of reification construed and fabricated to a tee
and labeled as a single taste. But they seem so timeless and lilting and I
found it fruitful to hear one again so far from home. It made me feel,
somehow, like a new man, one who could sail on to new, yet old,
horizons.

But we must remember that the «dirt moon» or «scarlet's midnight discharge», held in such high esteem in countries where morality has gone limp from trying, is nothing we Westerners need emulate. Take, for instance, the vulgar verse:

Forgetting the nominal forms of death-like semen,
Beware lustfulness in «spare-time» ladies.
Sucking humus from shining nether lips,
Enter the tunnel of the mother-figure
Through the flash-light of the father.

Gibberish such as this need not detain us here. Suffice it to say it makes you wonder if it's even worth bothering to visit «the other side of the world.»

Then old man Cayman came sauntering along the deck whistling a snatch of the old air «Marengo Nocturno». He was, by the way, a man of positively Mongol endurance; I mean day and night for weeks without end. What a monster! I'm afraid I'd have to fold my hand after only a few days. Well, these fishbones in my back, for instance! That's very debilitating. And this bandage of flesh across my shin. Now don't start telling me about pain. I've had more than my share of that. And don't tell me about freedom movements. Oh, I know all the touts and the boosters are well paid to keep the populace sufficiently distracted and off the case. Don't bother to tell me about it. I know the conventional wisdom here. I learned to talk double sucking simulac at my mother's knee. Don't think I was anywhere near the point of having any truck with a savage and his much maligned simples any day of the week. But the sun was just about to disappear when Cayman started giving me insider tips on the stock market. Something about Diamond Int. or maybe Engelhard. I forget.

"No, really, " he said, "they're in everything. Salt, matches, tampons, toothpicks, precious metals. A real family kind of business, real basic. You want in? I got a broker's open. I can telex. Maybe a split or a buy-out in the works." And here my mind had been high in the arts and his struggled with this low function. And at exactly the same moment. And he wouldn't stop there.

"Look," he continued, "I'll give you another tip. Sell A&P now, they're dumping. Keeping up with the latest Jones. Block-busting better neighborhoods. Pick it up later at a lower rate and watch it climb. You follow?" As if I would follow him! It turns out he was right on this one but I'm sure it's nothing your local recognized stock-broker couldn't have told you. I never bothered to follow him. Though he always managed to derail my train of thought.

Oh, yes, we were speaking of India, land of religions. And aren't some of those Hindi figures frightening? We certainly did see some poison-faced Siva figures in the sexual embrace of their naked consorts, naked save for ankle bracelets which became quite an obsession with me. And it is so difficult to shake some obsessions. But everyone began manifesting curious behavioral traits as we bore in on this capital of Maharashtra state. Deborah kept lifting one leg slightly, shaking her foot, and then putting it slowly back down again. The Captain had huge iron hooks dropped into the water on enormous chains. There they clanked against the hull as we ploughed through the water. He also had various lights implanted which vastly extended our night-time visibility. When I asked what sort of conditions would necessitate such a manoeuvre, he looked at me as if I were an idiot to ask. But in self-defence, I was most distracted at the time by two Chinese translations, being the prior half of an evocation written in the first years before the Mongolians were so strangely and permanently diverted by hatred, so he could have been pissing in a splatter pan for all the difference it made to me.

The first hint I had there was something amiss came when the Captain found a murdered cat on the fo'c's'le, the forward part of the ship where the sailors lived. What a shock! I tried to explain it to Cayman, my feeling about it, but his willful ignorance was so aggressively dumb I couldn't make him see a thing.

"That's okay," he said, "just don't show your ass out there after dark. Those guys don't know what they want if it ain't class warfare." Then he laughed a ghoulish laugh that sent chills up my spine. And it did turn out so cruelly auspicious, the augury contained in what he said. Oh, even boobs can utter such tragic forecasts. I crossed him again together with wife coming upstairs from the dining room where I had just eaten my evening meal. He drew me aside but Nan was right behind me and listening. He repeated his crack about it's being pot-belly or hunch-back for me and then added this little fillip:

"Right, I think I know your problem, maybe I don't. It's basic questions like why'd they slant the six. Stuff like that. Don't get me wrong. I want to spell everything out so even a dunce can read it.

"Stability, I suppose," I interjected lamely.

"Is that what you think, Des," he returned.

"Oh, go away, old man," I spit at him in something of a huff. I saw Nanette frowning as I turned on my heel. She never liked to hear me talk like that. We had moved up into the Arabian Sea by this time. With our twin screws and full heads of steam we were fairly cutting through the water. And you could see that the water was quite a bit redder in color than the deeper Indian Ocean.

Nanette followed me up the stairs and out on to the deck. She was in a trenchcoat of a reversed whipcord which looked like a high grade serge. She was quiet and looked quite smart, pressing a small handbag up under her arm.

"Dessy, I think it's time for us to talk, before it's too late," she began. But I cut her off quickly.

"Never mind about that, Nanette," I said, "just think of me as another world traveler, here today and gone tomorrow." Perhaps I was a little piqued, but I never let it show.

"All right, Dessy," she chirped, "have it your way. And have a good night's sleep. I'll talk to you tomorrow." And with that she disappeared into the bowels of the boat.

At last I was alone with my thoughts. I found all this business with the Caymen just a bit too much. God knows what they thought of me. And what they thought they'd do with me once they'd had their fill of having their way with me. I began to conceive quite unconsciously, and innocently I might add, several social and cultural contraptions, untoward chains of event, as it were, whereby they, the Caymen, might suffer and die and thereby free the world of a presence which had become noxious and irksome to me, the one no less than the other. It was almost as if I had taken a notion to kill them off. It was just a notion, mind you, nothing I would ever act on. I'm not homicidal, after all. I assure you, it was the furthest thing from my mind.

12

Bombay

I was so excited to be getting near a city I had heard so much about from my school days. There is a lot of mystery in a city like this, believe you me. A large part of it was made up from seven basaltic sisterlets joined together by British moon-bridges in the nineteenth century. That's Bombay Island. Nearby is Trombay where there is a nuclear reactor. She's the only natural deep water harbor in Western India. The sultan of Gujarat ceded it to the Portuguese people who passed it to the British way back in 1661. That's why it's so much like America. She took care of the world's demand for cotton when we blockaded the South's ports in the Civil War. She's still known for filling the world's hunger for tie-dye. Nearby is the small island of Elephanta which is noted for its antiquities. On Salsette Island there are early Buddhist caves from the days of Asoka and his grandfather. He was, you will remember, the first man to unite nearly all of modern India under one thumb. But then you've probably read all about this sort of thing in adventure books.

The next day at luncheon Nanette took me aside as she had promised. She had become rather pushy and I let her know in plain English just how I felt about it. We sat in lawn chairs on the sunny side of the boat. I wore my sunglasses and just stared up at the sky so she couldn't see if she displeased me. I owe this much to common courtesy.

"There is someone here in Bombay I want you to meet," she began. "She lives in Santa Cruz on Malabar Hill. It's a suburb. She's very interesting. And very influential. Will you come up with me?"

"Of course, of course, but leave me in peace until we're safely tied up in Bombay Harbor," I said shortly. So even here she knew the hob-knobs. Well, well, well, I said to myself.

"She's on the planning board of the All-India Atomic Energy Commission."

"Oh, really, is Ernest dealing her black market tube alloy? Is that how you happen to know her, Nanette?"

"Oh, Des, stop carping. I thought you'd be interested. She's Parsee, you see." Then, gripping my arm, she said, in a serious tone which made me want to yawn or chew gum:

"You've got to find your own place in the world, Des." Well, it didn't mean a thing to me but it appears the Parsee are a «religious» community believing en masse in Zoroastrianism. They are natty dressers, wear black hats and have big noses. You see how easily one accumulates this incidental information, how it piles up. And to think she'd think I'd really care who they were.

There are one hundred and twenty thousand of them, plus ou moins, concentrated in Maharashtra and Gujarat states, especially in Bombay. Their relatives immigrated here from Iran in the eighth century to avoid fundamentalist persecution. They make use of very ancient books, the «Pahlavi» scriptures, and are faithful to much «Zarathustrian» dogma. They heatedly deny the frequent assertion that they worship fire. And isn't that wise. Rather, they reverence it along with other aspects of nature, grain, certain microbial life-forms, water, certain metals, as outcroppings of the god Ahura Mazdah who is the good spirit of sovereign knowledge. It's too complicated to follow out here, all the way to the «bridge of the separator» and the «great Mazdah feeling». Suffice it to say it be sufficiently complex. One thing they do do, though, is to avoid air, water, fire and earth contamination and pollution. So they dispose of their dead in crude stone towers twenty feet off the ground where vultures eat them.

"Well, thanks, Nanette. I'm sure it will turn out quite instructive." She smiled at me with her typical condescension and, taking my hand, pressed the fingers together so hard I almost screamed.

"Don't grouse, Dessy. First we'll visit the caves and I'll give you the tour. Then we'll go see my friend." Here she gave me one of her «dirty» looks and was gone, off to a card game with some dead-heads in steerage.

That same evening we steamed into fabulous Bombay Harbor, rippling with ship and the stacks of giant refineries glinting back the last rays of the sun. What a sight! Everyone was on deck. That must be some sort of index of how wonderful a sight that was, in some crudely democratic cosmos, in the electorate of sensation. I think it is so wonderful for everyone, especially young people, to socialize and socialize and socialize some more. Go out to parties, talk to people, mix with the right sort. Make friends. Dance crazy in discos all night until they are nearly dead. That's all that's really left to talk about. That's the most positive thing I can say. And I really think that is the point, the single most important message I can attempt to deliver over this vast distance: to meet as many people as you can, go out to parties and dance until you drop, go shopping if necessary and be positive and appreciate the importance of positive thinking. Oh, don't talk negative to me.

After we had safely anchored, twenty tons of dead-weight clattering noisily through the chainspill, a launch pulled alongside our vessel's boarding ladder and two men came clambering up the steps. It turns out they were from the India Police and wanted to question us all. The chief of the two, Inspector Lallubhai Sulli, called us into the lounge and addressed us as a group. Oh, these port officials. Most men who have traffic with the sea are proud to proclaim it by some article of clothing, some salty gesture or dry word. But not these gentlemen. It was the boulevard and the café that turned their heads, the antique of the cinema and the television. But I must admit that contact with these men of action, thoughtful and intelligent though they were, lifted my spirits right off the ground.

Inspector Sulli, their chief, was a medium sized man wearing an English style trench coat. He smoked a cigarette, rapping out his words, glancing with his shining dark eyes which had the fixed expression of expecting the worst, a look men acquire from long contact with foreign troops. I put him down as an old soldier. But I was wrong. It turns out he had never had any contact with military life. He cleared his throat and spoke to us in very good English:

"I am inspector Lallubhai Sulli of the India Police. I do not wish to cause you any alarm but there has been a crime of some magnitude in the water here somewhere. We have found bodies floating. And so something is wrong here. I must, with your kind permission, question you each individually and find out why you have come to India and what you intend to do while you are here. I must know how much money you are carrying, if you have any relatives in India, etcetera. And please, if you would be so kind, be prepared to answer any other questions we, myself and my associate Mister Bowring Watcha, may have for you. Thanking you in advance for your most kind cooperation, I will wait for you in the stern section of the lounge. If you would come to us alphabetically. . . " Well, that caused no end of confusion but I soon had it straightened out. Then he and his partner, a tall man in very thick glasses, walked to a set of offices at the far end of the lounge. We were to be called in one at a time. Watcha read our names off from the ship's roster. I thought it a little silly and unnecessary since we were set to sail in 24 hours but they seemed like nice enough men.

So I sat down with a smoke and a drink at the bar and patiently waited my turn. Rory and Deborah were there but they didn't sit next to each other. Rory sat next to me. I must admit that I was happy with Rory by my side. Though Deborah rather queered it for me when she butted in. There she sat with her legs tightly pressed together. I kept imagining she was trying to make eye contact with Rory. But then she'd look away when I'd try to catch her and just be fiddling in the most annoying manner with one of her ringlets. When they called her for questioning she burst into tears but I don't think she was guilty of murder. Rory was friendly but seemed somewhat agitated. I said to him jokingly:

"Why, Bucky, you haven't committed any crime, have you? You're not sticking women with your knife late at night and throwing their naked, mutilated torsos overboard, are you?" That's the first time Deborah burst out crying. But that sort of woman always worries to death about her «catch» and fears his «readiness» itself is perhaps unnatural and cause for suspicion. And Rory just gave me a horrified look and walked away so he must have been upset about something. I did hope that he hadn't «let fly» in some inconvenient corner of Deb's physiognomy.

They called the Caymen and some others and then at last it was my turn. I had had them put me at the end of the list because I had something to fetch in my room. Or so I told them. It didn't really matter. In any case I had gotten so nervous I was sitting on the edge of my seat. Bowring ushered me into the office and I took a seat. I took each of their hands in turn but apparently that is not the custom.

"We shall not, Mr. Desmond," Mr. Sulli began, "keep you hanging on a string for long. Tell me, please, how long you intend to stay in our country?"

"Oh, not more than a day or so," I replied cheerfully.

"Ah, that is a shame, you do not like India?" I knew in the leathery heart of the traveller that this was just a bid to have me spend more of my hard currency in their lovely though depressed country but somehow I forced myself to believe him. Indian men have a peculiar quality of appearing absolutely sincere even when they are telling bald-faced fibs.

"Oh, I love India," I stated firmly, "it's like a warm blanket on the cold, cruel surface of the earth."

"That is very kind of you to say. I can see that you are a well-travelled man. You have been here in India before, I think?"

"That's nice of you to say but no, never."

"Well, that is a surprising thing for me, a man like you. But I hope you will come back to see us soon and perhaps, if you can, bring Mrs. Desmond." Well, I thought I would fall on the floor laughing at that one.

"There is no Mrs. Desmond, you silly!"

"Oh, I am very sorry, she has passed away?" he asked with concern for my well-being.

"Oh, my goodness no," I sputtered, "there never has been a Mrs. Desmond."

"Ah, you are a gay bachelor?" He seemed to be picking up some of my mirth, I was laughing so hard. Isn't it wonderful how a little good feeling like that can spread itself around the room and warm the spirits of even the most hardened heart. I assured him that I tried my best to be carefree and loving but that it was so difficult in these troubled times.

"Well, very good. But let us get down to brass tacks, Mr. Desmond, before the killer himself steals a march on us!" So there was a killer, that much, at least, was perfectly clear. But I could hardly see. All that laughter had brought tears to my eyes. So I let Sulli continue:

"We have reason to believe that these murders were not committed in Bombay proper. You see, the bodies were all found to have been floating for some time in the water before the curious beachcomber or man from a fishing village would poke it with a stick. Then and only then would he see what had floated to him for they were in a bloated state quite beyond your recognition. You see, my friend, they had been in the water floating for anywhere from three days to a week. Indeed. You see, the fish had been eating them. It was very ugly. I saw them myself."

"You didn't," I broke in. "That's disgusting."

"Oh, not really, in my line of work you see all manner of disgusting things, things more disgusting than these bodies, a hundred times over, every day."

"Incredible," was all I could say.

"We have further reason to believe," he continued, "these heinous crimes, not really even Indian crimes, were crimes committed aboard a ship, a ship at sea and then the bodies thrown afterwards overboard into the water. Mr. Desmond, my friend, I ask you what you think of that and what do you say?"

"Well, how many have you found," I asked lamely. I was hesitant to take on a case of this magnitude so far from home. And, despite my reputation in certain circles, I'm not really that good in that sort of a situation. I lack the thirst for consecutive detail that is the lash to so many. I mean, as the old bible song has it:

If I had it, I surely would

Slap the water, slap it good

but I don't feel I really should. There's enough of that done every day by professionals who know why they're doing it. Let's just let the amateur enjoy himself.

"We have found five: three female and two male. We determined their sex by means of autopsy. So, you see, it is a serious problem we have here."

"Yes, I see, someone is killing people and then dumping their bodies at sea, " I said. "This is very serious." And here I had thought it was only women being killed. I was silent for a moment while they looked at me expectantly, then, off the top of my head, I gave them the benefit, however dubious it may seem, of whatever insight came to me on the spur of the moment.

"Just let me say this, Mr. Sulli. And you, Mr. Watcha. If I were you, I'd look to the Saudis for trouble. Remember, life is cheap out there on the desert, the days long, the nights cold and they've got to do something with the women they've butchered. And remember this: like dead fish in a glass bowl, some will float and some will sink to the bottom. I hope I have been of some assistance to you in your investigation. You people are doing a wonderful job. I've never had any reason to complain." They looked at me blankly for a number of moments. I can't really believe they were at the head of their class in the police academy. They glanced briefly at each other and then Mr. Sulli said:

"That will be all, Mr. Desmond. . ." But as I lifted my arms to get up, Sulli motioned for me to sit a moment more. "Just one moment more, please, sir, if you don't mind." He stood up and started to pace back and forth in front of me.

"You should thank your lucky stars, my friend," he said, "you are not in Calcutta. Ooh, that is an evil place. There you would be forced to pay to the police officer in charge of the investigations a heavy bribe in order to be freed to leave the area."

"We certainly are lucky," I said, not thinking for an instant he was suggesting that I attempt to «buy off the gypsy.»

"Oh, yes, it is a very wicked place," he went on. "When your Prime Minister was here he was very upset and he was overheard saying to his mother, and I quote here verbatim, word for word, «I am happy I am here with you now, Mother, because now it will not be necessary for me to be here alone.» Those are the words from his mouth. So, you see, very great men like this are unhappy there." He began to pace more rapidly and searched in his pockets for something he could not fine. He continued:

"You know, the police in Calcutta are not like ordinary men; they are men who are capable, quite frankly I am telling you this, of putting on your boat with Ganga water, just so, and tying and binding little bits of string or some such thing like that and when that is done, you will not sail. I know you will be finding this hard to believe."

"Oh, go on," I said, "that's not possible!"

"You better had believe it is, my good friend, Mr. Desmond; you are not in your own country now. You are in India where anything can happen."

"Sounds like Disney-land to me," I joked. I was attempting to lighten the atmosphere a bit with some jocular note but he had never heard of Disney-land. I explained as best I could it was a world of animated fiction run by a mouse with three fingers called Michael, etcetera, etcetera, all conceived by a man named Walt who had had himself freeze-dried solid just before he died. It seemed so confusing to me but Mr. Sulli was very thankful for the information and even more so Mr. Watcha. These people want to learn; it is important to keep this in mind in our dealing with them.

"Good, good, you will see some of our city tomorrow," he said as he walked me to the door. "Good. You must go first to the caves. They will fill you with wonder. Don't doubt it. You will see many wonderful things, divas, sivas, near-boddhas, many naked people, much funny business. . ." And here Mr. Sulli looked to Mr. Watcha who inserted his right index into a circle formed by his left thumb touching the tip of his left forefinger. At that specific moment I had no idea what he was talking about, just a vague uneasiness, but have since managed to decipher his digital esperanto. Mr. Watcha dropped his hands and Mr. Sulli concluded:

"Just one more thing, my friend, before I thank you again and bid you good evening and good night. The local villages," he said sadly, "must be overlooked. They do not fit in with the idyll of palms, elegant leisure and sun and sand as we would have them. Outside each hut is a string bed, and on that bed often a man is resting with chores to be done lying all around him. When the villager's city cousins come out for a day's picnic, it's fun. Females of all ages and dimensions swim in the sea fully dressed and have a good gossip while their menfolk ogle other women on the beach." Here he lowered his eyes to the floor and slowly raised them up again. "But if you insist on going, then you must keep your eyes wide open for what may be the answer to our little puzzle here!" So I see he still thought they were swimmers even after what I had told him about white-slaving chez les sheik. But one of the wonderful things about this place is that the men love to talk and are very highly socialized. So much so I never thought they'd stop talking and let me go. Nanette grabbed me as I walked away from the office.

"Whatever did they want to know, Dessy, that they kept you in there so long? Do tell me."

"Well, there's really nothing to tell. Apparently the Arabians are floating a shit-load of corpses across the Bay to Bengal and no one's the least wit wiser. Why do you ask?"

"I, for my part, couldn't for the life of me discover what they were about. The tall one with glasses talked to me while the other closeted with Ernest."

"Well, what did he want to know?" I could tell she was excited by the way she talked. She just loved it when she felt she had made contact with natives.

"It's not what he wanted to know, it's what he wanted me to know."

"Oh, really, what?"

"He began by telling me that Hindooism was to blame for all the poverty, all the suffering, all the nakedness in modern India. Isn't that incredible?"

"Well, what did you say?"

"I was polite. I said, «but, my goodness, aren't you a Hindoo?» «Oh, no, no, no,» he said, «I am a Xtian just like you.» Isn't that a scream?"

"You, a Xtian, that is a scream. But perhaps he's right. I've heard India's full of nakedness." We both laughed at that and went down to the sauna which was empty at that time of day. And it wasn't much of a sauna with the rusting steel walls. But we all found it helped us to relax. Then later, over a drink, we continued our discussion for apparently he had told her quite a lot though I know she just made up some of it to amuse herself.

"You know, Nanette," I said , in a more serious vein now that it was later, "one of the main things that I have always related to Eastern philosophy and perhaps this is an ignorant opinion. . ."

"I pray not a consciously ignorant opinion," she interrupted.

"Of course not," I snapped. What do you take me for?"

"Nothing, Des, please go on." You had to keep her on track when you talked to her. She wasn't exactly senile but she did have a tendency to wander in the path of least resistance, a traditional female malady.

"Well, as I was saying, is a concept of incarnation into a new life every time you die. . . ." I was finding it a little difficult to think without crossing what professionals call the «meta-physical trestle». "Has he run into opposition, people thinking that this is the way?"

"Well, he said that you must remember that Hindooism is a religion of ladies. It is nothing but ceremonies, fast days, ladies' days. He told me Gandhi strongly believed in incarnation and therefore the people won't kill farm animals. They think that it is the last of three states before the human being."

"So if a cow was to be slaughtered, then it would end that person's ability to come back?"

"Yes, he would go back again and start from the beginning. It takes millions of years."

"What about people who have become Xtian out of the Hindoo faith? How do they see this idea of preserving the life of the cow when thousands of people around that cow are naked?

"He says that some of the Hindoos are very shocked if they suspect a neighbor is «eating beef».

"My, my. Do the people of India look at Xtianity more like just a popular thing to do for some people but nothing as more real?"

"They think it is following the Western tradition, the Western religion, the Western way of life. But, all the same, most of the educated Hindoos dress like Westerners do, they eat like Westerners do, they like to have homes like Westerners do. But when Christ comes, they say he is just a Westerner." I don't know why they would always talk to her about everything, philosophy, the life of the mind. To me it was all crime and criminals. Not even criminology. On returning to my cabin Murchison the Collared accosted me in the passage to the lower deck with the «good news» about Mr. Watcha. I shushed him up promptly with the information I had been told quite frankly all this hoopla about Xtianity was a ploy to draw out the killer who was still very much at liberty. This put a scare into him.and he hesitated to burden me with any more evidence of the miraculous nature of reality. I couldn't help but add as he attempted to slip away: "By the way, Doctor, is their a Lady Murchison to whom I should tell all should anything untoward transpire chez toi?" I got a little laugh out of him on that.

We did, per adventure, go to the caves the very next day, early in the morning when the sun was first peeking out from behind this golden land. A launch took us out to the islands where they are found. I had read about the rogue bull elephant, the tusks of which tourists had rubbed into satin, and there he was, his tusks rubbed smooth by the idle hands of the people passing in. And half-way up the hill a natural cave We gave the man a few bills and entered into the chipped out entrance hall in imitation architecture and prehistoric iconography. It must have been fun back then, just to live here and work everyday at some simple task. Stone-carver, say, or butter-sculptor. Anyway, I half expected to find a pile of library books and canned goods in the corner. Or that American Indian bad-man; what was he doing in the cave. I've seen such caves in the Hollywood Hills. Deborah was along. And Rory. Cayman had gone to the market-place, trying to find a use for frozen rupees. Nanette took my hand in the darkness of the «reception» cave and whispered:

"Oh, this is so exciting; it's like a time machine in here." Then, out of nowhere, she nudged me quite painfully in the ribs and hissed: "You men are so violent." And I hadn't said a word. I was trying to keep an eye on Rory and Deborah. They were far from being above suspicion. But Nanette trapped me in a side-chamber and let the others get ahead of us. There she once again had her way with me. I'm helpless in these situations. I just can't say no. And she wore a big full skirt for the express purpose.

"Oh, help me, Des," she moaned. "I can't think of anything but sex in a place like this. Just lie down, you big stupid silly, until I can collect my thoughts." What could I say to the woman! And I guess it wasn't all that unpleasant. Just inconvenient, really, what with hygiene and dress code. That's why you can tell with a really sloppy person that they have been «doing it» a lot. She had me lie flat on a slab of marble and exposed my «thing» to the air with her delicate white fingers. Her hands had not aged nearly as rapidly as her spirit. And she had become quite free with me ever since that night in the where-ever. Then she squatted down on top of me much the way you do with a primitive toilet on the fifth floor of a Paris walk-up. And it was hot under there, like a green-house. Of course the air in the cave was damp and chill so it was curiously comforting under the folds of her skirt and the silken bulk of her petticoats. It was so dark I couldn't see her face, just one small taper stuck to the wall. All I heard was the squishing of fluids, my own respiration, a faint wheeze coming from Nan, until she had quite finished with doing it.

"Let's Hurry, Nanette," I said when I had put myself back together.

"Oh, don't take it so personally, Des, anyone would have been just as serviceable."

"Well, thank you very much. But actually I'm worried about Rory and Deborah."

"How thoughtful of you, Des. It couldn't be you're sniffing about her little bottom just like everyone else. Even Ernie can't seem to keep his distance." This was the first hint I'd had that all was not well with that trio.

We quickly covered the rest. Some of the upper caves with sky-lights were all right but we soon suffered crippling claustrophobia. The outsides were deserted save for broken prayer wheels, fallen arches, hungry goats and picturesque but destructive little boys. We soon found our companions and returned via launch to downtown Bombay. Someone dragged us into the bazaar for an interview with a Nepalese jewel thief from Kashmir by way of Ladak. The purser set it up. It was really nothing more than a tupperware party. We were served tea seated on oily divans and ceremoniously shown what to me looked like bits of cut glass. The old dog, called Gratna, couldn't keep his eyes off Deb's bust and his hands off her lower back and upper bottom. I just abhor these feelers and their wily ways, their false promises, touching and touching until there is nothing left that is sacred. But never mind, it was really little more than a black market which is what so much commerce is these days. I couldn't be interested in whatever business occupied the others. Oh, I think anyone should be allowed to operate a side-show or drive a gypsy cab. I mean, what could I care about trade in precious objects. I don't know why I mention it. Though it is of more than slight importance to my possible defense should any of this go to court as wrongful death. Oh, this is about something else so I won't go into it here. I'll bring it up later. It has to do with certain court dates and flimsy, flimsy allegations which I hesitate to dignify.

When they had finished we left and hailed a taxi. We were lucky enough to get a sedan. After two or three left hand turns I saw that a huge crowd had gathered about us. On looking into the car and seeing me seated between Nanette and Deborah, the people went mad with joy. At least that's what it looked like to me. But maybe they were angry. I couldn't tell. A procession was immediately formed and the sky rent with shouts of something that sounded like «nasty gory» and then «inquilabzindibad», «good joke on him». Now I don't know if you know what it's like being caught in a riot of enthused Indians. But please believe me, it's a bit insufferable.

"What is this!" I shouted to the driver, "what is this!" But he didn't speak English. He turned around and shook his head in what roughly was a figure eight. Perhaps I look like someone else, I thought to myself, or perhaps someone else is due here at this hour in a sedan. Then we sighted a body of mounted police. Brickbats were raining down from above. I thought to beseech the crowd to be calm, not for my sake so much as for the ladies present in our company.

At Crawford Market we found ourselves suddenly confronted by a body of heavily armed riot police who had arrived there to prevent the crowd from moving any closer to the Fort, a huge red brick affair where city officials were housed. We were all clearly terrified out of our senses. We clutched at each other with hard cold hands drenched in sweat. The crowd was quite obviously out of control. There was hardly any chance of my voice being heard in that vast concourse. Just then the officer in charge of the police gave the order to disperse the demonstration and both the horses and the helmeted men charged the mob. For a moment I felt that I would be hurt. Believe me, I am not cowardly, just realistic. But my apprehensions were groundless, the staves they carried just grazed the car as the horsemen swiftly passed by. The ranks of the people were soon broken. The horsemen and the people were mixed together in mad confusion but our motor-car was allowed to proceed. I thought to stop before the Commissioner's office in order to lodge a complaint about the conduct of the police but Nanette screamed that her friend was waiting so I didn't bother to make a thing out of it. Anyway, they probably knew what they were doing.

The driver, shaken but still game, then took us to a stone bungalow on the outskirts of Bombay in the Malabar Hills. We turned into a long crushed-shell drive just as Nanette's friend was coming out of her front door. Nanette hopped out and ran up to her. They embraced elaborately like two overbred she-dogs. It looked so social and I'm sure they were very close. Then her huge face was at the window of our car faster than you could say Jack Robinson. She said:

"Oh, hello, and these are your friends. Welcome to our country." Then Nanette stuck in her head and I thought I'd gag.

"A terrible thing has happened. Gangabehn has been called away to a monster meeting of the Atomic Energy Commission. It's a terrible shame!"

"Oh, I am so sorry you must suffer like this because of me but I am on the planning board and must leave immediately." Nanette let out a groan of protest, as indeed did we all, but Gangabehn quickly silenced her:

"No, Nanette, do not raise a hue and cry. You are tourists here and do not see what we are facing. They think we stir our nuclear liquids with bamboo poles! You know that this is a lie, don't you, Nanette?" Nanette nodded her head, as indeed did we all. My, how those lovely Indian women show their teeth when they smile.

"Anyway, they have come from all over the world to tell us what to do with our atomics. I must go. My son is inside. You must visit with him. Good-bye." With that she left, off in a limo to who knows where. I'm sorry she had to leave so quickly. I think she and I would have gotten on. Not in any intimate domestic situation, to be sure, but somehow.

Well, her son was a big fat baby of twenty-eight or so whom we all found exceptionally repulsive. He was huge and had rolls of fat absolutely everywhere. He was seated on the roof of their house while a servant dusted his nearly naked body with baby powder. Sweat was just running off his belly in streams. We left almost immediately amidst a shower of protestations from the son. He even offered to put on a bathrobe and take us to the spice pavilion. I half thought of staying to listen to his record collection but just felt all tuckered out after the caves and the riot. We taxied to the wharf and back on the boat each and every one of us went straight to his or her room.

I lay on my bunk and read the local papers I had purchased coming off the cave-launch across the Irrawaddy basin. Oh, the news was so depressing. There was no mention of the disturbance in which we were involved. But then they wouldn't have had time, would they? And, oh, all those swastikas plastered all over the paper. But you must remember that here it stands for baby Krishna's four-bladed scythe. It was unscrupulously taken without permission by those dirty Nazi swine, inverted and twisted slightly. And they were so perverted, those leadership types. Bickering and fighting, bitch, bitch, bitch. And bang, bang, shooting each other in the heads. And that Hitler! Thinking he was so cute! It's just too bad we never had a chance to nuke Berlin. And Rome. Two thousand four hundred years of Western Civ. and all those broken statues, kabloom!

That is an outrageous opinion and I know it as well as you know it. But I just do it to shock you. I feel it so important to come to one's senses occasionally, to wake up and stand four square and toe to toe with what's what once in a while. I mean, I'll be the last one to actually recommend the complete annihilation of Western Civilization. Don't come climbing up my leg if that's what you want. Oh, some will say a perfect ass-hole wrote this but long life and happiness, I always say; serve the lord and he'll bring you joy in the end.

And while I'm at it I want to thank god for that great team who got us the A-bomb in the first place and let us fry those other dirty bastards, whoever they were. It really did prove that America was the richest country. And willing to sacrifice absolutely anything to get what it wants. They really showed the world what we can do with a little wartime control of our own.

That night at dinner the Caymen cornered me for what they called a «serious discussion» of my future. In fact it was just a long string of their assumptions plastered across my activities. My god, their companionship was little more than a marathon job interview. I've always found this true of the idle nouveau nearly rich. And even the well-to-do. The really rich are, of course, untouchably nasty and idle. And some job! I don't even know what it was if it wasn't house-boy. Even if I'm not «executive material» I don't care to be insulted.

After dinner and just before we sailed, Inspector Sulli paid me an unexpected visit. He stood in the door to my room with his hat in his hand, somewhat crestfallen, and told me the most outrageous story of crime on the street. It seems a certain «desperado» had savagely murdered and mutilated a gentleman of the first rank under the most sordid of circumstances. Apparently the killer had lured his victim into a «compromised» situation chez victime after having subverted his morals in a place of public entertainment. There, in the home of this same victim, after engaging in a variety of unnatural acts, he had murdered him, clove his male-member in two lengthwise slices, squashed his testicles beneath a jack-boot and taken everything of value. Need I say more? Even I thought it made a chilling story. Mr. Sulli said he was being taken off the «bloated bodies» case and put instead on the «stranger in the night».

"Just tell me this, Mr. Sulli," I asked, "what sort of unimaginable desperation would drive a man to do something like that?" Sulli stood dumb for a moment giving me the oddest look and then whispered:

"He must be a very bad man."

"Oh, worse than that!" I pitched in, meaning to help him out of the hole into which he seemed to have fallen.

"You are a very unusual man, Mr. Desmond, you seem to understand so well the criminal mentality."

"Oh, I'm a rank amateur," I assured him. "Imagine what I could do if I were forced by circumstance to throw my whole self into it." He seemed to shudder at the thought but I put it down to an oncoming sub-tropic ague.

I was sorry, so sorry, to be leaving beautiful India, land of unspeakable riches and indecipherable squalor. So many are afraid to visit here, afraid of what they may find here. And they should be. But, as I always say, what? Afraid of this? After some of the things I've seen come out of England?

Oh, there are those nay-sayers who deplore so earnestly the political situation, the chaos, the in-fighting, the assassinations. Wasn't that awful, their shooting that poor Gandhi fellow? I was so sorry when I finally heard about it. And after all he had done for them. But never mind. It reminded me of how they «popped our Johnny» and how much cold cash changed hands to get King killed. But then so many are gunned down in the streets these days. It just doesn't have the meaning it used to have.

The next morning Cayman had the nerve to say: "Look, Bosco, I'm sorry it didn't work out right. We're still friends. And I'll still handle your stocks for you if you want me to." Of all the poisonous interchanges I have had the misfortune to experience! If he'd held a silver chalice filled with cyanide under my nose his message couldn't have been clearer. I decided from that point on to stick more to myself and keep my own counsel. I had to in order to maintain any self-respect.

I went into confinement right then and there but before I did I had a nice little chat with Deborah in the lounge. She had, somewhat, tempered her attitude toward me as will always happen with a woman on the «make». It was quite by accident, meaning it wasn't through any plot or plan or design of mine. We started talking of this and that and nothing at all. She was drinking a tonic for its quinine. She never touched alcohol. I was having a bit of absinth in grenadine. I find a few ounces of a spirit taken in moderation before meals to be just the ticket for a traveller's stomach. Deborah, for some reason, perhaps insecurity brought on by culture shock, was again interested in what she called my «beliefs». You know what I mean. In theatre they're called «props» and lie about the stage to be fiddled with in absent moments when the actor forgets his line or when the actress feels she is no longer sufficiently attractive after time and lights have melted her grease-paint. And in society these props are called «knick-knacks» and lie about on shelves, bed-tables and walls. Well, I gave her a little of my old razzmatazz.

She was speaking of religious belief, I assumed. I believe we were alone in the lounge, it being an odd hour of the day. She came up to me where I lay slumped across the bar. I was weary and glum to say the least, not yet having recovered my appetite. I mean, think of all the chilling scenes I had been forced to endure: The conspiratorial ways of all my fellow travellers; those terrible and nasty detectives and their talk of murder and mutilation; my mortification at being little more than chauffeur to Nanette. I was pushed quite over the line and had gone through enough to justify anything I might thereafter have done or even what people say I might have done. And I think that to eat is human, that to want to eat is divine. Even if it be but gruel and come to you cold on a paper plate. So you see how loss of appetite is a sign of the unhappy, the lonely and the maladjusted. Love sick, the physicians say first. But my gloomy humor at this point need not and should not be taken as the barometer of all things. And I determined, as you shall see, from this point on to show an aggressive spirit toward what I wanted and from whom I wanted it. She, Deborah, expressed insecurity in so many words and gestures and then asked me with the usual dollop of her uncertain and over-generalized emotion:

"Desmond, let me just say this to you as a new but not unfriendly acquaintance. I feel, and don't take this wrong, that I can never get to know you as anything more than a casual contact on the boat because I feel that you don't believe in anything. It's that you're so negative." Or something like that.

"So negative, that's rich," I drawled. "Why I believe in everything."

"Do you really, Desmond, because if you did that would be wonderful. I'd really feel much better about everything. Tell me exactly what you do believe." I demurred as firmly as possible but she wouldn't let go of my bait once she had hooked on it. She practically begged me. Well, I couldn't tell her everything but remembered that she had an interest in things religious. I said at last:

"You're probably wondering about my religious affiliation. Well, I want to say this and put it very simply: Jesus is lord, at least in Western industrial civilization."

"Oh, Des, I think we might be friends after all. You put up a big front but underneath I think you're just like the rest of us." She leaned across the table here and kissed me on the brow, almost touching her bust to my forearm. To stop her from going farther I thought to throw the question back at her by asking:

"Well, tell me what you think." I wanted her to share at least some small bit of the revelation she seemed to have received.

"About what?"

"Well, about me, for instance." I knew this would be good for a laugh. I always love to hear what people think just to know how wrong they are.

"I'll tell you what, Des. I'll tell you what I first thought when I saw you on board, back when you were buttering up the Captain and trying to get a larger stateroom." She stood quite close to me and I could smell her provocative eau de cologne and something more, something musky, which I had not previously detected on her person.

"I thought you were very handsome. But conceited. And maybe, well, not quite like a normal kind of guy." I certainly hadn't expected anything this diverting.

"Not like a normal guy, how absurd. Of course I'm like a normal guy." Good lord, what more evidence could she want!

"Oh, I know, I know. But then, when I first saw you coming up the gang plank, I thought you might be a creep. I hope you're not offended because I don't think that now."

"A creep, how drôle !" Really, I don't think anyone ever called me a creep before. No one who meant anything at all to me. And some might here be tempted to say she was falling for me, falling for me in a big way. And I think she was. If only she had allowed herself to be more honest things might have worked out differently. Most women want to be more honest, but very few succeed. Nevertheless, she seemed so warm and understanding in that heady atmosphere it is easy to see how I slipped, unconsciously, into a more compromised relationship with the dear young thing. And I just know she went back to her cabin and pushed every button in the book.

After we sailed I saw no one for days except the boys who served me my food. I sat in the dark. It was terrible. I'd cry occasionally. I think I was experiencing something of a regeneration. I felt that from somewhere out and beyond me I had received the strength to carry on. With what, god knows. Endless travel, I presume. Lost in a forest of aimless peers, hearing their whisper at my shoulder, "oh, there goes old good-tyme Desmond again, down to the casino to blow his nose." What's left, a smoko with Rory, cribbage with Mr. C., a douche with his wife? And to know there were those aboard on their knees, repeto, on their knees, praying for an torpedo or an iceberg or both. But it's not really all that bad. A few hours in a tearful state, the land of exiles and homeless men without countries, men of reprehension, down and out on skid-row with their lips, cut and broken, scaly, plastered on to half-pints of fruit alcohol. I have no religion as such or social position to help me keep my head high. But I'm not, and don't think I am, begging for sympathy. I get more than I need of that from my good friends and close companions all of whom find me most congenial, sympathetic and compassionate. And I happen to think a stint at solitary can really steel you for an ordeal.

When I finally emerged from my room, as we were sailing down the inner curve of Sumatra through the Straits of Malacca, I caught sight of Nanette behind the frosted glass doors leading into the lounge. She burst into tears when she saw me and her hands flew into her face. I really didn't expect that sort of behavior from a woman of her age and breeding. But you can never tell with a female. They are so hopelessly erratic and flighty, always liable to jumping up and screaming at the top of their lungs. And then there is a scene and everyone is thrown into a brown funk. Give me a male any day of the week: so stern, so solid, so uncompromising and unfluctuating in the face of the blast. But a woman will feign weakness in order to entice you into a position where she can stave you in your face with her shoe or a heavy, blunt candle-stick in the parlor. And it is well known that all women really want is the tedious «double-teardrop» of normalized relations. As she passed me going out the door I whispered:

"Your feelings are showing, Nanette." I felt a timely reminder of a fundamental and unswerving rule of decorum would, perhaps, lift her from her melancholy. I must say I had caught her shifting her abstracts like dusty pieces of cultural furniture.

Then I discovered old man Cayman had paid an enormous bribe to the detectives in Bombay and was trying to pass himself off as our savior. That was just too much for me. I don't approve of bribery and payola under any circumstances much less these. And at a point off the coast of Singapore, to top things off, we had something of a navigational crisis, one that could have flared into a mutiny or intra-passenger strife had it not been for the cooler heads in our midst. Certain «cruise types» wanted to go straight to Bali, stopping at Singapore for fuel on the way back up into the South China Sea. Others thought that this was about the silliest thing they had ever heard. The entire issue was at loggerheads until Deborah caused a scene and threatened to jump overboard if she didn't get to Bali immediately. It was such a disappointment to see her back at her old tricks and I almost wrote her off as an incorrigible malcontent. She claimed she was getting old and more than likely had a female cancer as did so many of her generation, etcetera, etcetera. It was just awful with tears and screaming and foam, tearing at her clothing. A real snit-fit. I suggested she be forcibly confined but finally everyone just gave up and we set a course for Bali. And Cayman told the Captain, a man who was looking mutiny in the face, that he'd wire ahead and eventually got him a guaranteed load of cane or Hong Kong grass, some sort of mainland produce, for trans-shipment to the West Coast, which I thought very thoughtful of him. He must have been very well connected in those circles, shipping circles.

13

Bali

Now Indonesia is the only country I have ever visited where an actual turd was thrown at my head. Oh, it was a small turd, mind you, of no more mass than an Italian meatball and of a similar texture, but human excrement none the less. I didn't let it stand in the way of my enjoyment either, for these people can't possibly know what they are doing to every conceivable tourist. And, in truth, though the missile did hit me, I am convinced it was thrown at one of the women.

We landed but for an afternoon to set Deborah down under a giant Waringin Tree, sacred to the natives, and put on fresh fruit and vegetables available at local markets run by peranaken Chinese, mix-blooded people conceived when mainland menfolk left home without the mainland little ladies. And you know there's no chance of «biological containment» without them. You know what they did next. Don't make me go through it even one more time. Ugh! But they did it and then slowly rose to a sort of «entrepreneurial domination.» So that's where we stood in the food chain.

Our ship, unfortunately, was too large to pull right into Klung Klung harbor so we anchored in the channel and took a launch ashore. What a jungle paradise, though you can't see much of it from there. I mean from the launch with Deborah retching and smelling of spit-up. On landing, we hopped into a pedicab and the boy pedalled off to a café we had all read about in the guide books called «The Volcano». It was huge, outdoor, and jammed with smart looking Balinese. I just love the café life. All at once it's cozy, public and intimate, all at the same time. And it's so easy to meet people. Of course, who'd want to on most continents. But this was Bali, the left-bank of Asia, and we were all filled with high spirits.

Let me just say that the towns here don't look like our towns back home because all the trees are connected by high voltage wires strung through their crowns. I spoke to an electrical engineer once and apparently this is an accepted electrical practice. I was surprised.

We paid off our taxi-boy and found a seat on the vast veranda. We all ordered coffee which is so good here and a powerful local schnapps, known to be nearly total alcohol. At the next table was a group of typical Balinese youth. The oldest couldn't have been more than twenty-nine and the youngest a very sophisticated little fifteen year old. The boys in their chinos and letter-sweaters, the girls in their slacks and thin-cotton tee-shirts, just like college kids. They have the finest figures in the world, those young people. You see them sometimes walking up Broadway on the fourth of July. They were talking and laughing and drinking fermented pineapple juice as if they didn't have a care in the world. And of course, they didn't. Nobody cracks a book these days. They just lay around their dorms, water ski, sky dive, hang glide, lay in the sun and make like Cheeta and Jane any time they feel like it. Really, wouldn't we all have good figures if we lived like that!

One of them came over to our table after about an hour and introduced himself. Such a nice man, big and tall and muscular. And so handsome. He was on the team of the Trigger Research Facility at Bandung on Java. More a boy than a man; he couldn't have been more than twenty-five or twenty-six. So young and so bright. He had studied at the U of M. He was very excited because we had just sent over a big load of U235. He could hardly contain his enthusiasm:

"Just think," he said, "of what wonderful things we can do with this radioactive material. All for the benefit of humanity, of course." His English was more than adequate. With his friends he spoke a colorful «revolutionary Malay». They had all gone to «wild schools» together during the war. They all speak fluent French here, if only that restaurant pidgin we Americans be fed. And here Deborah was in her element. We were all in Deborah's element really and she was quite strange just now. I feel a little defensive for her, because she wasn't exactly at the bottom of my list, but nor was she at the top. I'm not «girl crazy» like Rory was. She stared off into space and licked her lips as if they were salty. Not that serious a symptom, I guess.

At the table in front of us sat four Japanese traders in their middle thirties. I understood them to say they had just flown in from Tokyo so I assumed they spoke English and introduced myself. We chatted for a short time about this and that. They were with four local girls, «daughters of poor families» I am told, who sat at a separate table somewhat behind them. After ascertaining they were in trade, I told them certain relatives of mine had been involved in trade. This seemed to establish a bond between us.

One of them, a regularly featured man with thick black hair and, of course, the more typically Oriental musculature about the eyes, confided in me that he had, quite honestly, just come here for the weekend to escape all the tensions of Tokyo. He owned a sushi bar, he said. "We need women and plenty to drink and masses of sleep to forget our troubles. I'll be honest with you," he added, "we come over here to get drunk and screw with the hula girls."

At a table nearby what looked to be a «bar-fly» had taken up her station on a chair within easy listening range. I didn't make anything of it but another of the Japanese indicated the attractive woman in her late thirties with his forefinger.

"It's a key moment in my life," he said. "We're set to make a killing, and now this has to happen." And he again pointed at the woman. Then he whispered, "She's a spy, you know; that's all these people know how to do, make love and spy." He gave me a friendly punch in the arm and smiled. He was just a little drunk and thought of me as friendly. Taking me by the elbow he pulled my head closer to his and said:

"But seriously, I'm in business over here. I can trust you. I got a crop of virgin brides three villages around the volcano.. We child-buy them, grow them up at home. The biggest problem is to keep them out of the clubs where they're let in young. It's the highest priced commodity there is today. Of course you couldn't put it on an exchange. Some places we're paramilitary. We do it ourselves. Nobody messes with us, Commy or Xtian. Here we keep them out back." I saw Rory perk up his ears at this. Moments later I watched him disappear up a staircase with an hostess. Deborah saw it too and I knew she knew what they were going to do.

"I thought the problem Moslem/Hindu," I let out, not quite having understood his last few statements. He himself had no religion he said but worshipped his ancestors who were traders.

"Well, that's not much of a religion," I snorted, not meaning for a moment to offend but rather calling before my mind the image of many of mine. But he got a little huffy then and pretended we were talking about something else.

"We take risks, you know. Sometimes we need cash on the nail-head here, maybe a telegraphic transfer. Swiss banks. Swiss banks. It all comes out of Swiss banks. Give you an idea of the price. But that means we take responsibility for the consignment quality. If it is wrong, then we can lose everything. And now this. This spying is all wrong. There is no law here. And again he indicated the girl on the chair. I have to say I don't think he meant real spying, but rather «spying», the much favored identity game played by «experienced professional women» in a cheap bid for attention. And I must say I don't blame her; their lives must be so desperate and lonely. He was even a bit drunker than I. He looked at me with slightly glassy eyes and sought to determine exactly how much of his «yarn» I had «bought».

"And you know who buys the best? Right. First the Saudis. And then fortune's five hundred." I wondered for a moment what he meant because his emphasis was so flat; as if he had meant what he said. I excused myself as politely as I could and went back to my table where, I soon discovered to my sorrow, everyone was drinking coffee and complaining about the heat. What a pack of grousers they were.

It was then we discovered the preacher was indeed and permanently missing. As I pointed out with no lack of emphasis, we had to be back on the boat by five, preacher or no preacher. Deborah was crying so and carrying on. I got some of the Balinese youth to help me get her into a pedi-cab. I told them she was my sister and had had a little too much to drink at sea level. They were very co-operative and didn't have to treat her roughly at all. I myself had seen him disappear, so it was no mystery to me where he was. Out of the corner of my eye

I had seen him whisper something to Deborah, I only caught the word «haunt». And then he dashed off into the brush like a wild-man.

Oh, there had been rumor about him before. Rumor he was not entirely continent, that he had been put out to pasture to die, that he and Deborah had been more than just friends. Rumor that he had planned all along to jump ship in this South Sea Island paradise. But gossip is like the news. One shouldn't react to the story itself, but rather to the fact it is mentioned as news. What kind of a person would tell a story like that. Truth or falsity, we all have to look out for our own societal profit and loss in everything we say. Which is why I wondered when Deborah said I stole from her. What possible motive could have possessed her to say something like that.

And what was he up to, this Murchison I mentioned. Well, given the history of the island, more religious strife I am sorry to say, that despicable counterfeit specie of mentation. But that «pope» of theirs does seem to feel something is afoot.

So, thanks to Deb, we were forced to return to the boat after only a few short hours ashore. And I had to pay the tab. It was downhill to the water so I had an opportunity to question our driver as he lounged in his bicycle seat. It seems the young man was drawn to the city from the country-side, lured by the cash economy and considered himself fortunate to rent a betjak, or pedicab, a three-wheeled affair with two or three passengers on top of the rear axle, @.75¢ per day to gross, on a good day, about $2.40 per twelve hour rental period. I was deeply shocked at the criminal exploitation of these taxi-boys whose country origin is betrayed by their unfamiliarity with the city and their shyness about revealing it. I really didn't mind the unnecessary ride around the dusty little town but Deborah was furious. She tongue lashed the poor fellow until he found his way to the launch where everyone was waiting and furious. So the preacher's fate nearly befell me through no fault of my own. I gave him a handsome tip which I felt would more than compensate for Deborah's lack of civility.

I happened to tell Cayman about the terrible oppression under which these boys labor but he had a good laugh on me. "Don't worry about them," he said, "just look at the mathematics of it." Then he explained it all in the most tedious detail. He said:

"Now, they pay .75 anythings and gross 2.40 anythings. That's 31.25%. That's what he pays those who control the means of his livelihood. He pays for his food, shelter, clothing. Since it's the tropics the later two expenses are sub-critical if not negligible. Plus extended family, he lives at home. And his body does the work so his food is his gas. You with me on this, Des?" Indeed, I was staring out into space. He paused hardly not at all, just long enough to take a big swig of his drink.

"I happen to know in a lease agreement for a licensed hack on the East Coast of the States you end up paying 33.50 anythings out of a hundred. Think about it, Des. Pretty pathetic difference when you figure out of this Joe Blow's got to pay gas, food, clothing and shelter, all critical. Plus he's driving a sophisticated piece of machinery prone to costly down-time. You figure it out for yourself from here, kid." And he laughed again. I'll have to admit I had never actually figured it out for myself. Not that it's important to us. If people heard I'd picked up my date on a bike they'd die. And actually I felt better knowing Billy Bali was so well off. But no, Cayman said, "you're a sucker. That's the joke. These spear-chuckers are a hell of a lot better off than Hal the Hack. It's so bad, in fact, I say we move in on these bozos, bust their bikes and make them drive Mercs. You and I baby, we could make it happen." And then he laughed again. What a strange and twisted mediocrity he was, now lucid and cogent, and again demented and drooling. I knew all about the economy and didn't need him telling me how to spend my cash. And I could have told him that the next thing here was going to be tourism and the University business. But I didn't.

Then there was a terrible earthquake hours after we got off the island killing twenty and injuring over two hundred. So you see sometimes it's okay to travel fast. I think we were very fortunate indeed to have gotten out of there when we did. We should all thank our lucky stars every day of the week. I thought about starting a chain letter for pin money but never got around to it. Those things can be such fun.

14

Sea Lanes

Rory went and got drunk on a bottle of something alcoholic he'd located on the island. He came to me in a severe depression. It always happened when he'd drink too much. I suggested, in a friendly way, that perhaps his continuous diddling of Deborah had had something to do with it.

"Oh, you've been with all the madonnas, haven't you," he said with a nasty snarl. He could be quite ugly when he lost his charm. But he rose to a new height of insult when he said: "Don't tell me, I've seen you with that old hag. You look like a sick mouse drowning in a bowl of cold porridge." I don't know who he thought he was to go watch people in the middle of the night. I could barely contain my anger and might have lashed out at him had he not wrapped his arm about my neck and whispered as if I were his fellow conspirator: "Don't worry, Dusty, you're secret's safe with me. And I won't tell them what you know of the acidic detonator fuse in the stomach of a Zurich Irishman in 1942." This must have been an allusion, but not one I bothered to ponder. Instead I said:

"Well, there must be some reason they call her Debby-one-fuck." I had intended for this to be the terminal remark in this dotty discussion for I did not wish it to continue along these lines. But Rory was not to be put off.

"Women," he said philosophically, "are so unsatisfying, finally, aren't they, really? I mean, a man like me, a man like me could have any woman he wanted, couldn't he?" I certainly couldn't deny him. He put on quite a good face in the right light. Then, after a short pause, he said meaningfully:

"Or any woman who's available, if you know what I mean." And here he gave me the strangest leer, as if I were a woman sitting across from him in a small stateroom on a boat eight hours out of Java. Or Bali, rather. These must be the DT's, I said to myself, and wondered what had happened on the second floor of «The Volcano.» Perhaps that shapely hostess had had something more innocent in mind than the menu of Rory's degeneracy. He continued on the subject of Deborah. He said:

"Do you know what that woman said to me when I asked the way to her heart? She said: «Mettez vôtre nez dans mon cul et vous etês dans les faubourg.» I was surprised. I hadn't known she knew the revolutionary period.

"Well, how do you feel about that, Bucky," I asked.

"Oh, I don't mind," he said.

"Well, it's all right then, isn't it, if there's no skin off your nose." He agreed but still seemed troubled.

"Yes, well, it's not easy," he mumbled, "but it's a labor of love." I just turned my head aside and stifled my annoyance. So it had come to this, nothing but this base object left between us. This was a turning point between Rory and I, one to which we never returned, and I was grateful for the opportunity thus afforded of becoming wholly my own man once again. Personally I think he was an honest lad lost in a morass of popular mysticism and back to nature slogans, but then it's not for me to say. I'll admit I was just too broken down, spiritually and physically, to give him the cold shoulder. I hardly had the strength to get him back to his room much less to deny his whims. And in fact I didn't. He confronted me suddenly face to face:

"Just let me show it to you once, Dust, just let me show you what it can do. Go ahead, take hold of it. It won't bite you, for god's sake, watch it now. . ." And he was off before I knew what to do. I just had time to remark, "what, Buck, having a little problem with the magic wand?" But I know he didn't hear me. And who but a monstrosity with ice water in his veins and a stone for a heart could deny a plea so pathetic? What red blooded person with a shred of decency left in his bones would turn him away with an upraised and cold hand, or a fist clenched in anger? I ask you.

And this is the full story of how I unwillingly and then hesitantly agreed to «service» Rory if that were his last life's desire. Who knows that, had I not, he might that very night have gone off and killed poor dear Deborah or everyone else for that matter. Well, after he had dropped his trousers to the floor and forced me to grasp it firmly in my hands, I couldn't help but notice his little «rod», proud and erect for all the world like a naval cadet. "Look at that," I ejaculated, quite in spite of myself. I held the stiff little thing what I thought was a safe distance away from me, telling him under no circumstances to splatter my person. But you know what a promise is worth at a time like that. It wasn't really as horrible as it sounds. I felt rather like a nun in a rabbit class, feeling it pulse and throb in one's hand gives one such a sense of life's ominous, fruitful, forces. Some wags have compared it to a severed turkey's neck but I don't think that's fair. It's not all that ugly. (It stained my pants quite badly, by the way, a stain similar to one produced by carelessly splashed bleach. No wonder modern young ladies are so delicate and downright chary in questions of its dissemination abroad. If I had it to do over I'd make him wear a condom and then throw it into the ocean. It's probably better these days to destroy as much of it as we can.)

He humped about on tip-toes a bit, the «apple» itself growing quite large and bulbous, and then he «went squirt» right away, great gobs of jizm spraying up and down my pant leg and dripping on the floor. That annoyed me. He stood still for a moment and moaned softly. I just stood there dumbly regarding the reality of his achievement. Then he tried to kiss me but I brushed him aside. Had I been a medicine chest he might have done the same. I have never liked kissing men and don't know why the custom persists. He mumbled his thanks from the doorway and left. Why he was so drunk he probably thought he was me. I read for a while after cleaning up and then fell into a good sound sleep.

As per what usually happens, the next day he wanted me to read some of his poetry. He slipped me a sheaf of it as I was leaving the dining room and then left me with nothing more than a meaningful glance. I tried to read it but it was so turgid I finally had to give up. All about people going off alone and running at the nose. There was one long work about some horrible curse called down on him by some old Scotsman, about his efforts to mitigate it through the use of antibiotic. But so many young men walking the streets today have come from families cursed by their ancestors during low moments in the war and the idiotic «roaring twenties» which followed. It read rather like a fairy's Mein Kampf, no love affair without dishonor, no «drooling the future» short of absolute redemption. I know that's catty for me to say, but I'm afraid I'm incurably «that way». I was so disappointed. There was a love poem to some cripple he'd bagged, calling him his «polio pony», so very crude. But, then, when he went so far as to call John Aldrich a «weak pimp. . .with ways women want», I just went west.

Now we all like a well-turned phrase and a cogent narrative leading to the full exposition of an insightful argument. Something to be read on a basic level and understood straight out. But there's something to be said, simply stated, for high art or nothing. You may question what I mean by «high art» but that's no concern of mine.

And I'll be the first to admit I found myself turning slightly vicious from this point on in time. I was finally bored with travel and wished,only a hearth somewhere, a cozy chair, a piece of bread with my meatball. It's the same with everyone, be he real or make-a-believe. But this fissure in my patience was nothing really serious, mind you, no case of the screaming stretcher in the night, but rather an affliction of spirit. We were so close to the bone out there and seemed so far from our ultimate goal. We were two weeks behind schedule and that did quite a lot to stop the time. There's only so long you can spend in a life like this. I put it to the Captain; I said:

"Look, we're always two weeks behind and we're always in a hurry. Why both?"

"The engines," he said, "the engines."

"That is the oldest excuse in the world," I shouted and stalked out. I was furious as we sailed into Singapore Strait, convergence of so many sea lanes down there. It was very hot. There are no exploitable natural resources in this country. And then, just as we passed a large industrial complex built on reclaimed mangrove swamp, the boat stopped dead in the water. Or so it seemed. I went out to investigate further and found from Cayman we had been refused permission to land in the city proper though we would be allowed to refuel at the estate, their word for gas station. I asked why, why would they refuse us, us of all people, permission to land? Cayman indicated that somewhere we must have picked up a reputation as a «party boat».

"What in the world does that mean," I asked politely, "and how in the world could such a terrible thing have happened?" He threw me a side-long glance and said:

"Maybe they heard this tub was lousy with queers."

"I demand an explanation of that statement," I screamed. "What do you mean by that remark, my good man?" I was livid. He didn't answer but turned and walked away to the telegraph room where he and the Captain attempted to get us a variance. Personally, I couldn't have cared less. Except that now I'll never get to visit Singapore. And I hear they are such clever and industrious people. I couldn't see much of the city from the harbor but I could just imagine all the interesting things they were doing in there.

There was no variance forthcoming and so we were forced to set sail after we had filled her up. They put on some copies of the Strait's Times of Kuala Lampur so at least we could read. While we were waiting we saw a junk sail by filled to the gills with men, women and children. Those must be the boat people, I said to myself. And there right next to us at the fuel dock were hundreds of the fiberglass cabin cruisers for which the Singaporians are so justly famous.

The heat was overwhelming. I went to my stateroom and stripped to my boxer shorts. I lay in a sweaty half-sleep for days on end. I imagine I lay there for as long as it took the Captain to navigate his way into Victoria Harbor. Nobody was talking to anybody so obviously there is nothing to report. The next thing I remember I was awakened by the sound of the anchor chain slipping through the hawse-hole and splashing into the water. At last we had arrived in Hong Kong, ten square miles of harbor in the path of the terrible East Indian typhoon. I felt so justified, just to have come this far.

15

Hong Kong

I'd be a fool if I didn't just get right out of there and take care of myself for a change. No more of this "oh, hi, Nanette" and "now that is a cute halter, Deb." I didn't see a one of them and they didn't see me. Only some of the crew who were banging on the bulwark and calling my name. I hailed a hack, threw my gear in the boot and got out of there. Three hours later I had checked into Victoria Hospital and lay feverish and bleeding in the emergency room. No, it wasn't an accident, I was quite sick. They were trying to test my blood and deliberately splattered it on the bedding and the nurses, on Doctor Chow and his associates. They said they were going to feed me in the vein but I think they did it on purpose, bled me, that is, and shocked me back into consciousness. After I saw the blood, I felt much better. It was so red and rich looking on that white linen. It was the shock.

They kept me there a week , in which time I got to know the staff pretty well. They were all real nice people and well trained in Western Medicine. So it's just like I told that boy back on the boat. I was right about that. The hospitals here are just like state-side. And even a little better because the Oriental people don't have any race problem to speak of.

After release I took rooms in the native quarter. Sue Mee, the sweetest girl from physical therapy, helped me find them when I told her I was interested. It was in a relatively less expensive section of town, needless to say. But they'll never find me here, I secretly thought to myself. Inside I was a whole new man without any desire to renew a perfectly deadly recent past. And it wasn't that I was financially embarrassed. Indeed, I wasn't. Greed is no motive with me. Oh, I love a first class suite when the mood comes over me. You know that. But nothing can match the charm and local color afforded by a boarding house. And a spendthrift is like as not to turn out a man of easy virtue. I found the most wonderful little place in Cowloon. They, the rooms, were distant relatives of the nurse Sue Mee, far from the legation compound. And that's not wrong, that sentence, for in China a place is people first; not like the states where postal and real-estate considerations are paramount. You come down a steep hill off the Lo Wu Road and there it is in an area called the Rialto, a nice middle-range place and not too far from the docks. I got what they call in Chinese an «empty-nest», something meant for an older couple with grown children and hordes of grand-progeny. But she got me something of a deal for a slight consideration. And that's different too. Here you have to pay a bribe to blow your nose. But it's just a slight bother once you get used to it and know how much to give so you're not embarrassed in front of the natives. The neighborhood didn't look dangerous, some show-business types and various young professionals on the way up. Nothing glamorous, mind you, but I didn't know exactly how long I'd be able to stay.

It really was a charming place and full of so many interesting people. The concierge was a steady old bag of sixty or seventy with perfectly deadly looking coal-black eyes known as Fuk Yu. She struck a no-nonsense pose and stuck to it. How I admire that in a woman. She pointed to the rickety old elevator after I'd paid my first month and then very clearly indicated with her fingers fourth floor. But then it turned out to be the fifth so I guess they don't count the ground. Mine were three rooms with windows on all sides. I could see almost everything that was going on all around me but mostly I didn't in these early days. Call it introspection, I was seized in something of a narcotic fit of nostalgia, the mental disorder, the great feller of women and molester of men. That's what they call her here. But don't worry. I shan't reproduce it. It is enough to say I wondered what I should do, who I should be, where, why. The stuff of journalism, really. And now I saw no one to distract me from myself. So I returned to a prior concern, my enduring interest in the seasons themselves and their constant repetition. How could I help it? It was their spring and I could appreciate it so much more never hearing English spoken aloud in my presence. Perhaps it is important to our sense of social well-being if for no other reason than it lifts us up out of this constant mumbling, incessant mumbling. And I don't flatter myself to say you just never know where you'll encounter it.

And so I turned inward, toward my work on the climate, both the large and the myriad of small. Perforce all our interests center here and endure. That's one idea, that only the mad-man wouldn't notice. Another being that another sort of man lives without it, in some atmosphere of his own. But I don't really believe that, do you?

It was their spring and that brought problems. I gave up drinking and smoking ,those nagging question of small climate. I was to relapse, of course, it's only natural, half-a-dozen times. But my mind was made up and that's all that's really important in these questions of abstinence and personal prudery.

Oh, sure, it's not the history of diplomacy or the story of democracy or anything like that. And I'm not claiming it is, am I? It could be as nothing as the teapot put on to boil in the young people's apartment downstairs, the fire and the steam wafting up through the floorboards. Or the flowers I cut by the side of the road and arranged in the vase on my dining table. Nothing, I admit it! Just the secondary weather, those living above and below, the rice, the tea, the herbs. You get good value here. Or the huge bowel movement suffered by the bellicose tenant in 5 EF, sniffed so clearly through the thin walls and ill-fitting doors and windows, up from the two seater in the courtyard below. I started an indoor compost pile in my sitting-room at this point, just a little thing tucked unobtrusively in a corner. And that's just it, isn't it? It's an inverted bell-jar, isn't it? Oh, sure, I was lonely, but everyone was doing it. And I wasn't looking for world-wide endorsement anymore. Though I thought some of the denizens of this quarter were less than generous in their participation.

There was a kitchenette. That's useful. And chock full of funny looking pots and pans. There was a sitting room with some chairs and a glass-topped coffee-table. A place for me to think and think I did. You can't for a moment think I am unaware that I have been something of a «bad boy» in all this, in all these stories, even in my light-hearted reminiscence of them. And perhaps you feel you have caught in these same some glimpse of what you may care to call an «unsavory personality», one of mere clinical interest, one which has now exhausted itself in a back-water and is soon to fade from view. Am I wrong in this? I think you must answer no.

Having entered a mode of general reference, I think I should say this: I have never been convicted of a crime. I say this for, at this stage of revelation, there is cooperative respect demanded by «readers of the whole cloth». («Cloth's readers» would be a cult, like «bible's readers», «radio's listeners», «times' people»). Oh, braggart, you cry! Indeed, not a crime, say I. But I have no desire to joust about with short swords and bucklers like «her majesty's highwaymen». Just put it down as the qualm casserole of intestinal uncertainty. But I claim to be no better than the precocious teen-age female in the prep-academy shouldering the burden-bag of plastic shrunken heads she's begged for since may-day. I came to realize how difficult it was to escape from genre. I'm not mincing words here. That's not what I'm doing.

A word about «psycho-pathology» in all this. I don't think this is a real defense. Oh, in the eyes of an «all-mighty one», sure. But in our everyday doings? I don't think so. What is the place of such disclaimers as «was upset» or «did not know what he was doing»? I don't think it is useful to think of insanity as separate from a more general psychology of «seven deadly sins» for instance. But even granted a certain gratuity in my posture, I don't think we need a professional here in my adventure story, there being no requisite expert in this sort of narrative. Slander, mistaken identity, these were a few of the problems I was dealing with. People saying they had done what I had done and I hadn't done the same. And never, never a scrap of proof. Far be it from me to dignify these charges. That I slandered religion and made it hard for people to get to heaven? My fault?! That I have aggravated the political climate? That I was a driveling drug addict, pushing drug paraphernalia to feed my habit? Well, you tell me if I drivel. And I have been more than frank about what I do for money. That I am a lurching anonymous alcoholic beyond insanity, exquisitely fantasizing a mission to savage myself and my relationships? That I make girls cry? Slut-slobber! I mean it, I'm that angry! That I was sexually deviate, that I violated my seniors, that I had an unnatural interest in the female posterior? Or a pornographer showing people what they want to see? You see how they contradict themselves. Why, I could tell you everything of everything I have done and you still couldn't say that. Your tongue would swell up in your head and the poison sacks under your lower jaw would swell up and burst. Ontogenetically speaking. I'm not saying we're the same as lizards, that we share the animal in them, as it were. You can see what happens when you try to answer a charge of slander, respond to bold-faced lies, counter presumption, etcetera.

And then later, calmer, after my period of bereaved fascination had passed, I did look out on my whereabouts. I had a charming view down-hill to the market square and the docks beyond from my bedroom. Out of the east sitting-room window there was a touching panorama of the courtyard where I watched the locals going about the business of their everyday lives. It had been originally intended for the guests, I imagine, since it was full of flowers and statuary but had been «taken over» by the «coolies». I'd watch them washing and hanging out sheets on cotton lines. I'd watch them feeding the chickens and exercising the ponies. Always a few stray «girls» and their «boy friends», merchants peddling opium and her derivatives to «the youth on the hill». Occasionally travellers would come in from Western Szechuan on scraggly camels and sell silver and gold objects from woven-wool saddle bags. It was very fascinating and I could watch it for hours. But I think people are more important than places and views, don't you? And then, inside, children in every room watching color-television sets. This is the future, I said to myself.

I was alone perhaps a month. Maybe more. It could have been a great period of time for all I cared. Even here there were very many very very interesting people. I'll never forget the little candy girl who had a stall down a little side street where she made those little «diverticulum». And the taste as she squeezed them out one by one. Back breaking labor. And of course there was a missionary who lived on the third floor. There was a Miss Woo on the second. I'd just see her in the halls and look into her room when I used the stairs. And sometimes I'd see her in the dining room where the punkahs swung wearily from the ceilings and waiters wore soft-soled shoes. There was a young Chinese man on the fourth floor with his Mongolian girlfriend. She was from Ulan Bator. We spent a good deal of time together after I was beaten so badly and before I went to California to recuperate. And in case I didn't tell you Deborah did it. She had lured me to her rooms with flattery, calling me «boy-toy» and other trashy endearments. I'll admit I fell for them hook line and sinker. I always do. I was so lonely. Then she said to Wang Chung: "Beat up that faggot and throw him in a canal." Yes, there is more than a little you don't know about Deborah. But not now. Maybe later.

In any case they enjoyed my company and I theirs. They questioned me quite closely on politics back home. I told them it was business as usual and so nothing really worth talking about. It never occurred to me till later they might be Red Spies but when I thought about it, they might well have been. I hope I didn't give anything away. But they helped me in a place where there were none of my own kind.

Just another word or two of my neighborhood studies. The toilets, which I have mentioned, fortunately had «comfortable seats». I had some trouble settling in, some binding and then a terrible loosening. But nothing life-threatening. I spent the first «little while», as professional travellers like to call the «period» of one's cultural transition, in my rooms but within days was able to venture out with a somewhat broader view than that of a cultural attaché or a touring ballerina. But I found myself having to «go native» in order to keep up my fiber count. This meant a lot of «take out» chop suey and cold noodles, hot dogs from street vendors, pop corn in the movies. And a locally concocted cough preparation distilled from rice wine never failed to put me to sleep in comfort. But I would wake somewhat anxious and disoriented for quite some time. The time difference between there and New York, for instance, is very great. Even greater than that to Los Angeles. It is often already the next day in Hong Kong before it comes to America. A little waking in panic, starting in fear when I would begin to nod, nausea, cold-sweating. But I was soon almost as good as new, and definitely on the mend.

16

Dissembler's Dissembler

And then the dreams started. Well, thank god bullets in dreams don't kill because if they could I'd be dead. Hideous nightmares of murder and mutilation, of dippings in vats of boiling sugar-water and other Kung Foo. They say it's the climate and the diet but I don't believe it for a minute. And they say this is a violent place, not like the real China, but only Hong Kong. But I don't believe that either. I'm just happy dreams aren't real. Finally, after I had completely settled in to my new life and almost completely forgotten everything and everyone, the telephone rang and woke me up. It was Deborah. She asked, with a slight catch of urgency in her voice, if I'd come right over and I, for some crazy reason, agreed. I guess because the hideous place she picked for herself, an amerikanisher trailer-park sort of motel out Nathan Road on the Cowloon side, wasn't too far from where I was staying. I thought for a moment that she was like myself and wanted to get away and experience the texture of foreign life, but she was just an «Army brat». So what could you expect.

By the way, really hideous place. Neon-lights, late model Detroit cars, a domination-disco at the other end of the parking lot where, it is said, youth «wang chung» until nearly dead, fatally absorbed in that low drone of the beat-machine. I knocked on the door of her room and saw her looking through the peep-hole. She said "just a minute" and then I heard her undoing some locks and chains. She opened the door wide enough for me to slip in and bolted it absurdly tight behind me.

"Why all the caution," I said lightly, not understanding just then that a single woman can become very frightened in a drug port such as this. She looked at me as if I were a fool so I asked her, quite innocently, why she didn't go some place safer, like Taipei or Yokohama.

"Why ever would you want to know that, are you the police?" Am I the police! Can you imagine that? Of course she knew I wasn't the police. She was just saying that to throw me off my guard. How could she have ever thought something so outlandish?

She slipped her hand under my arm and drew me closer to herself. We'd never been quite this intimate aboard ship so I half-thought for a moment she mistook me for another. The curtains were drawn and the only light came from a small lamp on a bedside table. The room smelled close and a potent mix of nervous sweat and eau de cologne came up from her body. She was in her nightclothing for it was well past midnight. It was warm and my white silk shirt was thin. Her shapely breast happened to brush the back of my arm. With that my ungainly «thing» thrust itself out in my trousers, a nicely pleated light poplin pair, and gave her a solid thwack on the thigh as I turned. She seemed to notice and tried to catch my eye but I avoided a direct confrontation and moved to her left. I've always been subject like this to the needs of a woman in distress, looking for something solid to cling to in the rising torrent of floating anxiety. But one thought of her shipboard exertions with Rory, with the Purser, with any and all Toms, Dicks and Harrys in pants, decided me against going «too far». I wasn't about to get caught getting physical. Or so I thought. That's when the business about «boy-toy» came up. I heard her mumble something under her breath as she walked away so I asked her what she had said. She wouldn't tell me but I just know it was «boy-toy».

Now this woman was a dissembler's dissembler. Further, she was what they call a «plant». I know this for certain, a «warm body» drawn from the «active element» of society, from those «funny people» who are not sincere for whatever reason of ideology or profit. My contact with this strata of the populace has been limited, to say the least. Oh, a waitress here and there, a divorcée, nothing meaningful or lasting. And nothing that would ever drag me down to «their level». Just a casual pick-up in a bus-station, that sort of thing. Or and encounter with some devious young single sorting her things in the laundrymat, laying her most intimate possessions on the formica-topped table, turning them right-side-out,trying to flatten her little panties with her palms. Really silly because only wearing can unwrinckle them.

Or our waitress on an off-night in a strange town, an outpost with only electronic connections to the main metropolitan centers. A diner on the highway; she drove there in her Bonneville. You'd see her in her white fit-right uniform filling a salt-shaker or a sugar-dispenser. She'd more than likely have a good figure. You'd see her under-clothing delicately outlined and sometimes fully visible beneath the nylon tricot. Those things can be so incredibly skimpy. She'd give you the «eye» with your cup of «joe», her name and address with the meatloaf, and then her specialty with dessert. And eventually you'd follow her home. You'd make the arrangements somehow, anyhow. Call the office, cancel the tickets, throw over an old friend. Brute curiosity will permit nothing less than an absolute of contact. Then you'd penetrate her to an enormous depth with virtually no effort what-so-ever while she'd diddle herself idly and give out with little squeaks and groans, humming casually when bored, bringing you, like a sexual engineer, to an ejaculation in about five minutes the first time and, in cases of multiple ejaculation, that times a factor of 2.3 for $X(-2)$ hours through the night up to a possible maximum $60 \div 5x(X-2) \neq 0$. And not bad, either, with each repetition slightly more pleasurable for the extra effort involved. I was young and strong, then, of course. I could go on all night. But not any more.

Then between each coming, you'd be forced to listen to her dry chatter about some bit of local gossip or «do» at the firehouse or the church social or the supper club or the amateur theatrical. Or perhaps there was some protest in the back room of a nearby tavern. She'd ask you to attend and you'd say "maybe". She'd ask where you were from, sometimes calling you names like «stranger». You'd say "out of town". She'd say "oh", wondering if you'd killed your wife. What people will not do to eat! And then she'd give you a «long look» complete with eyes for all the world like Mexican framed-velvet and say in a drenched voice, "you want to do it again?" And on and on like this all night for, you see, she enjoyed it.

Other than this sort of thing, nothing. Outside my relations to auto-mechanics and carpenters and tradesmen, craft-people, a tap-room hostess here and there, truck-drivers, show-people and the like, whatever you want to call them, the various peoples with more or less hereditary occupations in the Western world.

Well, that's where Deborah came from. Have no doubt about that. She was cruel, calculating and vicious and I know it first hand. She said she was a jeweller. Then an «artist». I don't know about that. She further claimed to have had some library experience but frankly I doubt it. That, or course, would have coaxed me to lend her some credence. After all, it is a relatively elevated position. All too often no more than warder, but then that too is relatively elevated. Some very wonderful people, very near, very dear to me, are like that. But some of them are such sillies. And so hopelessly lost in an idle lexical morass. The real «do-do birds» even believe words have meanings all themselves and, what's more, that they make perfect sense in just any old order. Even «foreign» languages. Can you imagine that? And that the chance of their meaning anything like what the maker thinks them to mean is mathematically nil. Now that is a waste-land.

But then again I have other contacts who think it all has to do with the flow and deformation of matter under enormous geo-physical pressure, with matter herself's orientation to the flow of water, for instance, such as a stream strewn under-strata of rounded rock covered with sod-bound silt. . . . But this too is bookish. And please, oh please, don't think me stupid or boorish or ill or uninteresting. None of this is fair, but meaning-wise, it is fairly realistic. This is but one story; you must give me the benefit of that doubt. Certainly the annals of men action are not written with such idle «j»s and «k»s. Snow-flake like, every movement has its distinctive «shape» on the face of the earth, as lightening, where every one in four flashes forks, petrified, if only on the surface of the eye. So, too, when a flood runs through you'll find things «arranged», though certainly not for your convenience. Nor are these arrangements easily understood though most easily sized in gravel technology. The chert, the stones, the cobbles. Indeed, most «news» footage of disaster victims finds them praying to the heavens for mercy and promising to rebuild by human agency.

But, what we have in this particular case is a question of willful ignorance in a conspiracy to defraud what is so natural and needless of explanation in nature herself by the sort of people who see the natural world, the soil-plant-air continuum, both our untouched and second growth forests, primeval and trackless prairie, not to speak of waste tracts and vacant lots, so singular and unshorn, as mere steam-generation paraphernalia, the heater and the holder, the kettle and copper coil. People of the boiler persuasion. That sort. That's rot. And don't think I'm calling Deborah names, calling her an eco-criminal or whatever, something silly because it's probably not illegal. No. I'm just trying to explain how it was I was so duped and bamboozled by a girl like that. Her kind. How ever else would I get into scenes like this, except with really dumb girls. Can you imagine the organization which could produce and operate an unwitting agent of that stature?

We heard noises next door, men laughing, women giggling, glasses clinking. We listened for a second and then Deborah motioned for me to sit with her on the edge of the bed. She looked nervous. She said: "Those men next door, you know, I think they turn tricks, Desmond. I didn't know men could do that."

"You didn't," I screamed. "Oh, poor dear Deborah, that's the sweetest thing I've ever heard you say." I was genuinely touched. I mean it. I thought to give her a kiss on the forehead but then thought better of it. She, however, had other thoughts on her mind.

"The Caymen came by," she said. You see, we all called them the Caymen because Caymans seemed so clumsy on our lazy, drawling tongues. "They were very distressed about you," she continued. "They want me to visit them in Cleveland. It was they who gave me your number. Des, don't ask me how they got it."

"Cleveland," I asked somewhat sourly, "I thought they were from California or Washington. Washington State, I mean. And what do you mean, distressed about me," I threw in. "I have given them no reason to be distressed!" And I hadn't. But she went on in all earnestness:

"They said they thought you were crazy and dangerous and feared for their lives."

"Feared for their lives," I gasped, "how could they have done that!" Can you imagine?

"But they are very serious, Des," she continued. "They think you have something to do with the tongs."

"The tongs," I shouted. I was about to laugh because I was confused for a moment with the kitchen pincers.

"No, no, the teenage gangs," she put in, "the gamblers and the pimps and the rickshaw drivers."

"Rickshaw drivers," I cried.

"You know what I mean."

"The Green Society," I asked. I didn't really know. A shot in the dark. Something I'd gleaned from reports. But she said she couldn't remember the color and fell against my shoulder. She began to weep softly.

"I'm so frightened," she whispered, "what if they laugh and hoot at me? They can do that, you know. They just don't stop their evil laughter until you leave town."

"Hoot at you! Don't be silly, people don't hoot," I replied gently, "but who? Who is this they?"

"Some people I've met," was all she would say. She stood up and went to the bathroom door and switched on the light. She wore black spider-webbed high-heel pumps even in her night dress. She had her jogging shoes, sure, and her penny-loafers but these were really her. They went clack-clack as she stepped on the tile floor for a drink of water.

"Well, that's very mysterious," I said. "Won't you tell me something about them?" Some people love a mystery but not me. I can't stand not knowing absolutely everything as far in advance as possible. But Deborah was a mess. And I'm not so sure she should have been drinking the tap water. The girl was in real trouble and I was just as positive as could be there was nothing I could do for her. Sometimes you just know something like that. Oh, sure, some gentle petting, anything like that is okay. But the stark and nameless terror of it! They were by now working on the necks of the Chinese girls in ;the room next door. This wasn't the first indication I'd had that there were women in that room. Somehow I just sensed it, and I had seen female rubber boots outside their door on entering. This isn't unusual because it rains frequently and unexpectedly in Hong Kong. We could hear the protestations and the cracking through the thin sheet-rock walls. They have the same building techniques there as we do in the lower

48. What a terrible thing to be a woman. Or to be thought a woman. Then Deborah said, quite incomprehensibly:

"You know what they do to little girls like that, don't you?" I didn't say I did but I don't know what she was imagining. It was then I decided she was really quite out of control and began to behave accordingly. I said:

"Well, darling, if you didn't seize words like instruments of torture I'd just love to continue this conversation." I sought to move it to a somewhat more neutral plane. She walked back and sat quite close to me on the edge of the bed. She seemed calmer somehow for what I had said to her. I put my arm around her thin, barely covered shoulders and said:

"I'm sorry, Deborah, but I don't exactly provide social services; I'm not what you'd call a charitable institution. However, I would not be adverse to hearing whatever sorry little story you may, perchance, have to tell." She looked at me blankly so I right away thought I was being a bit oblique. So I added, in an understanding voice: "Go ahead, what's this silliness in your head?" I had, at the time, no idea what was to come of this overture.

"But you know, Desmond, I know you know. Don't pretend you don't," she protested pathetically.

"If there is one thing I do not do," I stated flatly, "it is pretend I don't know what I do know no matter how many people say the opposite is the case. My personality is no democracy whatsoever." I was just a little more than miffed that she would even intimate at no matter what odd angle that I was in any way a fraud. She whined fetchingly at this point and whimpered ever so subtly:

"What is the opposite? Oh, Des, I'm so confused." As indeed she was. She again came up close to me and took my hands in hers, holding them at my sides. At this her nightdress slipped open revealing a good deal of the inner sides of her surprisingly large and well-formed breasts. I'll admit I was more than a little distracted by the sight of this poor defenseless girl when she suddenly stepped back and extended her hands, palms downward, out in front of her. This in itself revealed a good deal more. But I of course made no move to further my advantage.

"My hands have gotten so old since I came to China," she complained, "perhaps I should never have come. It's just too confusing and I'm overcome with fear. Danger seems to be all around me. The cries of those girls in the next room is almost more than I can stand."

"Oh, so you're going to chicken out, is that it, Deborah? Is that the kind of girl you are. Is that what you're made of, stuff like that? Is that why you came to Hong Kong?" I now took her hands and held her arms at an angle to her body. I thought that if I threw her on her own devices perhaps she'd respond in a more positive manner. Not that I was indebted to her in any way, shape or form. She was nothing to me really. Just a fellow traveller. I remember I gave her a little lecture right then and there about how it was a strange and wonderful paradox to me that in all the tediousness and temporality of everyday existence there lay the glory of eternity and the magic of connection with the joyous puzzle of life, over and over repeating and replenishing itself, always unique, always a laugh and a tear. Reminders like this are important when a person is very badly depressed. Then I said that at the top of a long list of wonderful things was friendship, the interpenetration of lives that forever change the energy of the universe. I told her, for the specific purpose of cheering her up, that our life together was beyond adjectives, adverbs and sundry other parts of speech and that «love» came nowhere near. I thought this would possibly help but she was stubborn as a mule. She had the audacity to suggest that I was somehow coming on to her.

Something like that just makes me «lose interest». I tried to calm her irrational and hysterical fears by telling her to think of where she was in the world, so far away and so cut off from what is normal and sane. Then I started listing things: teak, ivory elephants, incense, postage stamps, exotic spices, edible dog, cymbals, gongs, camel trains, bright hot deserts. I thought perhaps the matter would sort itself out in enumeration and cause her to turn a page on her obsession. But it didn't.

"I have the idea there are too many people," she came back, "a teeming plague in a bare, overcrowded existence. Darkly colored eunuch beggars wanting to grab me by the ankles and carve me like a piece of wood. Their gods get angry, an American girl can't stand something like that. They are different, the bind the feet of girl children, they are nerveless and indifferent to pain." I stopped her here and said:

"Oh, that old bugaboo," but she glared at me and said in a very authoritative tone: "Don't you believe it for a minute, Des. There are still plenty of «little sufferers» undergoing the wicked and slow process of having their tiny feet encased in metal clamps, tightly bandaged around and a little above the ankles, to prevent their feet from growing." She fell on the bed and sobbed softly. I came up behind her and sat next to her thigh. Rory had given her some very lovely yellow silk sheets, kind of a meaningful code with that type.

"That's simply amazing," I said, "where ever do you hear things like this?"

"It's true, believe me."

"Well, then, where did you hear it?" She was lethargic and I feared for a moment she would drop off to sleep. I struck a sober pose and waited for her to respond.

"Mr. Hung told me," she said with a slight edge of superiority in her voice, "and he was very nice and didn't make it sound low and disgusting like you would even though it is."

"And who is Hung," I asked, arching my eyebrows to make my point.

"He's a very nice man, Desmond, and you had better remember that." She twisted half way over when she said this to me and had as of yet still not fastened the tie on her robe. I would remember it, I told her. It turns out he is quite a character, known to some as a later-day «Chunking Charlie» after the wartime capital of that name. Some enormous fortunes still extant were started there under the most extraordinary circumstances. I've since heard his nickname is «Rad», short for radish, I imagine. Just another unscrupulous war-mongering, arms-merchant robber baron bandit, I thought, but Deborah couldn't sing his praises in too high a voice.

"He's a really wonderful man," she claimed, "despite what they whisper of his past." Not to speak of the source of his fortune. But I didn't say that.

"Well, where ever did you come on him?" I asked in all innocence.

"The Caymen introduced us. They said they knew we'd hit if off."

"My, they are well connected, aren't they. It's a pirate in every port with them."

"Oh, don't be silly, Des, even you would like him. He's offered to take me everywhere. He's already introduced me to some charming young Oriental girls who want to break into show business in the West and are working on an angle. I thought maybe you could help them, you know a little about things like that." A little, indeed; aren't we being coy with our attribution. But I didn't say that, either. So you see I can control myself and don't always just make trouble. But that she thought I'd care to show glamor tricks to show girls on any continent just galled me at the time.

"Well, tell me about the tricks he's taught you, Deb, that should be something." I'm not abnormally fond of that quizzical look girls get when they can't quite follow the drift of a conversation, but it does provide some amusement. This expression then faded into annoyance when she decided to answer a question I hadn't asked.

"He took me to Rose Hill, it's out on a island in the harbor." That would be the Roosevelt museum with the huge closets. She hesitated and then lay down again on her stomach. Her face was turned toward me. The lighting, from the parking lot and the bathroom, were just perfect for her look of puffy vulnerability.

"What's the matter, Deborah," I asked sympathetically, "you don't seem completely sold on the old slope. Or am I inventing again." Her face twisted up the way it will and she paused before remarking like a slightly naked school marm: "Don't call them that. It's not nice no matter how you look at things." I didn't need her to tell me that wasn't nice to say. And I said it more to elicit a response than to communicate anything. She paused again leaning on her elbow.

"What's the matter, Deb darling," I asked, smelling a rat.

"Nothing," she said simply, "it's just I don't really like the Chinese."

"Well, my dear, I'm not at all sure it is within the limits of human capacity to do just that," I explained. I was going to say it sometimes appears they are queer or different but I'm glad I didn't. For it wasn't too long before I discovered quite the opposite was the truth with little Deb. Then she burst in saying:

"I can't ever tell what they think. They never show whether they like me or not so I feel funny about them. . . ."

"You are such a sexual being, Deborah," I said with a certain tenderness. She was sitting up on the bed now, totally unaware of her appearance. For some reason she pretended to be cross with me, got up and went to the mirror. There she tied her robe and straightened her hair.

"That's what Mr. Hung says," she said, "but it's different when he says it." I thought it so charming of her to have said this, to be so forthright and ingenuous. Old Hung, it appears, was a wonderful old Jeffersonian, practically a founding-father, complete with his belief in a «natural» aristocracy. I had to hand it to the old boy, he surely had thrown his weight around.

"Well, what did he mean when he said it," I questioned. But I could see this colloquy was not contributing significantly to the absolute warmth of our enclave nor was it liberating Deb from her perfectly ludicrous culture shock. On her bedside table was the book Pure, White and Deadly, the mystery thriller from the fifties set in an atmosphere of intense racial hatred. In it a black photo-journalist, totally au courant, once spurned by the sister of a famous family, seeks villains elsewhere in London's own Scotland Yard. Spy trials are underway accompanied by poisonings of bent scientists and a series of hideous murders on the «where» wolf theme to bolster moral at home. The American hero, of course, is seen as generous and altruistic even while losing his wife and children when they are killed in a gruesome tenement fire in the building where they had moved to be closer to his roots. We see this in flashback. He, somehow, has the feeling he is being used. She, his dead wife, was of Yugo-Italic ancestry from Queens, New York where her people worked in simple trades, food service and light manufacturing. He, the hero, talks to some of them, her people, on the telephone and certain unavoidable racial differences are seen in bold relief. I could see it as a three hour special drama but definitely not a mini-series. Large sums of money are constantly changing hands. There are some finely drawn portraits limned of upper-class Israeli and English call-girls who manipulate ambi-sexual politicians for speculative purposes. I wouldn't recommend it for the faint-hearted and meant to take it away from Deborah herself. But I stopped myself, perhaps influenced by the average Chinee's generally held belief that fate pursues the sufferer and if one saves another, thus defying fate, the rescuer must assume the responsibilities of the saved. So I did nothing. It is so easy to lapse into sinophilic faddism here. But I wasn't just staring at her navel. I prayed, without much hope, that Deborah's «Chinese dream» would soon be over.

More screams were heard through the walls. I didn't think of them as screams of pain, rather screams of a somewhat too intense pleasure. However Deborah thought otherwise, apparently, for she lifted a heavy jade ash-tray off the coffee-table and hurled it with a good deal of force toward the wall. It left a deep gouge in the plaster but thankfully the ash-tray itself was unharmed. I have it with me today as a keep-sake of that woman's fury. Then there was silence.

A few moments later I heard a timid knocking on our door. She and I had remained frozen in place. It was as if her act had radically shifted the camera-angle on our tête-à -tête to a blimp or a fly's eye on the ceiling. I imagine we were waiting for just this response. At the knock, I crossed to the door. When I opened it I saw a handsome, well-built, youthful Chinese man in his shirtsleeves with a loosened tie. I took him for a weightlifter judging from the size and shape of his pectoral development. Nothing swells the chest quite so well as religious exercise on those dumb-bells.

"I heard a noise," he said, "are you all right in here?" I'll have to admit I was very impressed by his manner, the way he presented himself in what was potentially an embarrassing situation. The people on the other side of the world are unquestionably the most courteous, honorable, well-meaning and self-respecting people on the planet, hypersensitively attuned to other people in their relationships. In no way did I credit the oft-heard notion, so at large in certain circles, that they all eat rats and enslave white women in «sex-balls», poly-urethane prisons of endless carnal stimulation. However, it is true that when they say yes they mean no and when they say no they mean yes, somewhere in their hearts. He said his name was Wang and I had no reason to doubt him.

He thought, he said, that perhaps we had seen one of the giant rats which came up from the harbor in packs to hunt for meat. If that were so, he continued, he would understand the loud noise. "No, no," I exclaimed, "I haven't seen a rat." And then I laughed. I don't think he could appreciate my nervous sense of humor. He said some were as big as beaver but I think he was pulling my leg. He had a wonderful smile and a sort of subliminal wink. He explained that in olden times the rats in Hong Kong had been smaller and fairly timid but since the early sixties they had grown very large and very aggressive.

I thought it only polite to explain everything as best I could. Deborah just stood behind me and looked out over my shoulder with an expression of thinly veiled contempt. I'm sure you've seen this sort of thing at a country-club or wherever there are boats and boaters, boating people. So I just said that no, actually my arm had slipped holding a large tureen the remains of which have already been cleared away and deposited in the «carry-out container» which is what the Chinese call a «dumpster». He smiled slightly less and cocked his head in the meekness of questions so I went on to say it had slipped from my grasp, knocked the table and banged the partition somehow. And that Deborah had fallen down and hurt her knee. I offered to show him the knee if he didn't believe me. But he seemed satisfied with this explanation and I thought it very generous of me to have taken the blame. He apologized for bothering us if in fact he had and went back to his own room. Deborah went into the bathroom at this point and did whatever girls do in there. When she came out the screams had started again but were much muted. So at least on this level international cooperation is decidedly possible. Then I went in to empty my bladder. And when I came out she gave me a look that said she knew what I did when I was in there. So you see she was not a totally grown-up person. I returned to my question about Mr. Hung.

"Tell me, Deborah, what does he have that I lack," I asked. She had remained silent with Wang at the door and now proved somewhat hostile.

"You name it," she said sarcastically.

"Well, if I did, you'd just say I'm inventing, wouldn't you?" I waited but she didn't respond. Oh, that's a cute trick, I thought. See how far that gets you. Then I asked her more out of annoyance than anything else:

"Thanks a lot, Deb. By the way, what has happened to dear Rory Macallister?" I don't know why but it hit her like a wet sock. She again fell on the bed with a strickened look and a choked sob. The hem of her robe flew well up above her thigh, something she didn't think to rearrange. After a moment of this she said:

"I think he's in bad trouble. He's called me several times but I can't make any sense out of what he says."

"Well, is he hopped up on opium or anything dreadful like that," I asked.

"I don't know," she answered, "but every time he calls he gets more incoherent and I hear giggling in the background. Native giggling." Girls, I thought. I could have told you he'd fall for the tender trap. Certain guys never learn, they just keep going back for more and more fluff. I had her give me his address and said I'd check up on him.

I was tired now. It was late. Hong Kong can be very hectic if you're not a native which none of us are. I stood by her makeup table and studied the delicate ferrying in the mirror's antique silver backing, Deborah's image itself reflected on its surface. I had a message I was to give to her but I didn't think that now was the time. She was lying with her head down and idly wagging one foot in the air. Her robe was totally maladjusted and riding even higher. I felt it, the message, could wait until some time else. She was disoriented and I was weary. Little did I know what was to happen to us all. The message was, incidentally, something about a shipment of jewelry waiting for her in a godown in Kashmir. It was information contained in a letter of hers which I freely admit to having had in my possession. And remember, I'm the one who told you about all this in the first place. The letter is one which I had thoughtfully picked up for her from one of the commercial mail-drops in the city and had been inadvertently opened in an absolute deluge which had overtaken me on the street. But that's another story in and of itself. What I'm saying here is, sure, I read it. Who wouldn't. Like the first skin-book you ever saw. Sure you saw it! And I read very rapidly. Usually a single glance is enough for both sides of a letter. And I thought it was going to be one of those "so our little girl is on the other side of the world" parental kiss-offs, "the snow is starting to fly here again. What have you got for weather over there" sorts of things. So it wasn't exactly that. There is nothing fishy here, it was a matter of public record she was slated to inherit a great deal of wealth in the form of various large bijoux cached for her by her early-years father in various of the «eternal slums» about the world. Everyone knew about it. I swear she used to brag about it in front of the crew and everything. It's one of them who could have done it. And I claim to this day I don't know what happened to them.

She asked when I had last seen the Captain. I told her he told me he was sailing for California in a matter of weeks. And this was contact made with him before I left the boat, not after. I had had a final interview with him chez lui. Of course I couldn't tell him how much I wished to be off his bloody boat. But he insisted on telling my fortune. Not that I believe any of us has any access to the not yet. It's all I can do to keep faith with the past. I won't tell you what he said in any detail. I'll just give you the gist of it. He said, Mr. Desmond, you will be a very great business-man and a household word. But you never quite know what they're saying because there's another sense of it which talks about an eye, as useful as a bar of soap, which had been many places. It is impossible to explain. There is just no translating pidgin.

She seemed sad but we made no plans. Then she told me the Caymen had gone to Taipei but would return to Hong Kong by Thursday. How interesting, I said, and made no further comment. But from this time on I began to appreciate my Hong Kong situation less and less and resolved a change would do me good. She told me where the Caymen could be reached in case I wanted to, in her words, "make it all up to them somehow." Again I kept silent though it made me burn.

It was late. She was dithering and I was slightly bored. She invited me to a «chop-stick» dinner chez Hung at the end of the week. This was Tuesday and that was Friday. I accepted for want of something better to do. I'll admit I was nervous and felt a state of flux coming on. She came and stood beside me in the mirror.

"That man you saw at the door, Mr. Wang, I think you might have caused him to lose face. That's very bad, you know." She was looking up at me in the mirror with bright, knowledgeable eyes and slightly touching my elbow with her hand.

"That's ridiculous," I laughed. "How would I have done that?" I was flabbergasted!

"By lying to him in such an obvious way" she said, "and indicating by your tone that you didn't care he knows you're lying." She paused momentarily. "And by refusing every overture of assistance."

"Don't be silly," I stated flatly. Much has been made of the Oriental concept of «face» but my information indicates that it's just not so. Apparently notion has been developed in the East solely as an outwardly directed social convention designed to teach manners of Occidentals and to avoid the customary insults occasioned by unequal treaties. Among themselves, «face» is never spared nor quarter given. In fact the opposite is true. A great deal of personal credit accrues to he or she who most profoundly «rubs his nose in it," as they say. We could all go a long way toward the correction of this inverted view. And I told her so in so many words.

"Well, most of the lights were out. I hope he doesn't think we were screwing."

"Why should you care what he thinks," I said haughtily. "It's much more important what you think about it." I don't know why this made her pout. And how annoyed I was with her for having thought that up. But little did I know this guy was just the first of a horde of «natives at her gate». I haven't wanted to prejudice you against this fellow up until now, but that very man who stood there before me was Wang Chung, enforcer to Hal Hung. The guy who came and knocked, that was her Wang. And I didn't even know! And it won't really mean that much to you until I tell you the rest.

She had lapsed into a perfectly sibylline silence and I'll admit I felt half-dealt out. There she was, looking up at me with her broxadent smile, so chalky, so wan, so tight-lipped. She took my hand and sat on the bed. It was a small room. Then there was an incredible bolt of lightening and a deafening crash of thunder as a sudden storm blew up. We fell together and I accept that.

Now, I'm an honest broker where affairs of the heart are concerned and I don't want to say too much or too little of what transpired. Let's just say I wasn't exactly helping a lame dog over a stile. She squirmed around some and pretended to touch it by accident. Then she had a little cry in my lap. I wouldn't have minded except that it was a bit squashed and doubled over some under my belt buckle. I didn't want to discomfit her with any obvious manual manipulation on my part. Finally she seemed to loose patience and took me by the lapels of my shirt and said earnestly and without undue embarrassment, with just the slightest affectation of «baby-talk»:

"Des, do you want me to blow your nose?" And then she winked. She positively winked.

"Blow my nose," I cried in disbelief. If only I hadn't been so engorged. If not for that I might have ignored her.

"Oh, come on," she cooed, getting right to work on my buttons and zippers, "that's just what people say. You know what I mean. It'll only take a minute and besides, it's good for you."

Well, there are two schools of thought here. Being roughly the «do-bee» and the «don't bee» schools. Of course, I knew of the Rajasthani Doctors of Philosophy and their endless hours spent in the copulatory pose without the release of even the smallest, the most darting and daring «little wriggler». And who does not know at first hand some dripping scum bag with his «jelly-jar», his «flying oatmeal» and his running sores. And I don't know why the public at large doesn't rise up and do something about this pendulum swing.

"But what about your profession of faith, what about what you told me on the boat. What about that preacher fellow." Believe me, my hands were on my heart. I could hardly believe what was happening to me.

"Oh, that,' she claimed, "that was nothing. I'm so adrift these days." So that is one of the ways she masked her agenda behind a curtain of lust. You see too the pressure of observable appealing detail and where it can lead, should you too ever «pet a swan». And then after that we became something of an item for a number of days. Well, it was almost as if we were really dating. I felt so juvenile. And of course no one ever saw us or caught on. I'll admit I wasn't thinking about the future. It seemed to me Deb had two weeks to do something but I can't remember and it's not important. So it seemed we had some time together and I thought that was nice. I must have been a little bit on cloud nine. Nothing makes me quite so happy as a spurt of generosity no matter what provoke it, even this, this nibbled wedding cake. But I've come to regret this little excess of flesh. If only I had known then how much she would resent it. .God knows it's not my fault she was killed. I'm not going to be held responsible for the suicidal side effects of wry, not having had a good look at her jerked parsimony.

17

Chinese Theatre

As it happened I did go to the theatre the next day. They play every day and it goes on for eight to ten hours. I, of course, understood nothing so you'll just have to trust my rundown from memory. In some theatres men play all the roles and in others, women. But here it was naturalistic and both played both.

They're funny theatres and take place in lofts in the upper stories of garment factories. They are undoubtedly sponsored by special interests. The actors frequently turn their backs toward the audience, breaking out of the action and ignoring them completely. Then they are approached deferentially by an assistant actor or an «intern» who wipes their sweating faces with a steaming hot rag, hands them paper cups of gatorade, combs their hair. It's really very touching. Sometimes they use this interval to spit and blow their noses on the floor. The «intern» then scuffs his feet over the spot much as a hen scratches gravel. They also smoke a good deal of tobacco which helps them achieve their escape from reality.

The spectacle itself isn't much. You just see a bunch of people running to and fro on the stage. Or, glancing up, you see the dwarf, so dear to Eastern story, peeping from behind a lattice. Not a trace of art. Everybody claps them out of courtesy. There's a lot of frantic competition for attention among the troops, each one having a distinct military wing, stamping a certain «black line» into dramatic art and literature.

This one was about a dramatic re-education center for youth tainted by American education who had leaned too far into musical comedy and the jingle business. They were supposed to be teenagers but were all played pathetically by failed actors and actresses in their forties and fifties. As I say, they went on for hours and I can't possibly remember everything. But I do recall a couple of very moving scenes which occurred right near the end. In one a Professor Norwood appears in a vision to Chow, a snobbish and «sensitive» university graduate who can't take the discipline dished out by the spartan Commy thug party-people and harbors deep resentment against the «life of betrayal» æthenian liberal Kuomintang wimp assassins. It's a rich conflict but they never really live up to the explosive possibilities inherent therein. The lights surrounding the stage dim. These are mostly five gallon oil cans with a hole cut in the bottom and an incandescent bulb stuck inside. I've come a long way from curbside at the Majestic, I thought to myself. I can't tell you how many first nights I've seen. But this is China, remember, where «state of the art» is not necessarily the only æsthetic. Norwood, a kindly looking white haired man in a rumpled suit of the Bryant vintage, principal of Eastern Illinois College, appears. He's hardly wraith-like but we're asked to accept his ghostliness.

NORWOOD

Yes, we want to set up some schools in China, but we must understand why we are doing this. Any country that is able to educate the Chinese youth of this generation will be able to reap rich harvests, not only in things of the spirit, but in commerce and industry as well.

Somehow the playwright must have contacted Norwood's subliminal desire to confess all in a late night vision. I think they should have shown him staggering drunk and talking to his mother.

NORWOOD

If America could have diverted a flow of students to her shores thirty years ago, we would now be able to make use of the trickiest and most satisfactory methods of controlling the destiny and development of China. {He laughs dryly, then immediately becomes serious again. He fumbles for an out-sized half-pint of Night Train in his clothing. He finds it, drinks and continues.}

For the sake of increasing and expanding our spiritual and moral influence, money can be expended. I am speaking from a purely materialistic point of view. This would be better than any other method and would also give us a richer harvest. We should finance

China through education and control her through education. (He then laughs wickedly and screams pathetically.} Mother, mother, are these the pagan babies I bought?

Chow, the sceptic, grapples with the information contained in this vision. And I dare say he'd better. If for nothing else it should serve as a timely warning to crack the books before it's too late and finals roll around. Meanwhile, Chow's good friend Wang catches a certain Miss Li Mo vibrating herself in the lavatory and then putting on illegal cosmetics. And eating forbidden peanuts. This is the scene that follows:

MISS LI MO

{Excitedly.} Where do I have cosmetics? Where did you see me «work the nimble finger»?

WANG EHR

When you were in the bathroom, you were like a little thief. You watched yourself do it with a small pocket mirror. and you were in a hurry. I saw you rubbing your little clam as fast as you could with that plastic thing in your purse. You were sitting on the toilet. Then you came like a big stink bomb and put on rouge. You think I didn't see you? Give me that bag of peanuts.

MISS LI MO

{More excitedly.} You dead-devil, you dead-devil! You're rumor-mongering. You're rumor-mongering. I'm quitting. I'm quitting. {She pulls a long face and dashes off amidst laughter.}

WANG EHR

Hey, don't run away, there's even better yet!

MISS LI MO

{She turns around.} What? What now?

WANG EHR

{He brings out Miss Lee Mo's outsize diary.} Look everybody, this is what Miss Lee Mo wrote in her notebook: "Love, love, you have conquered my roomy sleeve. . . ." {He laughs in derision.}

MISS LI MO

{She dashes back.} Aiya! Dead devil! Give it back to me! {She beats on his chest.} If you don't care about your own loss of face, then at least think of me! {Here she should be really bawling.} Give my notebook back to me. Give it back to me.

WANG EHR

It'll cost you one package of peanuts, one package of peanuts. {He dashes off «wiping himself» with pages of her most intimate thoughts.}

MISS LI MO

Dead-devil. Dead-devil. {She gives chase but runs into Comrade Long Won and falls smack into his arms. Long Won lifts her up, fiddles with her skirt, and tries to kiss her. She pushes him away and dashes out. Everybody laughs.}

The obvious lesson to be drawn is that there can be no privacy, no secrets, in such a youthful environment. If the students are allowed to room together they will watch each other and pry into locked boxes. A pillow placed in an unusual position on the yellow silk sheets, a bed moved to the side slightly, a suicide note, all these are noticed, arouse prurient interest and will be discussed at large. The day is saved, however, by a timely and distracting confession from Long Won, the man who attempted to molest Miss Li Mo. The scene was one of their endless meetings or group discussions, sort of parties without the mixed drink, where everything was continually dragged to the platform and probed.

LONG WON

{He bursts out spontaneously into tears and revelation after several hours of being suppressed in an atmosphere of intense boredom. I think he was forced to watch folk-dancing.} I am a sinner. I am a criminal. I am one of those who should be dead. I am one of those terrible Special Service agents! {Everybody shows surprise. And they all seemed to know what that meant. Of course they educate them in Chinese history from the cradle so it's really something different. But audiences over there will put up with all this stuff because they never stop eating from curtain to curtain. I can tell you back home these guys would be dead in ten minutes.}

EVERYBODY

Long Won. How could you.

SOO MI

{She was apparently in charge of the actual political re-education for the entire camp but worked on a very intimate level.} You what? You really are an agent. . . .

LONG WON

I'm from the Sino-American Cooperative Organization. The Americans trained me for six months and then sent us to this school to try to wreck the program!

SOO MI

Holy smoke! I had no idea. But who is this us? I want to hear some names.

LONG WON

Well, I originally came out her with Miss Li Mo. But I suspect you have already doubled her up.

SOO MI

Right! Very astute calculation! She could have been very useful to us, most of all to those in the entrapment detail. She has many fetching details.

LONG WON

I could tell you about some fetching details but I don't think the people really want to know the truth about it.

CHOW BOY

Maybe, maybe not, Long Won. But that is not for you to decide. Tell us of the Sino-American Cooperative Organization and their camp outside Chungking where Chiang and the Americans tortured the comrades who were freeing China. Tell us about that, Long Won. {Thank god that China policy was punished and made miserable.}

MISS SOO MI

No, first tell us what you are doing here in the first place. What is your job?

LONG WON

Yes, well, my main job when I was sent to this school was to spread counter-propaganda, to create rumors, to start rows with everybody, create friction between fellow students, divide everybody and destroy unity and start factions. My main job was to spread anti-discipline and anti-organization propaganda. And to spread incorrect isms of freedom and democracy. I was ordered to spread love America and hate Russia views.

MISS SOO MI

Cripes! You really were a dog!

LONG WON

You bet. I singled out Chow without his knowing and used him as a spokesman for my plans. Wang, the juvenile delinquent, was also very useful. I used him to expose Miss Li Mo to public humiliation. When she fought back, started scrambling for face, I knew she had gone over to the other side. Punish me, I beg you, I'm not a youth. I'm not human.

By the end of this scene the women in the pit are openly weeping. It is really quite effective when properly staged. The last big scene shows Chow's conversion. He sees the light and the play ends real upbeat.

CHOW BOY

{Unable to control himself, he stands up abruptly and knocks over a chair.} Leader Soo Mi, fellow students! What else is there for me to say? I never thought, it never occurred to me. . . . {Tears start to trickle from his eyes, but he holds them back with great effort.} I have become what Student Wang Ehr said. He said: "Don't you think of yourself as Mr. High and Mighty. You're just the mental slave of the aggressive thoughts of the imperialists; you have become the spokesman of the foundation thought." This is something that I never before realized in my life. Ten, twenty years of slave education completely blinded my view, prevented me from seeing the truth and knowing and understanding things clearly. I thought that people who are like us, who have been given American education, we so-called democratic self-centrists, were the only ones fit to save the country. I worshipped America's material culture and advancements, strongly advocated self-centrism. I could not see the murderous blade lying behind the masks of the American teachers and para-professionals. I could not hear the bombs and guns behind Oklahoma, Leave it to Jane, South Pacific, The Music Man, Camelot. . . . {He continued to list the shows and people cheered loosely at their favorites. Finally he returned to his theme.}

There is no middle of the road today. On one side are the imperialists and their running dogs. And on the other side are the people. To want to become a free man, one must lean to one side, join the actual struggle, join the organized body of strength! {Everybody is moved and applauds. Then they all join hands and lean together, first to one side and then the other. It was very confusing. Finally Long Won and Miss Li Mo step forward and make the ultimate sacrifice.}

I have sinned. I want to be sent to the war's most dangerous sector so that I may pay for my sins.

MISS LI MO

Me too! I'm going. And if it's not rough enough out there I'll go somewhere where it is.

MISS SOO MI

Good! Fellow students. Internationalist banking-interest reactionaries destroy your youth! Comrade Long Won, I hope you will think over your past carefully and then criticize yourself thoroughly. From now on, you must build up your determination to become a new man and cast away your sins. But we must all realize and know clearly that it is we who have some of these faults, it is we who have done wrong things. {She had them eating out of the palm of her hand. You could see she was really talking about «troupe politics» and not anything big. And I could just imagine what would happen when she cracked the whip!}

CHOW BOY

Leader, fellow students! I want to tell everybody that from now on you have my guarantee that I will destroy the imperialistic and reactionary views and attitudes existing in my thoughts. From today on our entire self will be dedicated to the revolution, dedicated to discipline and organization. We will obey the call of the school!

MISS SOO MI

Good, Comrade Chow. {She shakes his hand. This, quite obviously, means a lot more in this context than it does in Peoria.} Fellow students, Chow's improvement is very important to morale. Remember, an army marches on its stomach! The painful path Chow has taken to change our thoughts should teach us what we need to know to solve our remaining problems and blow out our heavy burdens and clear the path of revolution. {Her meaning is quite graphically acted out here by the more gymnastic members of the troupe. We hear voices, music and drums. Then gongs and everyone raises his voice as one.}

Yo! A group of students is going on the path of the revolution today. They have all answered the call to work in the hard and rugged and down-right unbearable district of. . . . {And here each night a new name is submitted, almost all of them producing a storm of protest and a hail of laughter, for in China all areas of the country are considered equally unappealing.}

They are just about to leave.
EVERYBODY
Good, good. Let's go and give them a royal send-off.
CHOW BOY
I am going to be sent to the war's most dangerous sector so that I may pay for my sins and free myself of all heavy burdens which keep me from a normal life.
MISS LI MO
Me too. I am going to a place where it is so rough and tough I won't be left with a single remaining unclear and muddy view or attitude. {These two kept coming back every chance they got to do variations on the scant parts written for them. It made it difficult to determine the real end of the play. This was called The Red Handkerchief and is done all over the world. And it presaged somewhat the «chop-stick» dinner I attended and from which I never really returned.}

Any place in this wide world you would have known there was a climax coming on! They had a little brass section down front and some really effective amplifiers! A group of students carrying bags and sacks walks barefoot on to the stage under a send-off banner. On it is written: "Go where the revolution needs you most!" Following behind them was the send-off brigade. Some of them beat drums and gongs, some are doing the yang-ka, an Oriental mambo. Everybody in the cast comes on stage to give them a rousing send-off. Everybody sings: "Young China, yours is the perfect heart, you are the direction." Hands rise, all waving in fervor and enthusiasm. The curtain drops. Thank god that's over, I whispered to no one in particular.

Many think this a lot of crumby clap-trap which I am forced to admit be true but this in no way detracted from my enjoyment of the spectacle. And besides, they're so serious about the whole thing. I've heard the Chinese themselves regard these theatres as the playing fields of Eton.

On the way home from the theatre I made a brief stop at a Lotus House, a sort of museum for foot-bound girls. There, at my request, the host induced one of them to take the bindings off her feet so we could see what this habit does to the poor girl's anatomy. I must admit that her crippled toes and swollen feet almost produced an involuntary reaction of abnormal intensity. But the atmosphere was very reverential, so I stifled it.   For a modest fee this manager, really a maitre d' more than anything else, took me to a spy-hole where I watched an elderly habitué practice the art. It was very much like a feast at which feet were served. In this case the woman took no part other than to critically measure the quantity of discharge. Apparently prices are reckoned on the intensity of stimulation. The feet themselves are called lotuses and the toes half-moons. It's not for everyone but I would be forced to recommend it as an adventure for erotic tourists. They seem to be justly famous for carrying the capacity for extravagant pleasure.

One of the younger girls recited a sad little ditty before I left something to this effect:
See how big sister
jumps across the road,
while little sister sways
in the agony of every step.

They live in a very family type situation and I understand they have supporters in very high places. It was sweet to see this young lady perform this bit of verse though because the literature in this genre couldn't be all that large. Thank god we in the West have no such singularly barbaric custom and long ago learned to use our heads for toes. I far prefer the more modern cult, that of special sneakers designed to enlarge the muscles between the legs. But I'll admit it made me nostalgic and I thought of the old saying: There are no pleasures like those the living steal from the dead.

18

Cayman Island

I woke in a slight panic when I realized I had told the Caymen I would join them at their hotel for brunch sometime before noon. I thought they were so gone from my life and then, gee, only a phone call away. However service on a Hong Kong telephone is very unsentimental. Often if you take the time to say hello they will hang up. Then Nan answered and pretended it would be difficult to arrange.our meeting. Really, some people are so pretentious.

I washed in the basin provided and dressed hurriedly. I walked the short distance to the Star Ferry for the six or seven minute crossing to Hong Kong Island. I got right aboard because there is almost constant service. You can get the Ho Hum Ferry there too, done up in pink and green pastel neon, but I don't think it goes anywhere. And it's nothing like the movie when you get here because it is clear there can be neither sex nor violence in writing.

On the Island side the ferry maneuvered along the terminal in the shadow of the high, white Mandarin Hotel and the glass-encased City Hall. In the shadow, that is, at mid-morning with the sun half way up the eastern skyscape. Between the two, City Hall and The Mandarin, is Statute Square with its wide green lawn, carefully manicured privet hedge, War Memorial and the bronzed and mounted figure of Sir Thomas Jackson, manager of the Hong Kong and Shanghai Bank at the turn of the century and noted equestrian. It was said at the time that no one could touch his stable of polo-ponies.

The three most important banks, Hong Kong and Shanghai, the Chartered Bank and the Commy Bank of China, stand around the green. (The trading of «red money» for «green money» is quite brisk.) The astro-domed Supreme Court and the white stone turrets and balconies of the very dignified Hong Kong Club on another side of the square face the New Prince's Building, home to as many as 500 companies, behind The Mandarin. Next door to the Hong Kong Club is the telegraph office and the studios of Radio Hong Kong. Rising behind and a little above the Bank of China is the Sheraton-Hilton, the two great giants of the industry having joined hands in common cause here. And that spirit infects the whole place. For instance, there is no difference between coke and pepsi here. This is where the Caymen stayed and toward which I walked. There is a stylized double «SH» in blue neon on the roof designed, purposely I suppose, to look like a Chinese character.

I had the desk clerk, an earnest young Chinese from New York, call their room but they didn't respond to his buzzing. The clerk then suggested I try the coffee shop where they had already eaten. I apologized for being late but they didn't seem to mind. In fact they didn't seem to care at all and were quite cold toward me. It was as if they were not quite willing to recognize who I was to them. Well, I've played odd man out more than once. And this eating before the guests arrive is happening all to frequently in society today. It just shows a lack of will-power, what you need to get to the top. That's why smokers should never be allowed into positions of responsibility. At first I was a little embarrassed for them and later I became enraged. Quietly, of course. I never liked to demonstrate anything to those people.

Cayman kept holding up objects off the table and showing them to me as if I were a precocious toddler learning names. And he didn't speak any more Chinese than I. Nanette gazed off across the harbor with a vacant stare.

"You see this radish," he's say, "this is a red radish. See how red it is!" He was impossible that way. He was referring, I suppose, to the undeniable fact that it is necessary to import certain produce and butchershop items from the Commy populace on the mainland. He thought he was so clever and well-informed. I could have told him a thing or two had I felt generous.

"And you see this water," he said holding up a glass of it, "this is from China too. Big pipe full of it runs in along the railroad tracks.

Here, try some." He held the glass out toward me but I told him I never drink local water. He laughed and drank it down in a single gulp. I tried to say something to Nanette but she didn't even hear me. I tried to touch her hand but she pulled it away sharply. I said:

"What is the matter, Nanette, you look like a sleepwalker or a zombie or something like that." And she was frightening, believe me! She then cast me a beady look and said:

"What do you do when you get up in the morning, Desmond? What do you do? Who the fuck are you!" I had no idea what she was talking about and said so. And she used the expletive here with all the bitter, dirty viciousness that only women from the anglo suburbs seem to be able to provide it. It's really the only place the bad word survives these days. Then I said "we're the fucqarwee" lightly, thinking the old joke would bring her to her senses. Then her beady look went dark and her beringed hands flew to her face. She looked as if she were about to throttle me.

"What are you talking about right now, for instance. What. Tell me. What are you doing right now? Tell me. Right now. Tell me!" I thought I caught just a fleck of foam at the corner of her mouth, but perhaps no. When attacked by a woman unawares like that one tends not to trust to mere observation. Then she returned her glassy look to the window and mumbled, "never mind." A wave of her personal perfume wafted to me across the table. The odor of a lonely heart, I thought to myself. But I was upset by her behavior and noticed my own toilet water to a certain extent. Cayman was holding up the ash tray and pronouncing Japan as if it were an invocation. I believe we lapsed into silence.

Out of politeness more than anything else I asked if I could have the honor of escorting them out for a night on the town but Cayman said "not for what we've got in mind, sonny," as if I were absolutely insignificant. Nanette herself managed to mumble "prior engagement", barely suppressing her look of panic. But some quite acceptable arrangements have been made on just this starting note. And he mentioned that they had Chinese friends from Palo Alto who were very well connected in Beijing so they would hardly be needing my accompaniment here. I wasn't hurt because I realized they were the same sort of opportunists as myself. I find this deep inner knowledge of my very worst personal faults to be invaluable. To this I attribute my fabled ability to «stand off while others are committing theirs.» He stood up and said they were very busy and had to be going. They were leaving the next day, he explained and needed all the time remaining to shop and visit with friends.

"But where are you going," I stammered, trying in this way to express some sympathy for their situation before they went and did something they'd regret just a little way down the line. I certainly didn't need their company but found myself strangely prisoner to my own more generous sentiment. Nanette stood up and went straight to the elevator. And out of my life forever, I might add. Cayman put his arm around my shoulders in that annoying way he had and said:

"I'll tell you, kid. We're going to Taipei. Best sex in the world there. No question about it, from meter maids and librarians through the highest palace circles. Can't explain it. Must have something to do with the corruption. But I'm sure you won't be lonely, you'll find some piece of chink jail bait to keep you company." Then he too went into the elevator and was gone. And I didn't even get their home address. Oh, well, I said to myself, I never liked them that much anyway. And I didn't. But I know it went deeper than that, that somewhere they had deeply offended the finer side of my life and I would never forgive them for it. I stayed at their table for breakfast before I walked out into a Hong Kong afternoon.

Behind the «SH», up steep Garden Road, is the U.S. Consulate. It's not an embassy because Hong Kong is not a capital. However, it is larger than the majority of embassies because of all the intelligence and compilation work that goes on there. Opposite the Consulate is the Peak Tram terminus. I went in the opposite direction toward Wanchai and the Tiger Balm Gardens built by Aw Boon Haw and named after the famous ointment.

I started out on Connaught Road and did some shopping. Hong Kong is quite a good source for things because so many things are made here. And it is a free port. I bought a wrist watch. I needed it for my morning coffee. To time the percolation, that is. A good cup of coffee in the morning is so important in the modern world of elapsed time and compressed space. And not nearly bad enough a habit to end a relationship. Coffee is very expensive here; it costs over $50 a kilogram. But that's larger than a pound. At least it isn't rationed, I said to myself, imagining such a much worse scenario.

On the whole I found Hong Kong a pleasant, easy place to be. It was the perfect place to collect my thoughts and recover from that horrid voyage. All the color and vitality, the physical welter of smells, sounds and bodies, the antiquity and infinite ingenuities, the charms and the horrors of Chinese life engulfed me. It was all they said it would be in the brochures and much, much more. I wandered through a maze of narrow stone-paved streets and alleys filled with people running into me, always past red dragons, split cats hung on hooks and everywhere men selling the tresses of their wives and daughters. Cayman said it this way: "Here, a guys cuts off his hair, throws it on a newspaper and has a store. Hell, they find you, you've got something for sale." And those monks with their low-caste women of questionable venereal health. I could write a report on these «blades» and their «doings». But the natives are friendly. You'll have no trouble with the language. The weather is benign. Of course you can almost never see out of the windows because of the continuous fog which hangs over us. And the butter is corrupt, for instance, so I was forced to do without. I made the switch to peanut butter without any undue distress. Though there was good butter on Cayman's table in the hotel coffee shop. It's probably air dropped from Denmark.

Connaught Road runs eastward into Wanchai. Beyond this you run into Causeway and Repulse Bays. Wanchai itself is the rough and ready saloon area because of the Navy ships which regularly anchor here. The sailors come ashore at Fenwich pier opposite the Luk Kwok Hotel where Bruce Lee, the American film star, died amid a set of mysterious circumstances. The area is built on land reclaimed from the sea during the thirties, a time of great unrest in China's history. It isn't really very sinful. Beggar children are everywhere. If you ever come here don't, for heaven's sake, start giving money to the poor urchins. I've been asked to say this. If you want to donate money, do it through one of the big international welfare societies. Hong Kong, in case you don't know it, has a «people problem» and they don't need your input. And it is seen as corrupting; chocolate one day and gel in the hair the next. The local authorities deserve all possible praise for their tremendous effort to house the refugees in apartments with modern conveniences at moderate rentals. But god knows I'm not going to stay here and become just another Hong Kong businessman. Oh, I know, there are those smarty-pants who are buying up everything they can afford and think they can ride on the wave of the future. Not that I think of myself as a wipe-out, as may have been suggested in the words of others.

The usual gaggle of «port city» professionals can easily be found along the narrow streets or even in some of the bars. However, all bar girls are not necessarily prostitutes, though all are known as «kind». They are hired by the management to provide female companionship and dancing partners for the thousands of very heart-sick sailors who come ashore here. I went into a place called the «Suzie Wong» and got a seat at an uncomfortable booth at the end of a long plastic bar. The juke box was playing the latest rock and roll hits. I ordered a beer at a surprisingly low price. The «girls», in their sexy cheongsam, were very neat and slim. (The cheongsam has slits on the sides revealing much of the wearer's legs. Often their full shags of «short» hair are visible when they sit since almost none of them can afford ordinary cotton underwear. I guess it suits them though because having a full and richly luxuriant «rug» is a matter of great pride in this water-front neighborhood. They will occasionally fight tooth and nail over an imagined insult to this anatomical feature not to speak of the man-hours lost every year in its grooming and upkeep. It is said in their idle hours they will tirelessly comb it out. Nice girls wear their sams with sane slits, showing neither too little or too much. But the not-so-nice girls wear them cut well up the thigh.) They were quite young and sometimes pretty. A favorite trick or «ice-breaker» practised by the professional here is to give the unsuspecting patron a «stink finger» under the guise of holding his hand.

One of these girls sat down at my table and said, "hi, G. I.," or some such nonsense and made it very clear she did not wish to be thought of as anything other than a out and out professional girl. Having a few idle dollars and nothing else in my «dance book», I'll admit I took some «comfort» with her in a small room on the second floor. I really couldn't resist. And anyway, I thought, perhaps this is the final illusion of travel. And I didn't yet know all the particulars about Rory so in some ways I consider myself uncommonly lucky. She led me up a wooden staircase and lay back on an iron frame bed in a small cubicle. I had the feeling there were many others doing what we were doing in adjacent spaces. I really didn't mind. After a while you don't even think about it. She rolled her skirt above her waist, taking care not to wrinkle the fabric. The slits are quite convenient for this purpose. She had a lovely «ear-muff» and I complimented her on its virtues. She seemed pleased I had noticed. They are really very vain creatures. Not that it was in any way unpleasant. But I'm sure you do this every day with the «secretary» or the «milk-man» or whatever you call them. It's only the traveller is so cut off from ordinary life.

In any case, to make a short story as brief as possible, she «ground the round», as they say, neither an «open-pit» nor a «strangle hold». One rather noticeable variation encountered in this part of the world is a gentle reverse loop at mid-distance. This much trumpeted accomplishment is believed to result from some deep trickery on the part of the practitioner. I could just see her below me, dark, invisible, somehow menacing. We flew on steadily, she just clawing me occasionally with her long, curved and lacquered fingernails. Then there was a quick swoop with a bump and then a mountain of stars and a carpet of golden jewels in the velvet night. It is not wise to underestimate the power of these women, no matter how roomy your «airliner». A «still» of her final jactitation is forever frozen in my mind.

We stood up a moment later and shook hands. She was a very sweet woman and if she had any children I'm sure she was a first-class mother. Then I went downstairs for another beer before walking home.

I was very depressed and down but certainly not broken. And, anyway, as the ancients well knew, the male is always despondent and suicidal after coitus of any sort. I stumbled on for a mile or so in a «heartland fog» until I came again to the ferry. I got myself aboard for the five minute ride across the harbor from Victoria to Cowloon. I was quite done in by the short day on the town. There on the endlessly churning blue waters were the fishing junks with whole families, American destroyers in gray battle paint, the Commy freighters trailing red flags with five gold stars across their bulldog sterns. From Cowloon the road snakes past the Nathan Road, jammed and turbulent. The khaki- shorted police saunter casually with a quick eye for the street mêlée which flash up out of the turmoil of Hong Kong, the mysterious currents of her politics, the low water of her mobs. Lo Wu Road presses out to the New Territories but I didn't have the energy to go that far. I turned to the left to my rooms and quickly fell into a deep sleep, though it was scarcely past the dinner hour. This is commonly the fate of tourists.

I had something of a breakdown that night, a shut down really, or a lock out. I'm not sure it's a recognized mental state. But I know I'm not willfully obnoxious the way they say I am because I would be honest about something like that. I'm sure it was out of sympathy for Rory more than anything else, Rory who I found the next day on the 2nd story of a teahouse prostrate on a raffia mat.

19

Song Sisters

"Rory, oh Rory," I cried when I saw him there, little more than a limp rag-doll swept into the corner, saliva dripping down from the corners of his mouth, remains of «fast food» lying about his prostrate form, the smell of vomit and stale urine coming off him quite strongly. It was pathetic and I was deeply shocked. When he had boarded in Capetown just weeks ago he had seemed so vital, so fresh, so virile. As I feared, he had come to the worst when I found him in a Cowloon dumpling house lying on a raffia mat, and not through any lack of warning on my part. He attempted to sit up to greet me but I pushed him back down gently. I wasn't prepared to risk a fit. He appeared to be in some sort of geriatric trance.

I'll admit I wanted to leave, call in the «shimboos» and have done with it. There he lay, a little bastion of contagion I was sure. I took two steps toward the door but he looked up at me with those delightful little eyes of his. Then I remembered the pixie-like regard in which he held all things naughty, his «girl-crazy» strain, my own weakness on this avenue, and decided to question him a bit. Unlike most public people, I have no vested interest in a polarized populace. Far be it from me to callously abandon him marginalized so, with absolutely no hope of redemption. Anyway, the quality of mercy is not strained; nor should it be.

"Well, what are you up to, Rory, my boy," I asked with theatrical innocence and a quick wink. I think he managed to identified me at this point, for he started to reply. But then he began to choke to death on some of his own spittle. I patted him on the back, just in time. He began again, slowly at first and painfully at best. It turns out the place is run by the three Song sisters, refugees from the mainland, highly educated, very witty, very beautiful and thoroughly nasty and squalid in terms of morals and behavior. And that tea house they ran was little more than a Class A bordello even though they had pretensions it was much, much more, a salon or a Kunstbunker. Themselves, they were Kweilin girls before the revolution, the glamor city of South China. One, Fanny, the youngest, had had a son by a famous American fly-boy. They had all kinds of girls there but I could see they were in fact a specialty house, given over wholly to the wantonness occasioned by the broken heart. Make no mistake about it, there is good money to be made in this quarter! And I'm sure I don't have to go into these quite detailed classifications of commercial sex; they will be intuitively obvious to the sophisticate and forever remain a mystery to the «knee-jerkers» amongst us. As it was, I went into the office to complain about their treatment of my friend where they received me quite decently and served me a very tasty cup of tea. But the force of my protestation was somewhat diminished by the fact of their speaking a kind of King's English which would render my complaints, however righteous, somewhat incomprehensible, as much for the Americanisms as from their lack of managerial skills.

As I was saying, anyone who doesn't know the difference between «fag-shag» and «wet-witch» will never get anywhere in the interlocking worlds of diplomacy, heroic art and high-finance. Enormous billions of dollars flow in these channels every day of the year, down from the barren peaks of power around this globe of ours and into the hungry, sucking maws of Number 1 prostitutes. In the mind of the common man these women are little better than lavatory attendants but in the real world of after-dark interchange they are the proverbial «foxes in boxes». In the gray demi-monde of «slut mugs» and «challengers», of «ghost dancers» and «livery ladies», there are, quite simply, «the only orbits round the earth». Just for a moment I wondered what a person like myself was doing on the other side of the world, where mad passions ruled supreme. And afterwards I never stopped wondering that.

Not that they were unprincipled. Not at all. The middle sister, Maybelle, took me aside and pointed out that "free-wheeling with no-holds-barred liberty" was responsible for the decline of most men's earthly fortunes. She let me know in no uncertain terms Rory's dilemma was of his own making, that he had buttered his bed and was, indeed, at this very moment, lying in it. She further explained this concept of liberty led to the loosening and eventual desecration of traditional values. And traditional values were so important in her business. The genesis of this decadence, she said, can partly be traced to the misconceived concept of liberty, which is given too wide a latitude and an almost "at will" interpretation so as to be all-pervasive and all-inclusive. There in her office I could see exactly what she meant, it being so much clearer in her presence than in the sanitized version filtered out by her secretaries. In fact, she added, "spouting the word liberty on every permissible or possible occasion, attitudinizing license and permissiveness as such and defending them with fervent hypocritical rhetoric, immediately elevates one into the hallowed halls of the intelligentsia." She absolutely did not mince words; if men where to darken her doorway, they would do it her way or not at all. But I'm not sure this fabled impotence of the professional academic was anything more than a lost-leader in this whore house. Thus, she continued, for there was no stopping her, "the self-styled elite of every cast of mind strain to range themselves on the side of the so-called progressives and liberals, the darlings of lecture halls and saloons, favoring or championing tolerance of all hues and forms regardless of how ridiculous, spaced-out, reductionist, retrograde or obscene their namby-pamby theories may be, rather than cautioning with caveats of taboos, of common sense and of obeisance to time-tested traditional obligations." After all, this is the killing-floor where they "look for a dick's trigger, no matter what he thinks he thinks." She chuckled softly under her breath and concluded: "This is now true not only in the sing-song business but in all our walks in life, the primrose path, the vale of tears, the hall of thorns, the book of days, Claire in the afternoon, Maude in the morning." There were obviously many rooms in her father's house. On the whole I found this soiled woman in the chinchilla tippet quite a charming and delightful woman.

Their brother, the «house organ» I assumed, sat in the other room watching a television set. On the screen was a variety show featuring a pudgy, middle aged Chinese with a black hat, black rimmed spectacles, thin black cane, shuffling from side to side on a music hall stage. The oldest sister, she called herself Jeanette Ashburn, noticed my notice of him and said, "oh him, I've done everything but murder him; he should be down in his hong by now." She shooed him out of the room in her own language. Then, leading me into a side chamber, she quickly demonstrated a simple manipulation which showed the staggering «penetration power» of her intimate imagination. My knees shook so I almost lost my balance. She told me by such technique, then, "does one jerk the «jilted-jube» of dead romance and renew and refresh the «routes of the heart». It was over in a matter of minutes. Not an eye was batted when we quietly re-entered the company of the other sisters. All three wore lovely flowers on the front of their shoulders. I found it a most becoming style. I also noticed a charming little Cartier box with initials set in diamonds sitting on a table-top. I'm just sure all three of them were in it for jeweler's bars. They continued to chat politely but I excused myself after a matter of hours and went back to where Rory lay in a corner. And in this way, it should be said, a sick friend can be a big drag. When I found him in a somewhat supraliminal state I decided to put the question to him rather directly:

"What exactly, my good man, is the matter with you," I asked point blank. He perked up a bit and began to froth out an answer, rather the way unkempt people do.

"Dusty, Dusty, Dusty, I am saved. Help me up, Dust, that's the boy." There it was again, that fetchingly accented speech, a convenient loss of memory, the conspiratorial air of heavy drinkers. Some things we never lose no matter how much abuse be heaped on us or how much we be made to suffer. My heart must have melted just a bit at this point for I cried:

"Don't get up, Boopie, just stay where you are." Then I told him about his parents whom Deborah had contacted in Adelaire. They had refused him all assistance short of his returning thence and beginning again the quiet suburban life known of old by his people. Can you really blame him for the fit of blubbering which followed?

"Oh, Dusty, they've sucked it all out of me, every last drop, there's not a chunk in there I can call my own." I didn't at the time and I don't to this day think this meant he had compromised any «network», any «activists» on an «intelligence initiative». Nor has any evidence to this effect been released to the public. Oh sure, they say they know and it has to do with taxes owed etcetera, etcetera, alitalia! They always get you for that. What business man hasn't had this thrown in his face. More climate, I said to myself, throwing up my hands in dramatic exasperation. Poor Rory! He may have come in here as Sir Peter Honey but, if he left at all, it would be as Mister Dudley Clove.

"You're raving, poor fellow," I told him firmly, "try to make some sense or I'll commit you to the care of Dr. Chow!" I meant it. I'd had about as much of this silliness as I could stand. I was nice enough to come over there to see what I could do for a friend in need. I had given freely from my hoard of time and now did not propose to have it wasted right in front of my face. And I remembered the sort of brawny sex Ror was known for, big hunks of women, voluntary restraint, the barber shop. Well, you see what happened to him. And I trusted he would be duly repressed by my authoritative mention of the ultra-modern psychiatric facilities here in Hong Kong.

"Oh, you know what I mean, Dust," he claimed, "all the cream's skimmed, skimmed and gone. Pack your bone and go, Dust, go. I'm dead. Nothing happening any more. I can't make it go. It just lies there cold and limp, like a stick of butter. I tell you, Dus, they've had me every which way." I"m forced to admit this does happen, had happened, will happen again. Happens to some men and then it never comes back. Write-outs of history. Really nothing to be done about it.

"They all took money for it, Dus, honest they did. I gave them what I had. They say I didn't, but I did. I didn't promise them a thing. But I gave them all the money." A pathetic appeal to decency. By the way, I don't go along at all with what Prince Phillip says about them but, like all pretenders, he's a little gaga. And perfectly delightful in his own way, I'm sure, in any ultra-civilized situation. Anyway, what we heard was probably nothing more than pillow talk, all perfectly innocent murmurrings, something the girls here call «catching fresh flake» from the font of the exhausted male. Several young novice were peeping through the doorway and giggling and I was forced to shoo them away. Others, perhaps debutantes of illicit congress, lolled about in postures of interest, for this was as much a school as many an

American University. And they had many strange rites here too. Such as «scorps-a-lot» and «impulse excretion», the «tom and jerry» and «fox coffee». The «service of Serbian caviar» was something that required 36 hour advance notice. It was a perfect jungle of sights and smells and exotic sensation. Again I asked myself what a man like me would be doing on the other side of the world. Well, one of the reasons I am here is because I feel it has not been explained to my satisfaction and I know there are others who feel the same as I.

"Why, Rory, why are you doing this to yourself?" He was silent and restless and glancing into the corner. He then vomited a horrible putrid fluid all over his mat! There's some yellow sheets for Deborah, I said to myself, and some opium parfum as well. I left the room and crossed to a window in another.

Now, now I couldn't help him any more, of that I was sure. Yet I couldn't stand the thought of Deb having to deal with this filth. And I had more or less promised her. Well, what's a promise worth, I was saying to myself when Rory, stripped to a loin cloth, came up behind me. Except for his garb, he appeared reasonably lucid. He struck a pose and in his normal manner asked if I'd go with him on a «hunt» with guns he'd purchased from a dealer he'd met at some point in his fall. These too, these guns, are a matter of public record and any suggestion that they be part of a much larger shipment destined for some global sore-spot is exactly that, a suggestion, without the slightest possibility of confirmation. And if one hundred years from this date someone were to investigate this situation as thoroughly as humanly possible in all existing documents including this perfectly frank exposé, one would be forced to conclude the issue impossibly clouded.

Oh, the cruel irony, I thought. Then I thought that perhaps he had turned hostile and meant to goad me with more seemingly compromising indiscretion. You won't believe this but no, he seriously meant for me to go with him to a five hundred hectare shooting reserve in the New Territories where a certain number of "Ringnecks" were to be found. They were laid out beforehand by keepers so there was little chance of coming up empty. He became almost cheerful as he told me that one of the most beautiful game birds to be found in that country was the Chinese ringneck cock pheasant. Of course the hens are pretty in their own right, he said, but it's the cock with his long tail and beautiful plumage that is the stylesetter. Wherever "chinks", as he called them, are in season, you will find scattergunners out in droves, seeking them every available hour of the day. They're not only a glamorous trophy, he claimed, they're exciting to hunt and exceptional table fare. "We can rent dogs and they'll even clean the birds for us, pluck and gut them." He seemed almost ecstatic for a moment, but then fell into sadness again and said: "Like all the rest, ducky, they're aced out, no natural habitat, game birds and animals, swelling population. Constant loss of ground cover. It's only on the private reserve you'll find them these days."

I'll say it right out: No, there was no plan. How you can make this into a plan I'll never understand. It is not, repeto, it is not even worth the small mental effort involved. This was nothing more than a last desperate effort to salvage something of his investments in non-governmental brick-a-brack. And he hadn't been eating right. No matter how crazy you may get, you just must eat a balanced diet! I am who I am today because of all the hot and tasty «squares» I have eaten. And my dentists.

I will tell you right now that Rory is dead. There is really no reason to hope any more that he is not. I don't like saying it any more than you like hearing it. I don't want to call him a comrade fallen on the field because that would be silly but he is decidedly and not the only MIA. Even then he was fading and looked up at me with those big soulful eyes of his that seemed on the drop of tears and said:

"Maybe, just maybe, I've been wrong all along. Say it isn't so."

"Oh, don't be silly, Rory," I disclaimed, "how could you possibly think of anything as silly as that?" I didn't give him a chance to answer but led him back toward his room where a slight, brown-skinned man came up to Rory and led him to a clean mat. There he listened for his breathing. So I could see that they were taking care of him here and I never did call Dr. Chow. Rory's head fell back on the raffia mat and his eyes closed. He had unmistakably passed out. Then this fellow who was dressed in what looked like pajamas and had bare feet said:

"Leave the poor boohoo alone; he is a broken blossom. Don't worry, heaven-born, I will care for him." So I felt I had fulfilled my commitment to both Rory and Deborah. And all recriminations since are just that, recriminations. But what a wonderful and poetic language these Eastern people have, such a way of putting things just so and not pedestrian and plain jane. He was no doubt by now his catamite. But that's not the worst thing ever happened to a guy. And surely, surely this man was a cad at heart. Yes, Rory was a cad at heart. The literary temperament is only tolerable so long as it remains cowardly. Once it becomes inflated at all it is a beastly thing to behold. And nobody likes a doggy performance like this, no matter how cruel the market may get. So my conscience is as clear as conscience can be.

I left and went directly back to my rooms to wash thoroughly and rest before dinner. I hadn't intended to sleep but did and in this sleep began a dream. I remember myself and some other young men were lying about a «bunkhouse» or some such ranch type outbuilding discussing this and that, the production of «social fluff» in ambi-sexual situations, the effects of opiates on central nervous questions, ancient religious iconography, the folklore of «el rancho physico». I was telling some colorful stories to keep the boys on the edge of their seats when Deborah burst in and made quite a little stink. Of course a lot of the boys, «cow-punchers» I was calling them, were jay-naked as ball players after the game and in the «half-fat» state which they found comfortable. And I certainly didn't mind. I myself was wearing my gurkha shorts which are so airy and roomy and a soft flannel shirt plaided blue and green. But you should have seen the way her eyes lit up when she saw what was arrayed before her! I have seen some lascivious and vulgar women but never one so ungraced by delicacy and passivity of demeanor, not once she had «turned the corner». I don't want to talk behind her back and it is, I know, juvenile to complain. But her «truth» was worse than a contradiction, worse than an absurdity. It was predatory and that's why no one will forgive her for what she did. If she even did it. I mean, I'm a modern man! What is a court of law? I woke in time for dinner. But I'm not sure a nap in the afternoon is always a good idea.

20

Antique Usage

Returning from dinner I found Mola, the girl from Ulan Bator who lived below me with the Chinese husband who did secretarial work at one of the big banks, waiting for me on a straight-backed chair in the hallway. She said she had waited for me since she knew I was a traveller and undoubtedly, after the perils and fatigues of a long journey, in need of relaxation. I told her that I thought that just about the nicest thing anybody had ever thought. And I didn't doubt her for a moment. But if you could have seen the look on her face you too would have thought how sweet that was. She invited me into her rooms which were much the same as mine. Her husband was asleep on a straw mat in the other room. She fixed me some hot tea, flavoring it with honey and lemon. We sat on top of her bedroll where she talked to me of the customs of her people, semi-nomads in the wastes around Hami. One of these customs related directly to her behavior that evening. That's what I was led to think, in any case. And now you can surely see how far any of all this is from any «plot» or «executive action», something someone could play with in his mind and then reconstruct in a courtroom. That sort of thing.

The men of Hami, it seems, are addicted to pleasure and attend to little else than playing upon instruments, singing, dancing, reading, writing, etcetera according to the practice there and the virile pursuit of total amusement. When strangers arrive and want accommodation at their simple yurts, the men are very happy and pass the peace-pipe to one and all. Just like the American natives, once you smoke that thing, that is it. You break the peace then and you're as good as dead. They give orders to their wives, daughters, sisters and other female members of their families to indulge their guests in every whim while they retire to apartments they keep in all the major cities thereabouts. And then the stranger lives in the house with the females as if they were his own females. Of course they pay for what they have taken. This certainly wasn't a story about getting something for nothing. Apparently, nobody will believe a story like that. This one hinged on «religious belief» which I did not doubt for a moment. For she and all people like her firmly believed this wantonness, for I know no other word for it, not only did them honor and added to their reputation, but it drew down the blessing of increase from the «controlling powers», no matter what their stripe. It was no limited agreement with the almighty, some almighty blink at their behavior. Oh, no, what they did was fully responsible for the augmentation of their substance, their safety from danger and the successful issue to all their undertakings. I imagine, as well, they accepted the good with the bad, the bitter with the sweet, the contagion with the cure, as it were. But she didn't say anything about it. The women are, in truth, very handsome, very sensual and fully disposed to conform in this respect to the will of their husbands. There is some suggestion, furthermore, that it be the will of the wives themselves. Mola's animation led me to credit this suggestion.

I expressed amazement and she went on to tell the story of what happened when a high commy mucketymuck visited her province a short time after they were incorporated into the red orbit. He got wind of what was going on and issued an edict strictly forbidding the practice. He added he found this practice disgraceful to them and he forbad individuals from furnishing lodging to strangers who were then obliged to accommodate themselves at a «house of socialist resort» or public caravanserai. I don't want to write it all out in the rolling redundancy of old but, though it appeared at first the proscription was made on moral grounds, it was soon discovered the official involved had been unduly influenced by certain unsavory caravan types who had given him the wrong idea of the practice in order to advance their scheme to open a chain of desert inns. Under pain of death for three years the command of the commissar was obeyed but at length the earth herself ceased to yield the accustomed fruits, a lack of fertility vividly seen in the grief and sadness of the obedient inhabitants.

And here the crux of this inverted contradiction appeared as well. For why hadn't their custom of generosity brought down blessings from Beijing herself, set-piece of Eastern custom? Mmn, but I didn't ask Mola directly. I formed the idea nonverbally in my memory. I find my mind works best when I am silent.

They dispatched a deputation to the Chairman himself who was Lew Shao Chi at that time. They issued an original proclamation, the text of which is merely this story itself repeated. The Chairman replied in a decree which she then quoted: "Since you appear so anxious to persist in your shame and ignominy let it be . . .as you desire. Go, live according to your base customs and manners and let your wives persist in the wages of their beggarly prostitution." So it was clear he more or less deliberately misunderstood the ancient practice, being further angered by the refusal of the local women to hire on as «fuck-women» in the new hotels, regarding it, in effect, as an unhygienic jerk-off of a job. This wouldn't have been an insuperable difficulty to the brave entrepreneur save for their location in the Gobi which made recruitment of «circuit-wenches» impossible, none of these so called «state-slits» being willing to undergo the rigors of the desert and the discomfort of «sand in the oyster». In this light the deputies returned to the secret delight of all the women who to this day observe this antique usage.

I'll just put down what happened afterwards as homesickness in a festive season, it being so exotic an occurrence. We climbed into her bedroll where she firmly guided me through the performance of very athletic copulation. She was a very sweet, very dear person. She had only one slight quirk, an eccentric opinion that the continuous twisting of the scrotum of the male in the vise-like grip of her left hand was somehow influential in the speedy production of large quantities of jelly-like «twill». But on other levels of cultural exchange they are much the same as we without the feverish guttural articulation and comic facial expressions so closely associated with Western sexuality. There was no raucous shouting of "Give it to me good, boy-toy" or other such cheerleaderish endearments. Most often, in the heat of it, the woman will study a fold in her garment while the gentleman will gaze with clouded eye upon a rice paddy seen on a distant hillside. It can't be said to be at all as personal as it is stateside. And that is sort of too bad. But you must remember to take this as a preliminary observation with a healthy margin of error. Though I'm usually not wrong about things like this, there may have been other factors involved. For instance, some missing bit of fore-play, as the failure to blow the nose when needed, the proper application of a called-for force, a divergent view of the ridiculous. I'll just say I happily danced out that "latent tango of late-barbarism." And I would not continue on like this but that I yet hold these strong opinions, unseemly as that may be. What a wonderful life they must lead! But I'm sure they get something like this out in Scarsdale and Rancho Mirage. So too must our founding-fathers as they cut their way into the wilderness and tamed what turns out to be America in such pre-revolutionary strongholds as Flemington, Bricktown and Suckasona, fingering the thumbcocks on their flintlocks, rubbing their tinderhorns. But there are those of us who have made our choices and will never know that life.

As I was leaving she said I must be hungry and gave me three of the weightiest rice balls I have ever hefted. I barely managed to eat two later on that night.

21

«Ron-Day-View»

I stared at the young man sitting in front of me. He was thin and nervous with long narrow bones. His face was straw colored and his hair, naturally, was intensely black. His eyes were deeply set in drawn skin. But maybe it was just an expression he chose to look at me. Evidently in his late twenties, he was very much Chinese in spite of his European livery. He wore an open shirt bearing the Hung logo, short swords in front of a pottery vessel on a diamond-shaped gold escutcheon, slacks and desert boots with gum soles. He had evidently worn the shoes for some time, the heels being quite worn. And when he stood up I saw he carried his weight back there.

We were in a top corner room in a detached part of the Correspondent's Club from which I had two grand views. The nearby mountain seemed to elbow in at the side window and from the front I could see not only the grounds of Hong Kong U. but the busy harbor still farther down the slope. I could see trim little river boats on strict schedules sailing through the gap between the mountainous islands. My guide, Ah Bum, stood up and began to rock slowly from the toe to the heel and back again on his shoes, the bottoms of which, as I have previously mentioned, were rounded from the exercise. I just know he was of the sort known as «rice democrats». Hung had all kinds fighting on his side, I said to myself.

"I say," I said in a friendly way, "this seems like a highly unusual apparatus for a rendezvous, don't you think?" We had been there for about twenty minutes but it seemed like two weeks in protective custody. It was late afternoon, early evening. The sun had begun to set. I had walked over from Cowloon and found Ah waiting for me as Deborah had said. Deborah had said he would be waiting. We were waiting for Deborah. He nodded his head yes and smiled. We continued to wait. It got darker and Ah Bum lit a bare bulb, so unlike America where we have shades. And about as interesting as a diagnostic program, I said to myself. I never have been a good waiter.

A few minutes more and Deborah entered, dressed in a powder-blue cheongsam, very nicely slit. I hate to say it but I was happy to see her. Hong Kong seemed to have changed her somehow. Not that she had gone native, I didn't think that. But she seemed more «womanly» now that her «retentive» period had passed, something like a Scandinavian movie-star, self-centered, kind of pouty, a little stiff. What about «us», I thought to myself, but said nothing, noting her preoccupation with the details of our journey. Ah Bum stood at attention. I started to say, "well, hello Deborah" but she silenced me with a motion of her hand and said "let's go". We three were soon on the street where we boarded a waiting rickshaw and began our ride through the native quarter. I asked how far we had to go but no one seemed to hear me, each of us being rapt in thought.

We went down narrow, steeply falling streets with vertical signs hanging in front of almost every house. They are all in business to a man over there. Bamboo poles protruded from every floor with blue, black and white clothes hung out to dry. The Chinese seem to like to carry loads, usually on a bamboo yoke with baskets or pails hung at each end. Many of the buckets were full of night soil, something, I am told, the very poor use as a form of currency. And here only women clean the streets. I don't know if it were the falling light or what but the picture lacked color somewhat. All the houses were the same, all the people wore the same clothes, grayish blue or black. Perhaps I was disoriented into a temporary color-blindness. I don't really know. However, it is a curious and not altogether uncomfortable feeling to be pulled by a man as if he were an animal. For those who can afford it and do not like climbing up and down the steep streets, the palanquin is the usual conveyance. This is a wicker chair suspended from a bamboo pole shouldered at each end by a big, sweating coolie. They walk or trot tirelessly, always in step and at amazing speed, their heads covered by round, flat straw hats and their pigtails swinging from side to side.

We then passed deep into the interior of the native quarter. I was a little nervous but Deb and Bum seemed calm and confident. There must have been something between them. The streets were four to seven feet wide, which is why no one has ever been here in a car, sometimes cobbled but more often of dirt. There were walls on both sides up to thirty feet high and topped with broken glass fragments. Behind wrought iron screens I caught glimpses of red and gold lacquered doors and windows. The streets were packed with humanity and we travelled slowly. It's not like a rich country. Most people passed us by in silence. Some children ran around our rickshaw shouting «jubaku chow chow» or «hello, big merchant». Only rarely did I hear the hostile cry «fayn kwee» or «red devil».

On coming to an arm of the harbor we passed the so called «flower boats». These are houseboats of all sizes charmingly decorated and fitted out for an evening's entertainment. Bachelors give their dinner parties here and, through the services of a so called «dancing master», order girls to sing and dance for them. On some of these «flower boats»«dancing girls» sat waiting, each in her little doll's house on the stern, pink-robed and heavily made up. On the veranda of certain boats some people were smoking opium openly while others enjoyed themselves in various ways I shall not describe.

We passed a silk factory with three hundred women spinning thread from cocoons. I noticed our guide spat in their direction and I asked him why. What he sputtered was a little unclear but apparently these women were notorious throughout China as radical lesbian feminists who refused to marry. If their families forced them, they merely bribed their husbands with a part of their pay and induced them to take concubines. The most such a married girl would do was bear one son. Then she would return to the factory, refusing to live with her husband any longer. The government had just issued a decree forbidding women to escape from marriage by bribery but the women ignored it. They were often involved in social causes and just as often arrested and forced to confess. "I have never gone to a picture theatre," Ah said, "without seeing groups of them sitting together, holding hands." This was the only English sentence of Ah Bum's I could really understand.

We came to another of the numberless arms of the harbor and boarded a small though elegant mahogany cabin craft crewed by two stout bandit types each sporting mustache and stiff iron rod. For navigational purposes, I assumed. I further assumed we were headed for an island.

The life on the river was fascinating. Every inch of surface was packed with small rib-rigged junk jostling for place, even in this failing light. Every boat had two eyes painted on its bow, one on either side of the sprit. Being motorized, we cut through them quite fearlessly and to singular effect. Oh, how they scurried out of our path! I noticed some of the young children with barrels strapped across their backs. I imagine they use them for pearl diving. So shameless these children are forced to labor so.

We saw a man in a flat-bottomed skiff fishing with large black sea birds. He set them out in pairs with tight metal rings affixed about their long curving necks. They'd then dive with a frenzied flapping and quacking, catching a sunny or some such fish which they were prevented from swallowing by the steel ring. They'd been trained to drop the whole fish into an on-board hopper and were then rewarded with a bit of entrails, small enough for ingestion. This «debilitated domestic» mode of enforced labor is not nearly so common in truly civilized countries. Some dropped bread crumb on the waters and held netting aloft. Others raised duck on latticed decking and let them feed by the shore for small fish and snail and other tasty morsel. It was a singularly greedy scene, everyone jumping about for a bit of food. But it was grand to get back to the sea, even this littoral bit. I know that reading it can make you anxious for a simpler way of life but it wasn't nearly as bad to be there.

We at last landed at Hung's private pier and were led up a winding stone walk through dwarfed trees to the low main building of the Hung estate. What a thrill and at long last. It was nearly dark but torches had been lit. We passed a terraced garden full of traveller's joy, a wild clematis. I also spotted, in the faded light, a plot of traveller's tale, a rank weed in our country but highly prized here and cultivated for its pungency as a potherb. Then through a bamboo curtain and voilà: Hung himself.

22

«Chop Stick Dinner»

What a wonderful man to meet! He was the first person I'd met in China who dropped the utopian pretense that everything was perfect chez les chinoises. He actually sounded skeptical about his people and especially the young.

"The young people are soft," he said with a sad expression, probing my stomach with his fat little hand. "They have to be reminded of the need for struggle." I smiled and put my arm around Deb's shoulders thinking in the language problem he had said perhaps "snuggle". But it was immediately apparent from his expression he meant struggle because he became animated and vigorously jabbed his forefingers together to emphasize the need for struggle. Sure, struggle was just a word, but it was the underlying principle of his philosophy.

"There will be struggle in the party, there will be struggle between the classes, between the male and the female. Nothing is certain except struggle," he told us. Then suddenly he asked:

"What do you think?" His question was so unexpected that both Deb and I hesitated with our jaws dropped. I had no idea I was to be tested on this material. Then we blurted out at the same moment:

"I agree. . . ." There was a silence as Hung waited for us to say more. Finally he spoke again, as if dismissing us, that sad look creeping back over his face.

"It is quite possible the struggle will last for two or three hundred years." Looking at me again, he added:

"Maybe more." Then he walked over to where Rex Driscoll and his party, the young Australian with an implant in his brain, stood talking. Miss Coy was at Deb's shoulder saying:

"He was telling me for the tenth time this month that my hair would look a whole lot prettier in the sunshine if it were silver instead of brown." Already I felt a little lost in the swirl of people, even though there weren't too many. And I could see it was to be a «serious» evening and my work would be cut out. Then I heard Hung saying to Rex:

"Certain monied groups in your country, California monopoly groups and others, have a vested interest in a racial war. They would have you believe your class conflict is hatred of the black and latin. This would be a great tragedy for humanity and all effort must be directed toward it's avoidance." Well, that was forthright. I just hoped he'd dummy up, as they say, and drop the polemical slant or I'd just might have to show my fighting sides! Oh, I didn't feel threatened or anything like that; I'm at home at almost any depth. But I did absolutely demand an evening be at least that much entertainment. And to be fair, he had been rather articulate about a somewhat complex notion. I'll bet he says this to all the tourists who manage to get invited out to his place. I have since met others who have made that tragic voyage to his «impregnable shanty in the sky» or «War Shew Opp» as it is called in Chinese. Everyone names his house here; it's just like the Jersey shore.

He spoke through an interprête, of course. His own English was atrocious. He seemed to be doing some ectoplasmic translation of a language he didn't at all speak. And he said much more than I can tell you here. I wouldn't think of subjecting you to it, a veritable blood bath of superb subjects. However, I could see the «raw verbiage» lying about in the background. The grasp of his hand had been firm but with a lineage of the Oriental caress in it. I moved closer to his group so as to hear him say:

"Yours is a totalitarian society, ruled by aging sectarians who one day allow a show of democracy only to reverse themselves when speech becomes too free. The country is now poor, its soldiery intent on pillage of the public treasury, its weapons largely inoperative, its citizenry overweight, its leaders intent on a higher stakes competition." Well, I was a little shocked to hear this. I mean, I'm not used to having old glory taken for a roll in the mud. But, as I told all my students in the grammar school where I taught, an open mind is much more important than any old pledge of allegiance. And I'm still fighting that dismissal! We'll all just have to learn to be completely frank and stew in our own juices if we have to. I'm just fed up to here with infringement. Some say he was a very bad man, lewd and wanton and lustful, but I just won't listen to them. Not just for my own benefit. And don't get me wrong about him. This man was a very successful international banker of the first water. One look around his place and you could see it was true. And there was talk he'd had something to do with the triad, a low-classed secret society dedicated to the memory of something.

And what a beautiful place. I told him he had a very lovely place here and he said his place in Shanghai was much more majestic. This was no more than a rustic retreat to him. Though I can't imagine what he'd be doing with a place in Shanghai. But they all must get hungry for a taste of real «China dirt» once in a while. In fact I know they do. And I say it like this because you can buy it in the store. I've seen it all over Chinatown: two square feet in a lacquered box. And Hong Kong is so British I can't believe it. They sell fish and chips on nearly every corner.

Right off Deborah began behaving rather strangely, hanging at Hung's side as if she were one of his women. And there were several of these about. I wouldn't have minded had there not been a room full of people. Relatively few had been invited but rather more came. Not that it mattered. The old spook Hung didn't seem to care. And I can't really say for sure how these reputed tong people arrange their social calendar. He did, however, make the singular choice of Miss Veronica Coy, a striking woman in her post-youth period, oh, say 39, quite tall with full lips, dressed in lightweight ninon blouse very revealing of two erect dark brown nipples. Yes, I too was surprised to see her dressed this way. But this was a private party. Some would find this irresistibly attractive but I could say, quite honestly, I'd had my fill at that point. Plus she had a dogmatic streak in her a mile wide.

Now as I understood it at the time, she was with him. But she certainly didn't act it. And in one jurisdiction she was actually his wife, for what that's worth, the way they write the tax laws! I knew there was something between them and I think it was money. Let's face it, it'll pour a lot of cement into any foundation. Things can seem so complex at these international soirée.   She was speaking in that wonderful, chirpy, four-toned tongue I so love to hear. Though I didn't understand very well, I believe she was saying something to the effect that, contrary to popular opinion, they never drive their cars in the dining room.

Just then an effeminate-cheeked beggar-monk came to the door and rattled the curtain. I was so embarrassed for Hung and his wife. What a humiliation. And I was amazed it wasn't a private island, heavily guarded. But I found out it was loaded with people who flocked here to endure this mortifying relationship to Hung. Hung rushed out and cuffed him on the ear and the astounded bonze must have rolled ten feet down the drive before he came up on his haunches. What dirty yellow teeth he had in his fleshy mouth. Hung told me he was one of the fishskinned people from high Tartary who have been begging lately in the district. I was a bit disappointed to find out we were in just another neighborhood and not the fantasy land I had imagined. He said they came from a «khonghouse» or «third way factory» just over the next hill and were barely tolerated here by the authorities. He called him «frog» and the man went running off with his tail between his legs. You'd have to say Hung gained face with all present by dealing so directly with the situation. He said they sometimes descended like this to perform various party tricks but mostly their so called «factories» were merely havens for draft dodgers. They waste their time scribbling on bone, he said, though some have made good as apothecaries in downtown Hong Kong. They are known, apparently, to practice certain undesirable rites including the «blow it back», the «hundred pulse», the «cannot pant», the «lost soul» and the «dead pit». However they are most adept at the «whispered transmission» and indeed I was later to encounter many of them on the city streets planting soft undetectable references in the air like «clouds» and «G.Q.» and «executive» and «extruder». Some club. When they ask me to join, I'll say I'm gay. "I hope their roof tiles turn over," he murmured when the man was out of sight.

But I was given to understand that Miss Veronica had, as the blotter would read the next day, «mud on her sleeve from dipping too low in the paddy for her rice.» I can't actually say I am in a position to judge her though certain particulars did become clear as the dinner party wore on. Hung was again talking to the little radio brain from Bauxite, Australia saying:

"Of course I'm speaking of history herself here, not merely some interested person's interested opinion of what did or did not happen in the train of eventuality." It wasn't quite to the point but I agreed with him just the same. Though he had been less than solicitous in his manner toward me up till then and though his back was in fact turned toward me he suddenly asked if I would like to see the library. I gladly accepted and he led Rex and I up the stairs. But Rex excused himself to visit the lavatory on the first landing. The little jerk-off, I thought to myself, but I never let on to him how I felt. And with Rex gone Hung was much more polite and attentive in attracting my attention to various curious objects about the house and on the landing in the stair well.

Here's how Hung himself talked. I had to accommodate him au natural because the interprête himself had gone into the kitchen to check the maids. We saw a globe at the top of the stairs. He took it in his fat little hands and said:

«How bout date glate slalt wader sea, Elope an Amelica! How ken jonck ship make come finde China so fashion and no catchy locks? Ayah! Chinamans no ken do all date same-same.» Well, that was hilarious. I could hardly keep myself from laughing. But, all kidding aside, his taking me to see his «nomber wan book loom» was indeed a rare treat and an unusual favor to me being so recently arrived. But I'm sure he saw I was cut from a different cloth than the average tourist.

Now I shall attempt a description of what I saw. Of course it was more than just a library. It was beyond that a retreat and a museum, an office and sanitarium, so much more than a place to borrow. On the walls of one hall were block-stamped and painted drawings set in old carved rose and dark wood frames. Some represented ancient battle scenes which he explained as having been fought in the days when China was conquered by the Tartars who long reigned over the country and had their headquarters in Peking where their Emperor and his magnificent court were located. The troops on both sides were represented as drawn up in regular lines, armed with matchlock guns, spears, swords, and all with small shields buckled on their arms. They also had bows and arrows slung on their shoulders but I didn't see anything like cannon. Both armies were regularly divided into squadrons of cavalry and countless foot soldiers. The mounted tartars appeared to be dressed identically to those who march in Victoria on certain bank holidays.

Another large frame held an augmented photograph of a great battle on the Yalu river, China's elbow on the world, during the Korean conflict. There were the famed hordes with their pilfered rifles and stolen American artillery camouflaged on a ridge overlooking the river valley into which ambush marched an American regiment apparently intent on rape and pillage. Some of the Americans are combing their hair, others washing their hands, some younger men fill government-issue condoms with water in the broad slow stream. And they are all eyeing a village in the middle distance where women are seen in domestic exposure. Really, the lowest common denominator of international geo-politics. It was quite graphic and Hung seemed slightly discomfited. I understand, by the way, that reports of drug use among the American legions are highly exaggerated. Those nay-sayers who search for traces of smoke in G.I. urine are just so many prophets of doomed respectability. I don't think these statistics mean one single thing.

Some curious looking old Chinese maps of the world were hung on another wall. All of China occupied three quarters of one of them surrounded by nameless islands and seas bounded only by the edges of the map. Hung values them very highly on account of their antiquity. One in particular because it represented all the world extended as a vast flat surface or plain with the Chinese empire one half of the whole and the remainder a boundless sea studded with what could have been a peck of potatoes strewn across the floor.

The main or great library hall contained a large collection of books some of which, he said, are very ancient and «hab got too much plenty culious ting inside.» The books aren't bound the way ours are with stiff covers and spines. They're piled flat on shelves, each work by itself between two slats of ebony. It's so wonderful that, as the mystery of the language is every year becoming more developed, the day is not far distant when the contents of such curious libraries will be translated for the enrichment of all.

In a third room was a collection of ancient copper and bronze articles, principally vases, urns, house and field utensils, pottery, old china ware and teacups without handles. Some of it bore marks of being very old indeed. I'm sure I could have made some valuable discoveries were I an antiquarian. He showed me one vase which he swore to being over twenty-one hundred years old, from the tomb of the Marquessa of T'ai. He said that the first man to enter her tomb had been burned to death by her «marsh gas» when it was ignited by his torch. One of his fellows picked up this vase after the fire burned itself out and brought it out to the market where he could get the best price. Hong Kong functions for Chinese grave-robbers much they way New York does for the Aztec and Mayan art thieves. Incredibly enough, it bore hieroglyphic marks unknown to modern Chinese savants very much the way bug markings under the bark of trees be greek to us at home. Or the way beans in a necklace will sketch themselves to mystify the African scholar.

In a case at the end of this room and on a velvet cushion sat a crossbow made of laminated bamboo and at least a thousand years old. He said that the crossbow, when used to best advantage at fairly short range, fires a heavy missile at high velocity through a flat trajectory and that the shattering impact of the bolt is greater than that of a modern high-velocity rifle bullet. In addition, it is much easier to aim and fire than a conventional bow which becomes effective only after extensive practice. Its compactness and accuracy made it very effective for defending a wall against nomad horsemen. The short squat nomads, relative to the Huns, stuck to their stubby little bows which they found more convenient for use on wild horses. Then the city folk found themselves at a distinct disadvantage in combat with the nimble little fellows. And I know what followed was the blunderbust; they might as well have been using sharpened pens for all the military utility it has in the womb of time.

In the course of my tour the old gentleman was quite inquisitive as regards foreign countries and showed that he knew something of the philosophical disputes which have, over the last few centuries, convulsed the Western world. We were standing in his Shang bronzes when he wanted me to know that he did not esteem any one sect or form of worship as superior to that of others provided they acknowledged the One and his subordinate agent, the devil, "Josh" and "Kwee" to Hung:

"My flinde, all mans rib. All mans mus make die. So fashion, so long time as Josh let you rib and you hab tluly good mans, and bum-by Josh make you die. Do you tinke he Josh ken make catchy you for make you too much. . . ." He hesitated here and then used the expression which means «as hard in the hereafter as the angel who made Mary».

"Yes, sir," was my answer, much to his satisfaction. Then he continued:

"Now, one ting more like for speak, my flinde. Suppose you hab make rib all same same as date bad Kweesie mans and when Josh make you die, he can gib you Kwee for make bamboo muche too muche?" Again I answered in the affirmative, at which he clasped my hand and said:

"Ayah, my flinde, now no more occasion for make talke dat Josh pidgin. Tluly now can see you like me tinke all same same." It was charming to hear it put this way, to see the merchant's morality followed his profession as the penniless maid the troops. And how amused I was to think of those poor dead souls being bamboo in the hereafter. But it was all so anthropomorphic, don't you think? For instance, how silly to say something so patently false as «god is everywhere» when, obviously, he is only where he is even if this be «everywhere». It is perfectly meaningless in the ordinary sense and necessarily how much more false a notion in the instance of an indwelling deity, his omnipresence here being merely the cute contradictory stricture: "You will never find him because he is everywhere." As if he were a disguise artist or some fictitious adventurer rumored to have slept in many beds beyond his own. The truth is I'd just agreed with him to smooth the social path. I didn't really believe any of that stuff.

But it was a little scary none the less. Maybe I was being set up as a «Manchurian candidate» too, just like everyone else who went to

China. Not that I had any political ambitions. But what if I one day discovered I was the junior senator from Wyoming and had a bomb in my briefcase. I'd have to think twice. But I think all those tales of their powers of thought control are exaggerated. And in any case all these people here have been bottle fed on such notions as «life's a bitch» and «look out for old number one» and don't really see the suffering of the down and outers trodden underfoot. They are so inured to long bouts of intense boredom and mechanical submission to a mere ghost of authority that just one of our major networks could have them voting for tobacco subsidies tomorrow. And of course there is no real technology any more, just diversity and miniaturization.

But please don't give up hope; I'm sure there is an end to all two-bit reductionist clap-trap somewhere down the pike. We've got to stop being in so many ways mere reflexes of our own ways and prey to her so many woes, forgone in so many ways, misbegotten and woebegone, despoiled and over-reached, despatched and out of mind, out of sight, all in the shadow of the valley of no-hope. And please don't use this as an excuse to slip into the pomps and excesses of group-thought or other various self-help programs, not to speak of the quirky racialist notions implicit in reference to the «phenomenal» and the «numenal» nose in the singular instance.

Hung lit a match very deliberately and then said: "Well, let's go down to dinner and I'll show you what a real chop-stick dinner is all about. Then we will proceed with the rectification of names." I imagine he meant he'd introduce me to the rest of his guests. When we came downstairs the table was seated with eight or ten representatives of Hong Kong high life. Hung motioned for me to sit. This was the moment «the camel put his head inside the tent,» as the saying goes. They all regarded me with curiosity as I sat beside my hostess. And what should they be discussing but treason? One of the twelve Chinese wines had been poured and then a thin gruel was served in small gray bowls. We quickly wolfed it down. Miss Coy informed me this so called «rock-sugar lotus-seed porridge» had a millet base. Then «SamFu», something involving the manipulation of eggs and having the authentic taste of old Havana.

The next dish was something called «Pale Beets», served cold with onions and a piquant sauce. Then «100 Straw Flowers and Giant Prawn». There was an oil prism effect in this. I half thought to ask for a collateral appraisal before eating but, perhaps foolishly, one pays so little attention to the early dishes at a feast. With this was a stir-fry aubergine and on a small side-dish, a cat's tongue of chocolate. This last was served with a native beer from the old German province.

Then two kinds of crab were brought to the table, one salt and the other fresh. With them were served small red fruits with the drupes removed. Of course they were fresh. As you can well imagine, no fruit likes to be frozen, let alone a vegetable. And I still had my doubts about the egg plant. It might have been birds-eyed. Now your joint of meat is different, it can take a freeze. That goes back to what used to happen to old and sick animals in the winter. But god save the food supply from this ice age of ours.

All these dishes were served on old thin plates with a strange design, much like the stone bird seen on the surface of Mars and glazed willow-green. Miss Coy said: "Well, crabs are delicious but not very wholesome" and I thought that less than generous. But then she had been in theatre and you know how unbeholden theatricals can be. How many times have we all been forced to tell one or the other of them that they «need not apply». She spoke in the so-called «crystal English» so popular now-a-days on the disco circuit. She leaned her head close to mine and whispered:

"You know I am close to Hung so you couldn't be as foolish as you seem. Tell me, Mr. Desmond, what is your nasty little secret?" I assured her in conciliatory terms I had no secret worth keeping, save perhaps for some future activity I did not think politic to propose. And I gave her a big wink. Not that I was attracted to her on any but the higher levels of intellectual congress. But I appreciated her openness in questioning me. It showed she thought me important and respected me. But then she drew a finger across her cheek to shame me and I found myself again confused.

Let me assure you this seeming intimacy between us was not assumed. I mean, it's always like this at fancy parties, be they gatherings of journalists, politicians, diplomats, money-men, rich fools or just plain folk. And as even your most hardened apologist for Western thought will tell you, the Chinese are not really inscrutable and much can be detected from facial expressions and bodily gestures in conversation, although they are careful in what they say for the record. So, though we had not known each other for long, we soon found a common ground on which to communicate.

Then a feeling came over me that signalled only one thing to my consciousness, some urgent purpose akin to the transference of information. But information in the broadest sense of the word, even to the purity of numerals and syncopation's inducement to swoon. And transference to its fullest extension, up to and beyond transmission itself, electronic or otherwise.

I politely excused myself and headed straight for the bathrooms which I was told were at the far end of the house in the basement. Right there in front of some of the top brass of high life here, some of the real big-wigs in a world of over two billion people, I found I had to be alone. I just had to be. Can you imagine that, at a cocktail party? And a cocktail party which, I have since discovered, never stops and is probably going on at this very minute.

I found it and went into the porcelain and teakwood chamber. I say «chamber» for it wasn't so simple as a «john» on our side of the world and all the usage that has had in popular fancy. I could hear water gurgling about in the piping and that reassured me. And it was then I realized, having gotten myself all the way down here, that the feeling I'd had wasn't real at all but was just a memory. I mean, I didn't have to «go» or anything. It was one of those memories come back as a compunction. And now here it was, like a bee on the watermelon, flashing back to me in images the way most of us remember, the memory of a desire so persistent it could kill to think the thought. With me it took the form of an urgent need to relieve myself of a certain insupportable and insufferable excess of seminal fluids. So I was relieved I didn't have to throw up. And it's not all that unpleasant and so important to nervous health in the modern world. I went directly to the sink and picked up one of the scented bars of soap. I wet it in my left hand, twisting it on my palm to build up a bit of slip. I've often done this to shave if an aerosol can weren't handy or to wash the stains from personal items. But actually shaving cream is best for those persistent spots if you're in a dormitory situation and haven't time to make it to the laundrymat. With my right hand I freed my «tube of toothpaste» and in a few strokes had it «humming». There was a time I would have liked to have a pair of day old panties over my head for atmosphere and thought for a moment of searching for the laundryroom but instead settled for an imagining of our hostess bending over the toilet bowl, her skirt above her waist, her swollen black-haired clam throbbing and belching, my banana deep inside her, pushing and pulsing like the worst bully on the block, some fingers pinching her hard nipple, a palm cupping her breast. God knows how we had gotten ourselves into that situation. I discharged the over-load within thirty seconds, thought being as rapid as it be, some say faster than the speed of light squared.

I only tell you this in order to let you know I'm like everyone else, like the guy down the street, the fellows at the office, the club, the bar, the construction site, the ranch house, the bungalow. I want you should listen to my story with open ears and know I speak for the experience of the common man, the average joe of the dear john letter. I waited a minute for the last few drops of «malingerers» and excess lubrication to drip off the tip, shook out the absolute «refusenik» residue and put it back where it belongs. I checked my appearance in the mirror and returned to the party. I feel it is so important to be well-groomed and polite at all cost. Returning to the dining room, I retook my seat at table and smiled at the curry which had just arrived, a steaming ochre mélange in lumps and bubbles. I'm sure no one suspected what had been going on between Miss Coy and myself. And so what if she was his wife? I mean, what is a wife these day, I thought, but some pompous prig's fairy-god mother or one of a sort known as «poison ladies».

"Oh, food from the sub-continent," I cried.

"You don't like," questioned Hung from his seat at the head of the table.

"Oh, I love their spicy dishes, but aren't you at war with India," I asked, not remembering where I was.

"Oh, them," said Veronica.

"Yes, them," said he, "and their rubber tantrums."

"No, no, not us," she put in quickly, "but on the mainland, they are."

"Yes, the mainland is," he added helpfully, "but we here in Hong Kong may or may not be. Or do anything we want. We need room to manoeuvre. We don't let war stand in the way."

"Rubber tantrums," I asked, thinking perhaps there had been an error in translation."

"No, no, he is confused. He thinks you're talking about Liberia. He means rubber plantations."

"Oh." What else could I say but "oh, I see."

"And anyway," he added, "we have our own «curry». It came over the mountains 2000 years ago."

Service at table was peculiar. It was called tiffin style. Each of us had a blue clad «boy» behind his chair whose pigtail hung down to the floor itself. He proffered a laden platter from which you could pick whatever morsel or whatever dish struck your fancy by a motion of the finger. Then he would retire to his position of subservience three steps behind your back. One somewhat amusing incident in regard to this «style»: My waiter, Wing Fat, served me some Eastern bologny sandwiches on which the butter was hard and in lumps so I just mentioned it, sort of a little joking communication with the staff, and he said, "spread it with your tongue, dick brain." I was so shocked I just let it pass without complaint but realized there was not no alienation in this quarter.

"This is the yellow sauce," said Hung through his translator. I don't feel I have to repeat this, do I? I mean the part about the translator?

So who was at this table, you well may ask. Well, Hung and Coy and Deb and I. Then a sort of Chinese free-mason named Dik who had been born in Honolulu. Then the fellow from Kuala, Australia I mentioned named Rex Driscoll who seemed to be consulting a radio transmitter implanted in his head. A handsome young English sinophile whom I took to be Miss Coy's assistant. And a wisp of a thing called Arjuna, so small, delicate and blond, big almond eyes and red sensual lips. I'd never seen anything like it though I had been looking

all my life. And she was in Hung's «stable», as they say. At a certain
point he walked behind me and whispered:

"She's mine, don't touch." So. . . She called herself a model, that
back door on civilization. Not that this Hung wasn't a good deal
straighter than a Bogart, for instance, and though he'd spent far too
much time in «Arabia deserta » to be considered totally à droit, he could
be light and cheerful without slipping into a house dress. I think the
truth of the matter is he'd taken a farmer to wife quite early in life and
left the rest «hanging on a dead wire». And there was always as little
content in his thought as he could possibly manage. He'd just go for
the jugular. Not that he wasn't all he pretended to be. Many a man had
been forced to «eat a leek» in his company. But, as they say, «the moon
is rounder in China.» And then, as if on cue, we began to discuss Sun
Yat Sen. Little Arjuna said to me:

"You know, of course, that Sun was Xtian, don't you? Through
and through. And doesn't that explain so much about the modern
country?" I was forced to admit it did, but then so much of my
thinking these days is merely social. I can't really be bothered with
what they call «deep thought». I've always thought of it like french
kissing: If you're not careful you just may end up going «too far». And
then Rex, as if in response to some internal stimulus, said:

"Yes, wasn't he a great statesman after all."

"Great statesman, my eye," put in Hung. "Even his own
townspeople didn't like him. He was forever «leading an army against
the North», always failing, always hanging somewhere between
humiliation and absolute collapse. Finally he was made ill by shame at
failure. However, he was a confirmed marxian. And even today the
railroads run by his express command." I was flabbergast to hear such
talk. I'd never heard anything like this and I said so.

"Well," I said, "sir, if I may," for I was truly then on my high horse,
imaginary or otherwise, "if I may make so bold and I trust you won't
think me a schoolboy," for being thought a schoolboy I thought so
gauche on a social level, "pray justify this your expressed opinion unless
you intend your remarks to be taken with no more credence than that
of a page from a book chronicling the flight and suicide of a warlord
written by an interested journalist, either this or some other undesirable

document in a foreign library." I'll admit I was attempting to pander to their chauvinism, knowing full well how they loved to distrust the very ground on which a foreign well-wisher stood. And I wasn't frightened when I said this for I knew even the pope in Rome to be but another moralizing politician and I didn't at all fear a beating. Physical courage is often that, isn't it, no more than a faint taste for the hardened hand. Not that I wanted it, don't think that, whatever be said. And even then, just hours before my own thrashing at the hands of Debby's goon, I knew nothing of it.

Hung looked at me in that calm penetrating manner which a Chinese reserves for a white man, a sort of dispassionate, detached scrutiny as if suspecting lunacy and simply indicated with his fingers that he held my objection beneath comment. I was a bit miffed for I had always taken myself for a good deal more of an approachable Caucasian than that! I showed him how I felt about what he had said by flicking my ears slightly. Then he went on to describe Sun's liver cancer and his bedside conversion to «the old way».

"First they bled him," he said, "in Wellington Koo's house in the old Tartar city. Pus continued to drip from the incision on his side. The missionary doctors, jealous of their practice, were pushed aside «by the will of the masses» and way was made for the trinket mongers with their animist shakes and charms. Over the protests of Koo and Eugene Chen and Ching-ling and Michael Borodin, a young friend from Chicago, he grasped an old witch-doctor by the hand and said:

«I am Chinese. You too are Chinese.» Then he said: «I am a messenger come from God to help men to obtain freedom and equality. Many more will follow me and will be of all races; naked men, they may find in the creeds a cloak. . . .» He choked and faltered, large tears welling up in his eyes. All present were moved to bare their breasts in tribute to his greatness and beat on their chests with the clenched fingers. «Here was a peaceful man», some cried, others indulging in quiet wailing and open weeping. And finally:

«Don't make trouble for those Xtian buggers. Down South on St. Peter there is a mint. . . .» He wanted to say more but a gasp ended his speech, perhaps at the thought of what he was saying. Then a fatal dose of endocrinal bile poured into his bloodstream. They went ahead with the Xtian burial in any case. But he always said he wasn't a Xtian of the churches but of Jesus the revolutionary, son of a bird. After endless dickering the corpse was taken to an old style temple in a beautiful iron casket sent from Moscow by J. Stalin himself. After his death there appeared on the social scene the weird and cynically disturbing phenomenon of mass play-acting without belief, outward conformity and inward alienation, joining lines without intention, seeking sex without relationship." Hung seemed genuinely moved by what he had told me but it was water off a duck's back to me.

"One thing you can say," he said, "he was always involved in a continuous correction for contradiction, having grasped the true mode of oppression." And then Miss Coy jumped in to say:

"He believed in every man's and woman's ability to begin again and better his grand concepts and be born into the book of life in the body and soul and be free, be he what he be" for all the world like some preternatural spelling bee when on came the Sash Shag, "a cream that comes from the earth itself", said Hung with a laugh, "very tasty but finally debilitating. We bring food from all over the empire," he added proudly, "for instance, the Hami melon, the Sinkiang Kua, pink-tinged. But then musclemen don't really make good reds," he added with a smile.

And then they served a perfectly revolting plate of gray meat on ice, it might have been slivers of lamb from the way the fat congealed in little white balls. And sodden dumplings, delicious but rather moist, nested on the plate in marram shore grass. The remains of the previous courses were cleared away by fresh faced girls as more buxom young women carried in enormous platters of carmel colored roast duck to be served by our tiffin boys stationed behind us, though relations with mine had deteriorated to something just this side of «bad service». Then they retreated behind screens to dismember the birds, reserving the carcass for soup, the next to the last course. Miss Coy leaned in close to my ear and said to me confidentially:

"Isn't Hung boring. Don't you just hate his fractured history. I think people are much more important." Then she told me about herself. It appears she had been in movies.

Now, unlike the free world, these people use the motion picture as a political tool as well as a means of entertaining the populace. Films out of Hollywood, with rare exception, are so radically different from what the average person knows that to permit them to be shown would, in the view of the government, most likely create social and political unrest. .American films would be a mischievous influence. China can't afford to relax except at great risk to the controls it now has over the people. Unlike the free world, the indoctrination of the populace begins shortly after birth when infants are taken from their mothers and placed in holding-tanks and incubators. Then they are moved to day-care centers while the mother and father go to work. At this juncture the state has, if not total control, the greatest possible influence upon the mental and physical development of its future manpower. «Big Screen» TVs are set up all over the country where puppets, cartoon characters and ridiculous adults mime social and moral lessonettes which are burned into the children's control-panels. Thus it follows that commerce in motion pictures will be limited; so much so that the country's vast population will remain inconsequential in terms of potential box-office. For the motion picture is, as Lenin recognized, a more powerful weapon than police control because it can influence the mind itself. In this context it is interesting to note that, unlike the free world, even the ten or so film studios scattered about China have no control over their pix after they are made. The China distribution company in Peking determines how many prints are to be made and in what theatres they may be shown. It would, of course, be this state agency that would handle distribution of Hollywood pix if a deal were to be made, and regardless of payment, censorship would start in Peking.

Now as I was saying before my digression, this woman had a history in the pix. And some reputation she had! Immediately and justifiably suspect for possessing the ability to manipulate emotion (I mean, really, who would trust an actress; they're not like us ordinary people), she came under government surveillance. She did not seek fame in films, she continued more quickly, but after she had established a reputation as an actress, several film companies sought her out and tried to force her to sign a contract. Then great film impressarios (government agents) began to vilify her and threatened to kill her. Thus she was the subject of constant harassment. And her nerve, which had been like steel, was gradually eroded by the constant bombardment. Her voice rose in anguish as she said that all sorts of people and organizations had plotted to kill her. All the media were mobilized against her. The tactics they used were insidious and cunning though common during the «white terror». They spread the rumor that she was about to be kidnapped. They said that she was one of those who knew «the joys of sex», though she assured me it was not true. They were, in effect, trying to drive her into committing suicide. As an individual she had no power. Without access to the media she had no way of defending herself against her attackers, among them the very men who controlled the media. When she realized how truly isolated she really was, she lived in terror from day to day. Her health deteriorated and her power to resist disease became dangerously impaired.

The next dish to come to the table was a platter of large mollusk. This particular snail, she explained, was called by some a «french letter». The name, apparently, dated from a time when men dealt in cowrie shells, a form of money fashioned after the female genital organ. She smiled with ironic detachment at this explanation, that red detachment of women in their middle years.

After this, she went on to explain, she was forced to play «The Spongy Princess», low role on the horror circuit, a play on the silver dreams of capitalism, involving lip-smacking gossip-mongering, women's eyes that looked like they'd eaten ice cream, voluptuous flesh and quivering thighs, full bosom exposure and exciting make-up. This led her, she said, to «take a walk in the woods», which, for the sensitives of her generation, meant having repeated sexual congress with unknown partners. "During this period I did not, as is usual, «deny my dampness». Just to temper myself," she added, "and taste the peach of immorality. All this took place in the «red-titan» era, when those bon vivants who thought they had the people's proxy let the gold yuan go crash. Of course it wasn't real gold but rather an odd species of «flying paper»." She fiddled and faddled, confused and angry, with her bread.

By the way, the bird had been very knowledgeably cooked, showing all the know-how of an experienced «body-burner», knowing just when a stiff will «spring its dark juices» and always maintaining the proper flame-to-fluid ratio.

I was quite moved by her story and thought how too-bad it was, what had happened to her. But then once a thing has been plotted, it cannot be unplotted, as so many world famous «intelligence» organizations have discovered to their everlasting and international embarrassment. And it is just as true in «personal life» as well. The seeds of infidelity, for instance, being «in the bag» irregardless of intention and well before faith herself curls receptively on a corner of the carpet. I sought to comfort her in some way but she cut me off by saying:

"Oh, that's just show business, baby."

"Oh, pig-shit show business," roared Hung in Chinese, his translator rendering his statement: "The woman speaks with a diminutive «love apple» clinging to her lips." He may have been correct but I'm sure she intended it as something given freely in an emotionally charged atmosphere.

Next there came to the table torn strips of gray pork floating in a bath of liquid white sugar and red food coloring. Miss Coy assured me it was the only known cure for a malady described in the literature as «kraut liver», asking in the process if I "carried any German blood." "About as much as the Queen of England," I assured her but even her icy glare couldn't stop Hung from babbling: "Many Germans have come to us before. Your leader Hitler sent us Germans to train our armies. . . ." Again, you see, false ID, a perfect plague.

After the last of the «red sauce» had been spooned into our mouths the hostess passed her napkin around the table for each of the guests to blot his and her lips. It's an old custom, I was told, dating back to the stone age of matriarchy. I saw her smile broadly as I cleared away a large smear from below my lower lip. I'm afraid I've always been a slurper, having experienced since bottle-feeding some difficulty at the commencement of the swallowing motion, a motion which, of course, continues until excretion.

The courses seemed to come now in an endless stream. Next there was «three-yellow» ginger chicken, «pull-silk» bananas, the four inch sort caramelized whole, plunged into ice cold water to make them hard and inserted into edible orchid flowers, this being the «southern style». And then glass cake, white bread, fried chicken and mashed potatoes, chittlins, steak and french fries, collard greens, sliced ham with pork and beans and apple sauce, rainbow cloud jello and an ocean of creamy hot oyster-shell custard, fifty or sixty gallons of it. What would have caused them, the girls in the kitchen, to make so much custard, I thought to myself. It's at best a marginal desert, but done differently here. We didn't begin to scrape the surface of it. Hung informed me confidentially that one of his chefs was once a top man at Horn and Hardardts. He then zeroed in on my opinions under the guise of an interest in art. As if from nowhere he asked:

"Under what conditions would one need such «frigid irony and over-heated satire»?

"What irony and what satire," I started in unfeigned ignorance.

"Oh, you know," he drawled, winking. That pickled fish, I thought, and then said:

"Well, it's really the maintenance of a constant and absolute aesthetic, isn't it, really, at any expense. Something from which to pivot regardless of terrain or weather conditions or etcetera, isn't that what you're after?"

It was then he explained it to me. Another sledge part from the Finnish bog, that old vehicle, I said to myself. Apparently he thought art the ability of the human mind to enter into a representation. Aesthetics were, then, the nature of this representation. And the purpose of this representation was. . . politics.

"Oh, dear," I said, "next you'll be telling me the united states are paper-tigers." And do you know that's exactly what he did! The nerve! He said:

23

Cross of Gold

"The United States is flaunting the anti-commy banner everywhere in order to perpetrate aggression against other countries and insure its domestic oligarchy. It owes debts everywhere. The whole world, Britain especially, dislikes the United States. The masses of the people dislike it. Japan dislikes the United States because she lost the war. None of the countries of the East is free from its aggressions. The United States has invaded our Taiwan Province. Japan, Korea, the Philippines, Viet Nam and Pakistan all suffer from its aggression, although there are many conflicting alliances today. The people are dissatisfied and in some countries so are the authorities.

Everyone wants independence.

Everything is subject to change. The big decadent forces will give way to the small new-born forces. The small forces will change into big forces because the majority of the people demand this change. The United States imperialist forces will change from big to small because the American people, too, are deeply dissatisfied with their government.

In my own lifetime I have witnessed such changes. Some of us present were born in the Ching Dynasty and others after the 1911 revolution.

The Ching Dynasty was overthrown long ago. By whom? By the party led by Sun Yat Sen, together with the people. Sun Yat Sen's forces were so small that the Ching officials didn't take him seriously. He led many uprisings which failed each time. In the end, however, it was Sun Yat Sen who brought down the Ching Dynasty. Bigness is nothing to be afraid of. The big will be overthrown by the small. The small will become big. After overthrowing the Ching

Dynasty, Sun Yat Sen met with defeat. For he failed to satisfy the demands of the people, such as their demands for land and for an end to imperialism. Nor did he understand the necessity of suppressing the counter-revolutionaries who were then moving about freely. Later he suffered defeat at the hands of Yuan Shih Kai, the boss of the Northern war-lord mob. Yuan Shih Kai's forces were larger than Sun Yat Sen's. But here again this law operated: small forces linked with the people become strong, while big forces opposed to the people become weak. Subsequently Sun Yat Sen's bourgeois-democratic revolutionaries cooperated with the Commy forces and together we defeated the war-lord set up left behind by Yuan Shih Kai.

Chiang Kai Shek's rule in China was recognized by the governments of all countries and lasted twenty-two years. His forces, husbanded by greed and deceit, were the biggest. Our forces were small, fifty thousand Party members at first but only a few thousand after counter-revolutionary suppressions. The enemy made trouble everywhere. Again this law operated: the big and strong end up in defeat because they are divorced from the people, whereas the small and weak emerge victorious because they are linked with the people and work in their interest. That's how things turned out in the end.

During the anti-Japanese war, Japan was very powerful, the Kuomintang troops were driven to the hinterland, and the armed forces led by the Commy Party could only conduct guerrilla warfare in the rural areas behind the enemy lines. Japan occupied large Chinese cities such as Peking, Tientsin, Shanghai, Nanking, Wuhan and Canton. Nevertheless, the Japanese militarists collapsed in a few years, in accordance with the same law.

We underwent innumerable difficulties and were driven from the South to the North, while our forces fell from several hundred thousand strong to a few tens of thousands. At the end of the 25,000 li Long March we had only 25,000 men and women left to us.

In the history of our Party many erroneous «left» and «right» lines have occurred. Gravest of all were the «right» deviationist line of Chen Tu Hsiu and the «left» deviationist line of Wang Ming. Besides, there were the «right» deviationist errors committed by Chang Kuo Tao, Kao Kang and others.

There is also a good side to mistakes, for they can educate the people and the Party. We have had a good many teachers by negative example, such as Japan, the United States, Chiang Kai Shek, Chen Tu Hsiu, Li Li San, Wang Ming, Chang Kuo Tao and Kao Kang. We paid a very high price to learn from these teachers. In the past, Britain made war on us many times. Britain, the United States, Japan, France, Germany, Italy, tsarist Russia and Holland were all very interested in this land of ours. They were all our teachers by negative example and we were their pupils.

During the War of Resistance, our troops grew and became 900,000 strong through fighting against Japan. Then came the War of Liberation. Our arms were inferior to those of the Kuomintang. The Kuomintang troops then numbered four million, but in three years of fighting we wiped out eight million of them all told. The Kuomintang, though aided by United States imperialism, could not defeat us. The big and strong cannot win, it is always the small and weak who win out.

Now United States imperialism is seemingly quite powerful, but in reality it isn't. It is very weak politically because it is divorced from the masses of the people and is disliked by everybody and by the American people too. In appearance it is very powerful but in reality it is nothing to be afraid of, it is a paper tiger. Outwardly a tiger, it is made of paper, unable to withstand the wind and the rain. I believe the United States is nothing but a paper tiger.

History as a whole, the history of class society for thousands of years, has proven this point: the strong must give way to the weak. This holds true for the Americas as well.

Only when imperialism is eliminated can peace prevail. The day will come when the paper tigers will be wiped out. But they won't become extinct of their own accord, they need to be battered by the wind and the rain.

When we say United States imperialism is a paper tiger, we are speaking in terms of strategy. Regarding it as a whole, we must despise it. But regarding each part, we must take it seriously. It has claws and fangs. We have to destroy it piecemeal. For instance, if it has ten fangs, knock off one the first time, and there will be nine left; knock off another and there will be eight left. When all the fangs are gone, it will still have claws. If we deal with it step by step and in earnest, we will certainly succeed in the end.

Strategically, we must utterly despise United States imperialism. Tactically, we must take it seriously. In struggling against it, we must take each battle, each encounter, seriously. At present, the United States is powerful, but when looked at in a broader perspective, as a whole and from a long-term viewpoint, it has no popular support, its policies are disliked by the people, because it oppresses and exploits them. For this reason the tiger is doomed. Therefore, it is nothing to be afraid of and can be despised. But today the United States still has strength and hits out everywhere. That is why we must continue to wage struggles against it, fight it with all our might and wrest one position after another from it. And that takes time.

It seems that the countries of the Americas, Asia and Africa will have to go on quarrelling with the United States till the very end, till the paper tiger is destroyed by the wind and the rain. Or until they really understand what was behind World War II.

We are of the same nature as you in our opposition to imperialist oppression, differing only in geographical position, nationality and language. But we are different in nature from imperialism, and the very sight of it makes us sick.

What use is imperialism? The Chinese people will have none of it, nor will the people in the rest of the world. There is no reason for the existence of imperialism."

I was so embarrassed. He must have thought I was «someone», maybe a public figure from «Latin» America. He rose suddenly and left the room. Well, you'd think I'd expressed a willingness to eat tea-bags! I don't know who he thought he was! And anyway, I don't think he was a real commy. I think he was just capitalizing on it. I almost felt like crying. And my eyes did actually water. But I choked them back and didn't blink. I mean, why would he want to propagandize me? You'd have thought I was trying to date his daughter. But then Miss Veronica Coy took my hand and said softly: "But my dear, it's all propaganda. All of it." Well, I'm not really bitter.

Just then, outside our window, a deer came to lick at the salt gabelle, a small cone of calcium chloride put out for the wild things.

"Isn't it unusual for a deer to be about in the dark," I asked.

"Not here," Miss Coy replied, "for they are so frightened in the light, even in these wild parks and forest preserves. And they do so need the salt."

After dinner we watched to cooks retire to an outdoor court and expertly urinated into large pottery urns, casually and with a great show of indifference. And Hung sent word to the table that it was not for young people and teenagers to suffer such larger questions as above, that we were to go off and enjoy the city at his expense. Deborah indicated she intended to stay for a «private interview» and, the others not being about, I made my exit as politely as possible, not thinking it at all odd to be the only one leaving. I mean, I didn't think she was staying behind to plot and connive and «cook my goose». Little did I know! Ah Bum brought me back to Victoria where I stood watching while he and the boatmen roared away into the night.

24

Hollywood

Well, that was an ordeal but it's over now. That's what I say. How was I to know that the feeling, fantasies and emotions of a moment, things I may have imagined in my late night, sleepy musing on a Roman hillside, would one day present themselves as big as life? Well, I hope you see by now this isn't just another «green reader». As they say in all the books, you've never eaten Chinese food until you've done it «on location». It's all part of the novel experience of being there.

I feel I have dwelt too long in the intricate levels of the decision making process. Oh, it goes on and on and on, don't worry, but it is time to drop the technical talk and try, if at all possible, to make some meaning for us all, something we can cling to in the gathering storm, some simple message in it all, for all, perhaps too little, too late. And I realize it's a long time since the last time I appeared in these pages as anything but a narrator of a travelogue.

We've all matured, of this I have no doubt. Though some seem to have merely sagged and rotted in place, decayed as it were. Oh, the perils in this world of sensation. I had retired and was drawn out again, drawn out to do a favor, to offer myself as a buffer between a woman and the world. And where did it get me? And for what? So that she could later claim to the rooftops that I had the precious gems and she was empty handed? Drugs, diamonds, women's bodies: Is this life? Slander, misconception, innuendo: Are these the stuff of the mind? I know I sometimes seem to care but I don't. People say this is the way the world is but I don't think so. That I'm taken to a warehouse from which I never really return? That I'm thought of as having a «Viet Nam view»? It's the old sketch: Cut that story out of his head. And I don't know if they have or have not. They accuse me of posing as

Mr. Polo, of back peddling hollow spaghetti up and down main street. That was never my intention. Well, it's not just thumbing my nose at the public, but of taking them in and sitting them on my knee so they know how it feels. There is a terrible breakdown in an Occidental life which occurs no matter what you do, no matter how you live, no matter what your station be in life. There is no preparation necessary and then it happens. A casual package carried ashore for an even more casual acquaintance; then the spine crushing accusation.

Just one last word about the fabled Hung's rhetoric powers: Oh, sure, he could talk, but in Chinese. We'll never know what he really said unless you care to trust that gang of shady translators. All those braggarts boasting the size of their bloated larders. Let me tell you I take it with more than just a little grain of salt. But Hung was an old, old man. Natural causes would soon settle his hash. And time would overthrow our ideation of him. But he did seem intent that I should take a message to the democracies about the will of the people.

These are the only gifts I have on my person. And about the charge that all this was done on orders from Hung, that it was all Hung's fault? That these be dispatches from a prior contract, stuffed with intrigue and unregistered lobby? There are those who will find a plotter back of every grassy knoll, in every book store window. Why don't we just, as a nation, grow up and ignore the obvious, live in the never-never land of what we're told? Not that there is anything illegal in any of this. This is not just another Bohemian Republic. Even a man such as myself can be made to throw up his chin, the way you say no in the East. Only fools and naïfs give power away.

But I didn't give another thought to anything, to the trip, all that discharge on the road to nowhere, my memory, my tears, the theatre, my dining experience, returning to my rooms in a cool Pacific rain. But, as I struggled up that last hill, I swear I was walking through water, slow-motioning through our mother, the wine dulled mind, killed in that freak accident, past Farren's casino on Fuzhou Street where the doormen stood in postures of Albanian salute.

I half thought of ending the evening by «burying» a couple of «cheap pearls», as they say, in a house I had discovered right in my own neighborhood. It wasn't expensive and I didn't think it too debilitating.

But I'll admit I wasn't up to it. And, alas, that was my last chance. I realize now it was a sign of age, not wanting to feel the «jelly jewels» course through channels and disappear forever in the cavity of a hot little «gem case». But all that is past. Believe me, I don't even think about it.

A sudden chill overtook me on the walk back, my walk back to the residence. Think of me on those mean street, alone with my heartbreak, in my solitude and my situation. Perhaps I imagined it, but the locals seemed to scatter as I approached their little knots. The lobby of the apartment house quickly emptied as I entered. I knocked on several doors thinking perhaps to rouse up some warm body but there were no answers. Maybe they knew something I didn't know but I doubt it. These stories of prescient natives are all exaggerated. I went to my room, slipped on my dressing gown and sat in the cushioned bamboo chair. I was about to open a bottle of claret when. . . .

Let me recollect myself. After all, it is now but a faint raster left on the projection tube of my past life, no more, no less. I know it was wine bottle in one hand and flickering TV on the table before me. Of course, Hong Kong TV leaves much to be desired, being much the same fare we get stateside, blather covered serials, newscasters looking as if they could cry, commentators claiming they are saying what I have said they said. And then a kiss of crackling glass on the window behind my head. Someone had broken one of my windows. And then a knock on the door.

I tensed involuntarily. Then I heard Deb's voice whispering through the thin mahogany. I opened quickly and there she stood, looking fresh and radiant, dressed in local evening wear cut Las Vegas style, revealing the «blossom-scar» or navel as it is known in English.

"I thought you had stayed with Hung," I started to say, but then saw she was not alone. Wang, the handsome man from the next room in her motel, the man she claimed not to know, stepped from the darkness and stood behind her with menace in his look. The horrible thought crossed my mind that perhaps I had caused him to lose face, that perhaps he had discerned my obvious lie and was here to even the score. I looked back to Deborah and then I knew. Well, you can imagine my discomfort on learning, to know for the first time, incontrovertibly, that she had lied through honied lips. «Private interview», my eye! Why that whole boat was little more than a privateer. They had all conspired against me and not the other way around. And now I had to pay.

"You Judas cow," I screamed. "So you've gone over," I started to say but Wang slapped me with his pistol, very hard, and the first of my teeth fell from my mouth. I tried to appeal to Deborah but she turned on me viciously:

"Don't talk any more. Do you hear me. Just shut-up. And don't tell me what you want when what you want is a piece of turkey! I'll tell you what you want." Wang grabbed me from behind and put a break-lock on my arms. Deborah came two inches from my face and added mystery to insult by saying: "And don't tell me it's just happening when you've got all those fingers in my pie." With this she spit, splattering spittle across my face. I know to many this is an ultimate humiliation.

I don't know what gave Deborah the idea she had a right to anger over my behavior. Is there something I didn't understand. I mean, is the sub-text a secret or is it not just a constantly present thing, like the weather, or the love sickness or the heat of unidentifiable passion? I mean, really, did she have a right to accuse me of «being unfaithful», as if «Lord Silly» needed her grudging ministrations in order to know his part. Or was it my having witnessed her «hieroglyphs of sensual perturbation»? Was I now to be blinded to sight for what I had seen while I was with her? In truth, I never even gave it a thought. I'm not saying she was supposed to «let me down easy» or any thing in the rudiments of dating handbooks, because I don't think that. I mean, sex is just a coffee break with us humans. We're not really animals no matter what they teach you in school. But of course I had the obvious intellectual advantage of hating her, of hating her for turning me into «Lord Silly» in the first place.

I was forced to submit to several acts to which I would not voluntarily admit, committed not by Wang alone but by Deborah as well. Oh, so much that is malevolent can be accomplished with a simple hard rubber rod, but nothing, nothing like this! It's the general misfortune of getting personal. That's what gets me all this heartache in the first place. Having stripped me and tied my hands to the headboard, they went about their dirty work, Wang with his six-inch black plastic stump, Deborah with her horse-hair cat-o-nine-tails. Wang broke into some very abusive pidgin but Deborah begged, more for my benefit than hers: "Don't say anything more, Wang Chung, this talk of slicing him to death by inches gives me the cold shivers!" She was just trying to scare me. They're utterly godless, you know, and capable of starving to death with supreme complacency. And then leaving you, divorced and despondent. At one point she whispered: "This is for the rest of them and what you did to us, you jerk-off artist!" To me, can you imagine? Well, I've got her number even if she did better me in a contest of brute force.

It was then she made her claim. She claims to have lost ear-rings and other precious stones. Well, what an unfounded claim. Ha! I'll tell you what she lost: her virginity, that's what! And her moral stance. And after that a girl's only worth two cents these days. And I want to say right here I didn't, repeto, didn't filch her silly dish of precious gems, her filthy little baubles, the ones she claims I stole somehow from the go-down in Kashmir, the post-box in Vermont, the safe-deposit in California. How would I gain access to all those places? That's right, that's ridiculous. We've all been to the Smithsonian and everything's all right there! Psychologically, the very fact that I am innocent makes the nightmare of these accusations even more paralyzing. The charges against me build up a circumstantial picture of a man who might have existed. I am not that man but these are the charges I am forced to refute. If I am not careful, I might fall into a trap. People might think I am trying to defend myself against real charges! And I remain hurt to this day the Caymen have denied my existence, saying they merely lunched with a disturbed young man. Even though no normal person could believe such a farrago of absurd charges, mud always sticks, and the revelations, however false, may always prevent me from ever rising from the humble station into which I was born. Now I hope they're happy!

Why, oh why, these recriminations for tourism? I am not an operative for any «international police» organizations. What purpose would that serve? I was not involved in a «crippling campaign» against

Cayman's «mule». I mean that stooge Deborah, that ringer. That woman was a dissembler's dissembler. She was what they call a «plant», I know this for certain, a «warm body» drawn from the «active element» of society, those «funny people» who are not sincere for whatever reason of ideology or profit. And why would I want to «cripple» his «mule», his beast of burden? For jewels, you say? Humph! Who am I, the Queen of England?

And where would I hide said stones when I travel so lightly? In a few slim documents? In my poetry? In my toiletries? On my person? Don't be a fool. This accusation is absurd, a calumny, a gross and willful distortion of the known fact, spit in the eye of all reasonable people and carefully measured argument. It's about as silly as thinking I could corner a piece of the oil-lamp market in deepest Cathay. You're free to step right up and look inside my wallet. I have nothing to hide. And who says those stones of hers were worth anything to begin with. Glass, I say, glass.

I was prostrate and passed out. Before they left, of course, they had sandbagged my arms and legs, leaving shattered bone from trunk to toes and fingers. And pushed my face well into the brown vinyl couch smelling of my own low fear. It's a wonder I survived.

And there was something worse which I hesitate to mention. Oh, if someone could but make me whole! To think, then, that I, of all people, will never pass those furry gates again. Now there is nothing separating me from the black-eyed-susan girls of paradise. But as long as other men continue to «get erections and go to war», I will never cease my struggle and give up the ghost. And who does she think she is to so impugn the «straight phallus» of ancient mysteries? She's just a spoiled brat and that's that!

These people and their ideas! And, I'll tell you this much, it was all a ruse to fleece the very rich. My word! Dishonest, of course, and therefore useless to an honest man and harmless to truly wily wealth. But there are others who will fall for it. And don't think that guile won't keep you in some comfort for some time. But at such a price! I ask you, really, what is it worth.

In any case, they all end up silly having to invest so much in the power of mendacity, that old high-upkeep bungalow and the associated sanitary distress of piss-elegance, the calcium deposits, so indicative of re-doubled hatred, seen in stressful moments, moments of death, and in such phrases as «the corn is for the nurses» or, more likely, «the nurses will lift this from your body as you die.»

One may, it is true, assume a coincidence of corn and imagine long-toothed gals in white snitching a cadaver's ears. Or toes. Stewardesses perhaps. I believe I remember some drop of creamy liquid left behind, perhaps I imagine it glowing in the dark, like a heavy metal scoria radio-activated. I'm sure he suffered some morbid hardening, that disease, so imitative and contagious. I mean, he wasn't really «hard». And there's nothing doesn't go away. But enough. I left the university long ago intent on my pleasure, seeking it in every hill and billy of the senses, determined not to think on what I was being told, even in the farthest fetching of a phrase, such as: The radio was given to the dead boy; Women in white come in his dreams; He has had a hard attack; The oatmeal steamed in her bowl. Ah, but are not all these thought but a sober seaman's wetter dreams, left high and dry in a better world? Are they not?

So there I was left chained to the door, as if attending, for all the world, a dream cure. Oh, these torrid lotuses and the will they can work on a man.

After my release from the clinic, I recovered somewhat in a bodycast at the boarding house under the care of others. Then I flew direct to Hollywood. After all I had suffered I felt it was the only place I could make any real contribution.

Notes on the 2015 Edition

ABOUT THE AUTHOR

Jim Strahs was a playwright and novelist based in New York City. His work has been performed by the Wooster Group (*North Atlantic, Oil Rig*) and Mabou Mines (*Wrong Guys*). He co-wrote *Cowboys and Indians* with Richard Maxwell, and his short plays (*Jane Dorch, How to Act, Producers of Fiction*) have been presented at Little Theater. He has written the books *Seed Journal* and *Queer and Alone*. Strahs died in Vermont on October 1, 2011.

HOW ALL THIS CAME TO BE

Queer and Alone was first published by PAJ books in 1988, and was introduced to me in the autumn of 2006, a season of much Whiskey and very much Tit. In August of 2011, I approached Jim about re-releasing the book, a project in which he took immediate enthusiasm, proceeding to send many shiny baubles of his writing through the ether, all of which I hope to be able to share soon. Jim died a few months later and I took on other projects before whipping the book into shape. But here it is, at last, never again to disappear from the canon.

ABOUT THE COVER

The cover illustration is by Ken Kobland was and reprinted with permission of the artist. Cover design is based on Kobland's 1988 Queer and Alone hardcover design. Ken can be found online at http://www.kenkoblandfilms.com.

DEDICATION

This edition of *Queer and Alone* is dedicated to Emma, Jameson, and Rowan, with much gratitude from the publisher.

LOOK AT THE PUBLISHER'S BIG GRATITUDE

Whiskey Tit thanks Emma Strahs, Scott Halvorsen Gillette, Ken Kobland, Jon Frankel, Erica and Henry Heilman, and Sedsel Grit Gillette. And, mostly, Jim.

www.ingramcontent.com/pod-product-compliance
Lightning Source LLC
Chambersburg PA
CBHW070919180626
46817CB00003B/1134